Sharing HIS NANNY

A *FOREVER OUR GIRL* ROMANCE

TORI CHASE

BOOK 2

all rights reserved

Edited by Julie K. Cohen and Zoe Neft

Cover Designed by Christley Creatives

Publisher: Chasing Dreams by Deborah A. Garland

https://www.deborahgarlandauthor.com/blog/tori-chase-romance/

why choose romances

by tori chase

romances by deborah garland
(in order)

Wait For Me

All For Me

Live For Me

His Christmas Surprise

The Good Billionaire

Daring the Billionaire

Bossy Billionaire

Rebel Billionaire

Accidental

Unexpected

Convenient

The Cowboy's Forbidden Crush

The Cowboy's Last Song

The Cowboy's Accidental Wife

The Cowboy's Rebel Heart

The Cowboy's Christmas Bride

The Cowboy's Wedding Planner

romances by deborah garland
(cont'd)

dedication

To all the Book Tok Girlies who made this book my
best-selling release ever!

prologue

STELLA

My lips pucker as I prepare to blow out the single candle dripping wax onto a mouthwatering slice of cheesecake.

"Don't forget to make a birthday wish, Stella!" my design assistant and best friend Bernadette says, holding her phone to take a picture.

I consider the challenge until my brain inwardly whines: *Where do I start?*

"Wishes are for dreamers. I'm a doer," I say instead and blow gently because Bernie and I are sharing.

The servers who sang Happy Birthday to me leave and when I don't see anyone sneering over their shoulder as people often do here in L.A., I lift the fork for a bite.

Cream cheese, vanilla, and lemon flavor goodness explode on my tongue.

"You really didn't wish for anything?" Bernadette slides a piece across her bee-stung red lips.

"Yep." But that's a lie. I wished for my fashion line to be a success.

"Where is James tonight?" my bestie asks cautiously

about my boyfriend.

James Pace is funding my line. Some men don't mix business with pleasure, but James is a rebel. A rich one. No one knows we're sleeping together or that I'm moving in with him so Bernie's question is valid.

"He has a late meeting." I shrug and lavish on the hefty piece clinging to my fork. "That's the trade-off when you date a working billionaire."

Bernie pushes thick glasses up her adorable button nose. "Do you think he's the one?"

"Maybe." I smile. "I'm only twenty-five and I want at least four successful lines under my belt before I even think of getting married. Or having kids." I love babies and always feel that tug when I see one.

"Did James comment on all the preorders we got from the showcase?"

"He didn't ask about it. He trusts me." I pinch my ruffled sleeve. It's my design, a yellow low-cut wrap number. "He keeps telling me how much he loves my look. How polished and sophisticated my dresses are."

Growing up curvy, I had limited clothing options, all of which I despised. I watched Project Runway as a young girl and taught myself to sew. Eighteen months ago, I caught James' eye at a gala I attended with my wealthy stepmother. The V-neck red dress hugged me in all the right places and showed off my curves. I don't hide a woman's hourglass figure, I accentuate it. Nope, no mu mu dresses for me or my customers. The ones who haven't discovered me yet. But they will, as soon as I get my money.

When I met James, I was in my senior year at the Fashion Institute of Design & Merchandising here in Los Angeles. James gave me his business card. He gushed so much at me, that Katherine, my stepmother, lent me the start-up cash to create a sample line. With those funds, I also hired a photographer, a videographer, and a PR company to put my name all over the place. Stella Raven Designs.

"If James doesn't finance my line for some ungodly reason, I won't be able to pay Katherine back," I add. "She's family, but she made me sign a very strict loan agreement."

"Sounds more like a step-monster," Bernadette quips because she knows my story.

My father, a handsome Hollywood model/stuntman married Katherine Harlow, a wealthy heiress, when I was eight. My mother had passed away three years earlier. Katherine loved having a tall, beefy stud on her arm. Just not the bratty kid he came with.

"How much money do we have left?" I ask Bernadette, who I met at FIDM. She studied merchandising and works double duty as my finance manager. I trust her completely.

She's also plus-size like me. "Only about five grand," Bernie says, sounding guilty. "That will cover my salary and your rent next month with a few bucks to spare."

I gave my landlord notice after James needled me to move in with him. Time to announce *that* development.

Smiling, I reach into my bag and take out the square hammered leather box. "Make that two months' salary for you. James gave me this last weekend."

Bernie gasps. "Stella!"

"It's not a ring. He knows I don't want to get that serious yet. Look." I lift the lid and watch Bernie's face as she peers inside.

"A key!" Her big brown eyes lift to me.

"I haven't used it yet. Most of the house is electronic with codes including the gate and front door. The key's symbolic."

"Now if he'll make good on the funding."

"I know. He's making me dot my i's and cross my t's more than anyone because when I move in, it will be announced we're in a relationship. He has a board to answer to." Even though investing a mere three hundred grand into my fashion line is a drop in the bucket compared to his other venture capital projects.

Bernie and I finish our shared dessert and walk to our cars. "Happy birthday, again!" She hugs me goodnight.

"Thank you, darling." I watch her long red curls bounce on her back until she gets inside her car.

It's close to ten p.m. and James still hasn't called me for my birthday. He's busy, I get it. Thinking of that key, I figure I have a birthday pass to drop in on him.

In my Ford Edge, a car that is thankfully paid off, I head toward Brentwood to use that key and get a birthday kiss.

Driving through the lush neighborhood even at night, I twitch, thinking of Katherine's Beverly Hills mansion, where my dad moved us after they got married. Tall white columns, manicured lawns, and perfect red roses made it look inviting on the outside. The inside, however, was cold and unloving.

I haven't heard from Katherine today either, but I never hear from her. Or Charles, my much older stepbrother who barely knows I exist because technically we never lived together.

Then there's my dad... *Gulp.* The only person who I

forgive for not calling me. He hasn't spoken in years since his head and spine injuries from an accident on a movie set left him a quadriplegic with barely any memory.

But I don't feel that alone. I have Bernie and James. Plus, soon, I'll launch my design company.

Think positive. Think positive.

I'm chanting my affirmations when I notice a line of cars in James' driveway. Is he having a party? Holy crap! Is this a surprise party for me? Did I miss a text or message from him?

I punch in the gate code and park behind the last car, which I guess I'll have to move because now I plan to spend the night. Are people watching for me? I check my hair and makeup, then smooth my dress, inspecting for cheesecake crumbles on my boobs. Nothing, good. The fabric still looks as fresh as it did when I got dressed this morning. That's why I chose a wrinkle-free jersey blend for all my clothes. It hides flaws.

I hope someone at this party takes pictures and posts them to Instagram! I can use the free PR.

While digging through my bag for business cards that include my socials, I tiptoe to the back of the house and slip in through the kitchen. I normally come in this way since I usually park my car in the back next to James' Porsche Cayenne.

Walking through the front door would be too obvious now that I know he and his friends are hiding in the living room.

The key is for the kitchen door. When I use it and pop in, I wait to hear shouts of *surprise*.

Nothing.

The kitchen looks like a food and alcohol bomb went

11

off. A painfully thin woman breezes in, dressed all in black. She's touching her mouth and looks flushed. I guess she's a server. A server who may have just gotten banged by one of James' playboy friends.

"Oh," she huffs, seeing me. "Who are you?"

I roll my eyes. "I'm the…"

It dawns on me this is not a surprise party. She'd know who I was and someone would have yelled Happy freaking Birthday by now. James is having a party *on my birthday*. Not only is it not for me, I wasn't invited.

Unless this is a business event and he knew I'd be bored. Or one of his asshole friends asked to use his stunning estate to schmooze clients. I debate leaving because James hasn't yet figured out that I'm here and clearly, I'm not supposed to be.

But I'll toss and turn all night if I don't at least know what the heck is going on.

I have a key. I'm *allowed* to be here.

Slowly, I walk through the elaborate kitchen and duck into the butler's pantry, which leads to the dining room. From the mirrors on the far wall, I see ten or so people dressed very casually, milling around the living room, talking and laughing. Not the business event I pictured earlier.

I finally spot James turning the corner from the hallway that leads to his office. He brushes his hair, looks in a mirror, and smiles at himself. I take a step to make my presence known, but he sidles up to a woman I don't recognize. She's thin and beautiful like most women in L.A. James almost looks…bored.

I'm ready to take a step when her voice stops me.

"Where's this Stella you keep talking about?" she

asks.

Shivers run down my spine at how she knows me, yet I don't know her. What has James been saying about me if our relationship is supposed to be a secret?

"Working as usual." There's no spite in James' voice. He sounds proud of my drive and commitment even if he's never come out and actually said so.

"Did you tell her?"

I freeze and feel so guilty for eavesdropping. But I can't turn away now when a question like that hangs in the air.

"About the investment?" James asks, sounding bored and not excited as he usually acts when we talk about it.

"Yeah, I heard you tell the board it's for her debut fashion line."

"You're a nosey assistant." He smiles at her, my worry kicking up. "I haven't told her the board approved her funding. I'm waiting for the right moment."

Approved? I've been approved! I do a happy dance in my head, wishing I could do it for real, but then I'd knock over the glass display case behind me and they'd hear me, think I'm spying. Even if technically I am.

"She'll be thrilled," the assistant sounds condescending all of a sudden.

Fuck *her*. I'm getting the money! Well, I knew I was getting the money. It was just a matter of when.

"Of course, she'll be happy."

"I guess *those* girls need clothes too."

I shake my head in disappointment at how women can be so vicious against other women. James doesn't react. I know L.A. sees us as an 'uneven' couple. He's tall and skinny, and I'm neither.

"She's big, so she knows what looks good on girls her size." His words sting, but I bury the feeling because I know I'm big. We've established that. It's the marketing angle for my line. "But hey, I dodged a bullet two years ago. I need some good press." He finishes his scotch. "Besides, who else would invest in that stupid line of ugly clothes?"

Wait... Stupid. Line. Of. Ugly. Clothes? *What the fuck?* Say what you want about my waistline, I won't have my clothes insulted this way. By my boyfriend/*investor* no less.

"I'm sure the line will get a lot of press." Now the bitch sounds jealous!

"That's the point. I *want* her to get press. Stella. We just need to be romantically involved when she launches. After that debacle two years ago with a model, dating a fat girl will help my reputation tremendously. No one will care that I also invested in her shitty clothes."

Fat girl!

I lurch back. James is dating me for a P.R. stunt. He's *using* me.

James finishes his drink and gives the woman a once-over. "You want to see my bedroom or not? I assume that's why you're hanging around."

She smiles and off they go. Up the stairs.

Holy hell, he's cheating on me too. The room spins as I lose my breath. What if I hadn't stopped by?

I back up into the display case and consider smashing this entire collection of expensive vases behind me. All perfect. Like the woman he'll be fucking in five minutes.

That prick!

The fighter in me wants to confront him, but I don't know who these people are. Someone is likely to whip out their phone and next, I'll go viral on TikTok. With no context, I'll just look like a lunatic screaming at my boyfriend. I'll be 'canceled' before my line even launches.

That scum isn't worth it.

I can fight back my own way, take the high road. Pretend this means nothing and let him wallow in his skinny-model controversy. Let him keep banging his assistants until eventually, one tries to blackmail him.

I turn and leave through the same door, not even making eye contact with the server, who I now suspect was his appetizer.

When I get to my car, I throw on the Bluetooth and bark, "Siri, find me a bakery that's open."

I need a whole cheesecake this time. It's my fucking birthday after all, I deserve it.

one

One Month Later
STELLA

Someone else's moving men show up after I reach the lobby. Done. I don't live in this Glendale apartment anymore. It was a dump, but it was big enough to double as a studio for me while I poured money into my fashion line.

I gave it up when I got that stupid key in a stupid box. The landlord rented my apartment a few weeks before that disastrous night of my birthday. Now I'm homeless thanks to a cheating, scheming, pathetic, manipulative boyfriend.

And I still need three hundred grand for my fashion line.

Trudging away from the building, a Town Car screeches in front of me and James jumps out. I ghosted him right after that night, not giving him a hint of what was wrong.

"What the fuck, Stella? I saw you on my security cameras spying on me." He opens with that line, skipping any pretense that he misses me.

It's no coincidence he's here *today*. He knows I gave up my apartment and have nowhere to go. Cunning bastard.

"You gave me a key. It was my birthday, James. I showed up there because I thought maybe you wanted to see me."

"This silent treatment is all because I forgot your

birthday?"

I glare at him. "You really haven't figured it out? Or do you just tell everyone you speak to that I'm fat and my clothes are ugly? Then go fuck."

His left eye twitches and my heart sinks, thinking I didn't hear him mutter those awful words just once. Or that he hadn't been cheating the whole time. "*That's* what this is about?"

Stunned, I respond, "You think that's not a big deal?"

"No. You *are* fat and your clothes are ugly." He folds his arms and the collective gasps of people walking by make him glance around. Concern grows in his beady eyes as he attempts to backpedal. "I mean…"

I hold up my hand. "Forget it. Your ruse is exposed. You were using me to repair your reputation and make yourself look inclusive. Not on my back, baby."

He pinches his chin. "You need to grow a set of balls if you want to make it in the business world. The only reason anyone will take your circus tents seriously is because you belong in one. This is L.A., I'm not the last guy who will call you fat."

I can take being called fat. Just not from my boyfriend! "Anything else?"

He scoffs. "Now that you know the truth, I can stop pretending. Stella, just take my money and pretend to be my girlfriend. We'll both benefit. Besides, you don't have any other options."

I hate that he's right about that last part, but I won't sell my soul so he can repair his reputation. The very idea makes my skin crawl. "I'd rather sleep in my car for the rest of my life than let you touch me even if it's for show." I know the fashion business is ruthless, but I trusted the man who supposedly loved me.

James angrily grunts, "Never mind. I knew you didn't have what it takes." He gets back in his fancy Town Car and screeches away, giving me the finger.

I wish I had my phone out to record it. The confrontation shakes me up and I don't think this is the last I'll see of him. Any thoughts of revenge are on pause. Now I just need to survive.

I consider using what's left in my bank account to stay in a hotel. James is gunning for me. But I need to keep Bernadette working while I search for another investor. I can't lose her and I refuse to accept this line won't happen. A factory in Kansas stands ready to produce my clothes. I don't want to hire cheap labor in China. If I don't get my investment in thirty days, I'll lose my window with that factory. Then I might as well chuck the entire line because trends come and go like the wind.

Bernie offered me her couch to sleep on. I'm deciding what is more humiliating, sleeping on my assistant's sofa with her two cats, or asking my stepmother for help. More help.

She'll never give me more money. Right after she and Dad got married, she sent me away to boarding school in Oregon. During breaks and the summers, one of her housekeepers took care of me since Dad traveled a lot for his stuntman job.

Then he got hurt, bad. Fell off a horse filming a western and hit his head so hard he became paralyzed from the neck down. After the accident, Katherine put him in a rehabilitation center. But as years went by, he slowly lost the ability to speak, so she moved him to an adult-disabled facility in Santa Monica. Most days, he doesn't know where he is, or who I am.

I get to my Ford Edge and glance in the back filled with boxes, wondering if I'd fit between them to sleep there tonight instead of crawling to that woman for a place to crash, on top of everything else.

Key in the ignition, I pray it starts and consider where to go when I reach the light on the corner. A car horn blares behind me and I cross into the intersection looking for a place to pull over so I can make the dreaded call to Katherine.

I allow myself one more escape from reality as I pull into my favorite coffee bar. Even though it's late June, I order a hot caramel macchiato. Then it happens.

"Let me guess, you want whip cream?" the cashier asks with a rude once-over.

In the grand scheme of my life, one dollop of whip isn't going to make much of a difference. But why the fuck is everyone in this town so rude to anyone who's not a size two?

Some people just want a fight, so I answer calmly with my head held high. "*Extra* whip, please." And hope it doesn't cost more.

Sitting in a booth, charging my phone, and hoping my sim card doesn't go down because I haven't paid my wireless bill yet, I call Katherine to ask her for a place to stay. That will inevitably lead to the investment discussion.

"Katherine's line," her assistant answers.

"Hi, it's Stella. Is she there?" I expect Michaela to tell me no because usually Katherine brushes me off.

"Stella, Katherine's—" She's about to launch into her mountain of excuses of why her boss won't talk to me, but she's cut off.

"Wait!" Katherine uncharacteristically blurts loudly from the background. "Give me that. *Stella?*"

The utter frantic tone of her voice sends ice down my spine, making me think something happened to my father. And I hate that I don't know if she'd be devastated or ecstatic. My father's been in that adult home for seven years. That's got to be tough on a marriage.

"Hi, I'm here."

"Oh, thank God. Where are you? What are you doing?"

I pull the phone from my ear to see if it's still connected, worrying I've been given horrible news. Like I might have suffered a heart attack because she actually sounds concerned about me.

"Well, funny you should ask. I... I..." My throat quivers as I drawl, "I need some help."

"Really..." Her voice turns steady. "What kind of help?"

She doesn't know I was dating James and therefore has no idea we broke up. How else can I explain why I'm not taking his money? Money I need to pay her back. "I'm sort of in a bind for cash."

"Michaela, cancel all those appointments," she says to her assistant in a muffled voice. "Stella, how soon can you meet me in Malibu?"

Malibu? What the hell is in Malibu? I hoped to meet her in Studio City, the office where she and her assistant plan out all of her fundraisers.

Then I remember my stepbrother Charles has a beach house there. This time of the year, he and his two friends host wild parties for a month. I follow him on Instagram and the videos he posts should be on

PornHub.

"Um…" I mentally calculate the traffic all the way down to the beach from Glendale.

"Are you even in L.A.? Do you need my jet?" She has a jet and I'm eyeing dumpsters of five-star restaurants for my next meal.

"Yes. I'm in L.A." I don't say *home* because I don't have a home anymore and I'm not even sure she knows where I live. Lived. "I'll be there as soon as I can." It's noon on a Friday, but here in L.A., it's rush hour, all day, every day.

"Fine, Stella. Goodbye."

"Wait, Katherine, what's so urgent? Is it Dad?"

"No," she scoffs. "I'll tell you when you get here. Drive fast!"

The line goes dead.

I finish the macchiato and amble back to my car. I worry about speeding, thinking if I get pulled over and arrested, no one would bail me out. Except Bernie. Oh, James would come get me and use it as leverage to make me take his money.

Maybe it's stupid pride keeping me from giving in, but at least I *have* some pride left.

*

The traffic gods smile upon me and I make it to Charles' beach house in Malibu by three p.m.

"Jesus," I mutter at the gate, getting a peek at the palatial estate behind ominous bars. It looks amazing in his online photos and videos, but in person, it's dauntingly big.

"Who's there?" a voice I don't recognize rings out from the gate panel.

"It's Stella. I'm here to see Katherine."

No response, but the gate slides open.

There's a hilly driveway with pine trees on both sides. The smell of peppermint fills my senses and makes me hungry. When the ski-house-inspired chalet with teak siding comes into view, it hits me just how out of the loop I am in this family.

Coming home from Oregon for the holidays felt like staying in a hotel. The room Katherine gave me wasn't mine. When I got into FIDM, Katherine refused to pay my tuition. I took out a student loan at eleven percent interest. That should be paid off when I'm ready to retire.

Looking at this mansion on the water, I push aside how much money *Charles* might have while I scraped to survive this last month. But all of this will build my character. I take nothing for granted and work hard. I have to.

I park next to a massive, creamy-white stone fountain with a cherub boy in a loose toga holding a pitcher of water in the center. The driveway is all tiny, crushed stones except for manhole-size shale blocks that lead to a set of stairs in front of the house.

From a massive oak double front door, Katherine emerges onto a wraparound porch with a metal railing. Greeting me in the courtyard instead of ushering me to the back means whatever she needs from me, she'll tell me here then send me on my way.

Looks like I'll either sleep in my Ford here in Malibu or in a fleabag motel up the coast because I don't have enough gas to go much farther.

I smile, wave, and get out of my car.

Katherine, dressed in white pants, a blue, strapless top, and sparkly sandals, sweeps down the stairs. She's utterly gorgeous for sixty-something. And thin as a rail.

"Hey," I say, acting cheery, and move in for a hug.

She bends at the waist, and air kisses me on both cheeks. Giving me a concerned once-over, she says, "Have you gained weight?"

Biting my lip, I reply, "Lost weight, actually." Not having money for food helps.

"Really," she utters in disbelief like she's picturing me being even bigger.

"You look amazing," I say in hopes to get something positive in return.

What I get is a roadmap on her face of all her latest Juvéderm injections. She sounds ready to move into her hair treatments and massages at the spa, when I cut her off.

"What did you need me to drive down here for?" I fold my arms, acting business-like.

I have to stop thinking of her as my stepmother. She's a creditor and nothing else. I have to treat her with stern indifference. Then schmooze my way out of paying the current debt while asking for a little more money until I find a new investor.

Katherine narrows her eyes on me and then straightens her back. "I need a favor."

I nearly blow a gasket. "What kind of *favor*?"

"What are you doing this month?" She twirls her hair and if I have to beg for a place to sleep tonight, I'm going to yank those blonde extensions right out while doing it.

This is my do-or-die moment. My time to come clean. See what she's made of. Force her to deal with me. "If you must know, Katherine, I'm in a financial bind. I moved out of my apartment this morning and I have nowhere to go."

"That's wonderful!" she cries out.

"Wonderful?"

"Yes, I need you. I have a *job* for you."

"What kind of job?"

"Something right up your alley." She pokes me in the ribs.

I resist an eye roll, thinking she needs me to dress her for parties coming up. I drop all pretenses and let her know I'm pissed. "And what do you think is up my *alley*?" Other than a sleeping bag because that's looking like a possibility.

"Oh, he's here!" She ignores the question, and brushes me aside.

The gate's hydraulics hum and seconds later a shiny, black stretch limo crests over the hill.

My heart seizes, thinking she moved my father out of the facility and now wants me to care for him. Something I'd gladly do, but he's a quadriplegic. I'm not strong enough to lift him, bathe him, or move him around.

When the limo stops and a man gets out, I recognize the golden blond hair and the wide shoulders immediately.

It's Charles. Katherine's thirty-eight-year-old son and my first crush. The irrational kind of crush an eight-year-old girl has on a twenty-one-year-old. My immature desire was based solely on his looks. All I ever got from him were distant aloof glances from the other side of the Chippendale table during the holidays.

He's barely said a dozen words to me. My entire life.

Half of them being, *"What's your name, again?"*

Charles didn't live in the Beverly Hills home with

Katherine and my dad. After graduating from Harvard, he moved to downtown L.A. This is his beach house.

He steps around the limo wearing a finely-cut, charcoal Armani suit that probably costs more than the Kelley Blue Book value of my car. If it's possible, he's more handsome than ever. His hair hasn't thinned one bit and sweeps up from his forehead. It sits longer in the back, and brushes against his collar.

He looks a bit frazzled. I'd like to think a rich-as-sin playboy CEO concert promoter has some stress in his life. God, I could only imagine how many women he fucks a year. The summer videos alone make my head spin.

My body heats up, watching him pass the back-end of the limo. But he doesn't walk toward Katherine and me, he goes to the door on the other side.

A pit forms in my stomach, and I brace myself, expecting to see a gorgeous, thin woman step out and fly into his arms.

I blink again, thinking my brain is playing tricks on me. It's a female all right. And she's in his arms.

But…

He's holding a baby.

two

CHARLES

It's been the longest seven days of my life. Seven days since Ana showed up at my office with a four-month-old baby, saying the child is mine. And that she has a photo shoot in Alaska for several weeks and can't take the baby with her.

Then she left. She fucking left!

All the work at my office came to a grinding halt. My assistant's been helping me take care of the baby and has been an angel, really. I considered inviting her to my beach house to help me this month, but I think she has a crush on me and I didn't want to send the wrong signal.

I don't do relationships. Or screw people who work for me.

I turned to the one person I can always count on…

"Mom!" I wave to her standing at the base of my front steps with a woman I don't recognize. I ignore that and unbuckle Giana from her car seat. "Come on, princess."

I could question if she's mine, but Ana left me Gia's birth certificate, which has my name on it. Based on Gia's birthday, she *has* to be mine. During the time Ana would have conceived, she and I were in Hawaii.

Fucking like rabbits. Without a condom because she told me she was on the pill.

Somewhere in my brain, I considered asking a doctor to swing by and take DNA samples, but who would drop a baby off to someone who's *not* the father knowing he'd get a paternity test?

Jesus, I'm a father. I have a daughter!

I only wish I'd had a goddamn heads-up.

Gia coos lovingly in my arms as I approach my mom with a diaper bag slung over one shoulder.

"Why are you out front and not in the back? Hello," I address the woman standing there, looking gobsmacked.

Probably someone on my mother's staff. From the way this beauty dresses, Mom at least pays her people well. Something we have in common. "I met Stella out here, she's—"

"Stella?" I glance at the woman again and step back. The crunchy gravel under my feet sets me off balance. I hold Gia tight, fearful I might drop her.

"Your *stepsister*," Mom reminds me and I notice she's not addressing the baby in my arms.

"Hey, Charles." Stella smiles at Gia. "Who... Who's this?" She reaches out and immediately my daughter wiggles to get out of my arms.

Stella, with her curly blonde hair, doesn't look like Ana, who sports an asymmetrical dark bob. Gia can't think that's her mother. And... The next thought enters my brain and I hate myself. Ana is stick thin. Too thin. Stella... Stella is curvy. But Jesus, she's beautiful. Was she always this gorgeous?

"This is Gia," I say, keeping my hand on her back as she snuggles against Stella's ample breast.

Lucky baby.

Fuck, what am I thinking? That's my damn stepsister. I can't even remember when I last saw her. Five, six, seven years ago? What a shit I've been. She's my sister. Stepsister. We were both only children and we should have been closer. But I'm thirteen years older than her. Even full-blooded siblings with that kind of age difference aren't close.

"When did you get married?" Stella asks.

"He *didn't*," my mother hisses.

"It's a long story," I say to cover up how when we got back to L.A., I ghosted Ana like I usually do with the women I fuck. I'm a hard-working CEO. I wake up at six a.m. every day to work out with my trainer Alex for ninety minutes and *then* work a twelve-hour day.

"We don't need the sordid details." My mother waves her hand. Still not approaching, looking, or commenting on her granddaughter.

Gia is an easy baby. As easy as a four-month-old can be. At night when she sleeps, I go on YouTube to watch videos. Of all the paperwork Ana left, she didn't mention anything about food or a feeding schedule. Or how to change a diaper. That was the first video I watched.

Thank God, Gia's very go-with-the-flow. I would think a baby so young would scream bloody murder being away from Mommy. What the hell is Ana doing? I can't ask because she's not answering her phone.

"What are you doing here, Stella?" I expected my mother to be here to take delivery of all the furniture and baby clothes I sent a personal shopper to Rodeo to buy. I couldn't get down here. I had my hands full, to say the least.

"Stella is going to be your nanny."

"What?" Stella and I bark at the same time.

"What on Earth did you think I asked you to drive down here for?" my mother sneers at Stella and something visceral kicks up in me.

"Drive down from where? Where do you live?" I feel like a piece of shit for not knowing any of this.

"Glendale," she answers, smiling at the baby, who glows in her presence. Heck, they both glow and something stirs in me.

Holy hell, what was that?

When Gia starts to fuss, I reach for her because she's *my* responsibility. "I'll take her. She needs a diaper change."

Mom slaps my hands. "Stella can do it."

"No. Wait…" I scoop Gia back into my arms, feeling very possessive. I had my own plan and my mother is bulldozing me in a different direction. "I don't need a nanny. No offense, Stella."

"None taken." She fixes the neckline of her cute dress and I catch cherry-red lace. The seductive dip of cleavage makes my heart pound. Christ, she's sexy.

"Of course you need a nanny." My mother folds her arms, still not even looking at Gia.

Or noticing that I look like hell. Or that I've barely slept. I haven't had sex in a week. For me, that's a long time. I usually bring a woman home to my penthouse every night. It's how I cap off a long, hard day, driving my long hard cock into one of the many nameless beauties who use me as much as I use them. This past week, though, I've been too tired to even masturbate.

All these thoughts sour my stomach when I glance at Stella, who looks innocent and sweet.

"I have it covered, Mom." I turn to go inside, but stop when I hear the buzzer for the gate. "My help is here."

"What help?" Mom huffs.

"Open the gate," I yell, hoping Willow, my house manager, can hear me.

The gate opens and a red, vintage Dodge Charger peels in, hurting my ears. I cover Gia's head, ignoring my own pain. I glance back at the steps and Stella too is covering her ears.

Gia starts to cry again. This time it's piercing. I hear steps behind me and I want it to be my mother, hoping she snapped out of whatever denial she's in that she's a grandmother. No, it's Stella.

"Come here, peanut." Stella takes Gia in her arms again, and our hands brush, igniting a fire under my skin.

The heat moves through me like a powerful wave. I catch Stella watching me and only then do I realize how blue her eyes are. But my daughter is fussing.

"It's okay, princess." I stroke the back of her head then wave to Alex to cut the engine. "It's only noise, Giana."

"That's a beautiful name." Stella meets my eyes. "Where's—"

"*These* two?" my mother scoffs, breaking the tension between Stella and me.

Alex hops out of the car and grabs his leather duffel. Jordan, my General Counsel, follows.

"It's our month to be here at the beach, mother. They're gonna help me." Since getting Gia, I counted the hours until my annual vacation. This will give me the opportunity to take care of my daughter properly. I also have to catch up on the promoter deal I'm trying to close for Tyler Pace's two-year world tour.

"You're kidding." My mother shakes her head.

"Not kidding, mother."

"No. This won't work." Mom wipes a loose hair from her perfect forehead. "Stella needs a job and a place to live."

"You need a place to live?" It stings, hearing Stella is in dire straits. "You said you live in Glendale."

"It's a long story," she says with mischief, mocking my earlier cagey answer. Rocking Gia, she turns to my mother. "Katherine, this is why you wanted me down here? To be your son's nanny?"

My mother folds her arms. "Yes. I'll knock twenty percent off your loan."

"Loan?" I ask her. "What loan?"

"A business loan," Stella mutters with lush pink lips on Gia's forehead. "I needed money for my business. I was strapped with student loans."

"You didn't pay for her college?" I screech at my mother.

"No. She didn't." Stella eyes my mother. "Fifty percent."

I step back and realize she's negotiating for a job I don't need to fill.

"Twenty percent is ten thousand dollars for one month's work." My mother stands her ground.

In fairness to Mom, that *is* generous.

"She feels warm, Charles." Stella rocks the baby, steely-eyed at my mother. "*Thirty* percent."

Quickly calculating thirty percent of what I've figured out is a fifty-grand business loan is more than a decent wage.

Only, I *don't* need a nanny.

Then Gia projectile throws up all over me.

31

three

STELLA

I stifle a laugh as Charles' expensive suit jacket is soaked in sour baby formula. But holy moly, fifteen grand knocked off my loan and I get to live in this palatial beachfront estate. All to take care of an adorable baby for one month? That's a great deal.

Charles stripping out of this suit jacket and crisp white dress shirt in the kitchen we quickly moved to is something I'd pay money to watch if I had any to spare.

"Charles, your sister is in the room," Katherine snaps.

Gawking at his naked chest, I'm caught in a peculiar vortex here. I'm frustrated with Katherine, but she's offering me a lifeline when I need it the most. I could have argued more for the fifty percent, but I might hit her up for the full three hundred grand if I'm left with no other options.

Charles has been aloof, and even a little rude to me since our parents married, but he seemed genuinely annoyed at his mother's treatment of me just now. So I stay neutral. A single dad needs a nanny. I'm not sure why he thinks he doesn't.

Two hulking figures waltz into the kitchen, stealing my attention away from Charles getting undressed.

"Yo." Hulk One, with dark hair and a neatly-trimmed, sexy beard, eyes me strangely while I balance Gia on my hip. "Who is *this*?"

"Stella, this is Jordan Sawyer," Charles introduces

us. "My company's GC."

"Nice to meet you." I don't offer my hand because I'm holding the baby while going through her diaper bag looking for a change of clothes with the other.

Hulk Two wearing blue and white seersucker shorts, a black tank top, and a baseball cap steps out from behind Jordan. "What's going on?"

"That's Alex, my trainer. He runs the gym in my building," Charles says, washing his hands. "Alex, this is my sister Stella."

I cringe at that word, considering the way I'm looking at his body. "Nice to meet you, too. Where're the rest of her clothes, Charles?"

He crosses the room still shirtless, and his cologne hits me. With his sexy musk setting alarm bells off in my brain, I glance at his sculpted arms and chiseled abs. His dark pants with a leather belt sit low on his hips, exposing that sexy V cut. He's not hairless, but the light catches golden fuzz against his tanned chest. He looks so smooth, I want to lick him.

"I have two sets in the bag, and there should be dozens more upstairs."

"Upstairs?" I ask, lifting my head.

"There's a beautiful nursery set up with an entire wardrobe for her," Katherine says, leaning against the sink, looking annoyed.

"Her?" Charles barks, taking Gia into his arms. "Do you even want to hold your granddaughter?"

The way Katherine's right eye twitches at the word granddaughter is priceless. "No need. Your sister is doing fine." She sends me a stern look. "Take her upstairs and get her out of those wet clothes."

"Stop." Charles waves a free hand. "Stella, honey,

33

I'm sorry. I don't need a nanny this month. If you need money, please give me a few minutes to get the baby settled and we'll talk in my office."

I can take a payout from Charles, but that doesn't solve my living situation.

My eyes stray to the two alphas standing in his kitchen. I don't mean to be sexist, but these two beefcakes and a rich-as-sin, detached manwhore can't take care of a baby. I've seen what goes on during this month-long vacation here at the beach house.

Not that a four-month-old is a lot of work, but these three guys party hard when they're here.

"Charles, let me give you a hand for a few days." I take Gia back from him.

"Fine." His body relaxes and he squeezes my arm. "Thank you, Stella."

He showed up looking frazzled. Once he sees what kind of help I can be, he'll want to keep me around. With Gia in my arms, I take in Jordan and Alex again. Their eyes are either glued to me or the baby.

"Charles, you and I need to talk." Katherine's shrill voice sends shivers through me.

"Mom, you're not in charge here. Thank you for getting the house ready and for calling Stella. But I got this."

I tiptoe to the kitchen island to slip the diaper bag on my arm, but it tips over.

"Hey, I got it." Jordan catches it and slowly drags the strap up my arm, his fingers grazing my skin.

I snag a look at him and his green eyes are right on me. But I'm triggered at the moment. I fell for James, another pretty boy, thinking he felt the same about me. He was using me. Not that this Jordan has an agenda five minutes after meeting me, but I'm not ready to open up at the moment.

"Thanks," I say, holding my breath.

"Anytime," he purrs at me.

Before leaving the room, I glance at Alex. Trainer. Hmmm. I'm sure he'll be bugging me with tips on diet and exercise. I nod with a snarly smile to get the thought out of his head, but he bites a full lower lip back at me. What the hell did that mean?

Gia cries out, hurting my ears with a piercing shrill. She probably needs to eat again since she threw up. "Charles, do you have a bottle ready for her? I think she's hungry."

"No, I fed her on the way up here." His words put a picture in my head of a man in a five-thousand-dollar suit feeding his daughter in a limo and my ovaries scream. "Mother, did you get the formula I told you to buy?" He starts opening cabinets.

"Good grief." Katherine pushes off the sink and goes to a floor-to-ceiling pantry next to the Sub-Zero double-door refrigerator. She removes a container and turns to me, her eyes narrowing in on my breasts like she might ask one of Charles' friends to knock me up so I can be a wet nurse.

We're all silenced, watching Katherine make a baby bottle like a pro. Something I should pay attention to because I haven't a clue. I hope there's Wi-Fi in this place so I can watch some videos.

Shaking the bottle, Katherine eyes her son. "Go put a shirt on already."

"Yes, mother." Charles grabs a bag his limo driver snuck in while we were talking. "Guys, go settle in your rooms. We'll... We'll...order in dinner."

"I need a drink." Jordan grips a stunning Louis Vuitton pullman and smiles at me. "Welcome to the party, Stella."

"I'm gonna have a swim." Alex tosses a leather duffle over his wide shoulders. "And I'll take the pool house for this month. No offense, I'm a really light sleeper and a screaming infant will keep me up all night."

"She doesn't scream all night, but, yeah, take the pool house." Charles runs a hand through his hair. "Stella can stay in your room."

"I set up the guest room in the back of the house, next to Willow's room for her," Katherine says as if I'm hired help. Which I guess I am.

"That's for the house staff, mother." Charles shakes his head like he just met this woman. If he only knew how she treated me from day one.

I take Gia and the bottle to follow Charles upstairs, but stop to gaze out the wall of glass on this side of the house. I catch the sun's rays dappling across a calm ocean and can only imagine the breathtaking sunsets.

I sure hope he lets me stay so I don't have to sleep on the beach.

four

JORDAN

"No," Alex whispers to me and grabs an apple from a tower of Granny Smiths on the kitchen island.

"No, what?" I ask, reaching into the fridge for a beer.

"You *know* what." His perfect white teeth rip through the fleshy surface of the apple, then he chews around his explanation. "She's your best friend's little sister."

I stop mid-pour into a frosted glass, astonished at how well Alex knows me.

We both read the writing on the wall a few minutes ago. It looks like Stella is staying here to help Charles with the baby.

I'm a Dom with an eye for a woman who needs complete and utter adoration in her life. And some discipline. I sensed Stella was a control freak. They make the best subs. Not at first. But when they find I can break them, they clear their mind and just take my direction. And my cock. God, those women come harder than they ever had in their life because I get them out of their heads. They'll stay on their knees all day if I ask them.

After a sip of the ice-cold beer, I say, "First, she's not his sister. She's his stepsister."

"Same thing." Alex has the apple damn-near cored and throws what's left in the trash with extra oomph.

He's on edge because our plans have been upended. We come here once a year to fuck our troubles away.

Charles brought his troubles with him. I doubt he'll let us screw women non-stop the way we usually do with a baby here.

And his sister.

I'm on edge because my most recent Sub safeworded out of a shibari scene and I've not heard from her since. To lose a submissive so close to the end of a contract left me with a perpetual stiff cock needing to be deep in a pussy. I must look like a live wire ready to blow because Alex's 'no' comment meant I wasn't too subtle in sizing up Stella.

She gave me a vibe that suggested she might like being tied to my bed and throat fucked until tears leak out of her eyes. Until I'm screaming and sweating. But just for this month. My D/s relationships have an expiration date according to the contract I make them sign. Submissives come and go on a schedule for me, so my heart has been turned off to the possibility of a relationship for as long as I can remember.

If I make a play for Stella, that leaves Alex out of the fun. Maybe.

"Have you heard from Pierce?" I ask him, feeling bad that Alex lost his fuck buddy, a guy he let rail him from time to time.

"No," he says, and looks out toward the pool with empty eyes. Alex is primarily straight, but likes guys on the side. This thing with Pierce was more than that apparently.

"What's going on with you?" I ask him.

He exhales sharply and says, "Word around my gym recently is that he fell in love with an ER doctor, a client he was training. Not just her. He's also screwing Cooper, the running coach from JG. They're living happily ever after in her house in Beverly Hills."

The news hits me in two ways. One, I feel for my best friend and wish he told me this sooner. Two, I wonder what that would be like. Living with and sharing a woman with Alex *and* Charles. Permanently.

But Pierce is not only banging the doctor, he's banging this guy Cooper too. And planned to *forever* it sounded like, if they've all moved in together.

A shudder runs through me looking at Alex. Damn, is that what *he* wants? And with who? I never considered having sex with a man. But Alex? My best friend?

I finish the rest of my beer in one frantic gulp, watching his ass over the rim of my glass. The guy's a personal trainer and his body is nothing short of phenomenal. I kept my eyes on him longer than I should have in the past, but my brain told me that I really wanted to know how to get an eight-pack instead of a six-pack. I work out regularly too and have a cut body, but Alex…

"Shit," I mutter to myself feeling my cock growing in my pants. Five minutes ago, I couldn't stop seeing Stella tied up, sucking my cock. Now I'm picturing both her and Alex sucking me off.

With the beer glass in the sink, I reach for a cut crystal lowball tumbler and pour three fingers of whiskey, then down it.

That should keep my dick in check for a few hours.

Maybe.

five

STELLA

I follow Charles to the second floor where he keeps turning around to make sure I'm all right on the stairs. Not me, per se. Me, the woman holding his daughter.

OMG, Charles has a *baby!* And I agreed to be a nanny.

The last thirty minutes passed by like my life flashed before my eyes. Mostly because I was hanging on by a thread for a month and spent all day worrying about where I'll sleep tonight.

Katherine makes the trip upstairs with us, calling out all her hard work to create a nursery. It's as if I've stepped into a photo shoot. She decorated the enormous room with soft pink walls, a bright white crib, and a celestial mobile. A wall unit in the same white finish takes up the entire opposite wall. It's filled with books, stuffed animals, and fake plants. The bottom half of the wall unit is drawers, which I'm sure contain expensive baby clothes.

In front of the window with a white, raw silk honeycomb shade and a pink, velvet valance across the top, is the changing table.

Nodding, I bring Giana over and start to undress her. Charles took the brunt of the vomit, and just a few dribbles landed on Gia's cute pink and white polka dot onesie. She's calm and lets me pull the stained clothes off. It's like she senses I'm nervous and gives me a break.

Katherine and Charles exchange some hushed, but heated words, and without even looking my way, she saunters out the door to leave.

Feeling feisty, I say, "This room looks amazing, Katherine. You did a great job."

She stops abruptly, but doesn't turn around. Instead, she glances at her son, who's emptying the diaper bag. He peers at her like she has ten heads. Like he doesn't know this side of his mother at all. The rude bitch.

And she still hasn't held the baby!

"Mom?" Charles probes her.

"Thank you, Stella. We'll…talk." With that, she disappears.

"Does she need a nap?" I ask a bit loudly because I think Charles is still on the other side of the room emptying the diaper bag. No, he's in my face. "Oh. Sorry."

Before responding to me, he brushes his hand across Gia's head. "After she eats, yeah."

"What time does she go down at night?"

"Around seven. After her bath."

Nodding, I see where the rest of my day is headed. "I'll take care of that."

"I like to do her bath." He looks around. "I put a tub on the list for my mother to buy."

I see this nursery has its own bathroom. Lifting Gia into my arms because I don't know everything about babies, but I know you don't leave one on the changing table, I push the door open and my brain spasms, staring at the most luxurious bathroom I've ever seen.

The sweeping countertop with two sinks is made of light gray and gold marble striations, the wavy pattern making me dizzy. The stand-up shower has matching marble with glass tiles down the center. On the far wall is a jacuzzi tub that I plan to borrow when Gia's asleep.

Tiptoeing that way, I see a bright-yellow infant bathtub. "It's in the jacuzzi."

"Stella, thank you," Charles says, sounding hesitant. Like he doesn't say thanks very often.

"You're welcome. I'm sorry your mother didn't warn you that she asked me to drive down here and give you a hand." Not that I knew the reason either.

"Yeah…" Charles runs his fingers through rumpled golden hair.

I bring Gia back to the nursery and sit in the rocking chair to feed her a fresh bottle.

"Yo, Chuck." Jordan struts into the nursery. "Alex and I are heading down to Pedro's for margaritas and tacos. Come on, Friday happy hour starts at three down here." He seems to have gotten up to speed on the situation.

I'm the nanny and will be minding Giana while these three enjoy their wild, annual vacation. But I'm getting paid well, and I need a place to sleep while I figure things out.

"Go ahead, Charles. You look like you need a drink," I say, needing one too, and food. "Gia is fine."

Although, I passed starving a few miles back and now my body must be cannibalizing the donuts I ate a month ago.

I can miss a meal. I'm sure that guy Alex, the trainer, looked at me and thought that. His life's work is to sculpt bodies.

Sure, I should be paying more attention to my figure like that, but I'm happier eating a bag of potato chips and drinking a few beers. I seem to love my body more when I'm tipsy. Maybe because I feel sensual then. I chose to design plus-size fashions because everyone deserves to wear beautiful clothing that makes them feel sexy and powerful. Being stuck wearing oversized hot messes that look outdated, drab, and cheap, can kill a curvy woman's confidence.

With Gia's big eyes watching me as she happily sucks on the bottle, my desire for a drink disappears. I can't be drinking this month. What if she wakes up in the middle of the night?

"Are you sure, Stella?" Charles looks hesitant to leave me alone with Gia.

Or does he want to be alone with me?

"You heard the woman." Jordan gives me a wry smile and leaves, sauntering in a sexy catwalk strut. God, the man is stunning with jet-black hair and brilliant green eyes.

"I'll be down in a minute, Jor." Charles gapes at his daughter in my arms.

When we're alone, I ask, "Where is Gia's mother?" I'm dying to know where this baby came from.

"Barrow, Alaska. Photo shoot." He paces the room, checking out the furniture. "It's Midnight Sun now. Supposedly, there's a glow photographers love."

"I bet you miss her," I say, hiding regret in my voice because my first crush never noticed *me*.

"Who?"

"Giana's mother." I glance at his hand, sans ring.

Charles lowers his head. "I'm not dating Ana. I didn't know Gia existed until last week."

This news utterly shocks me. I have too many questions, but I want to get Gia fed so I can raid that refrigerator downstairs.

Looking at frazzled Charles, I realize he needs someone strong right now because his life is probably spiraling before his eyes. "Is there food in the refrigerator?"

He takes out his phone. "Let me check."

"I think I saw your house manager leave."

Laughing, he shows me his screen. "No. The fridge has a camera. It's hooked up to the WiFi." Where the hell am I? "Looks pretty well stocked."

"Can I see the freezer?" I ask, hoping there's some pizza.

"Not hooked up. It's a separate freezer, but I'm sure that's stocked too." He glances out the window.

"Go out with your friends, Charles. I got this." I squeeze his arm and his jaw jumps.

His conflicted eyes glaze over. "Can you give me a two-minute summary of why you're here? How do you have a free month to take care of a baby?"

Checking the bottle, I'm glad I don't have to look at Charles because it's so damn hard. He's breathtaking and I'm too old to have these irrational feelings for him. I'm an adult and we can do something about it. Which is utterly wrong, but just thinking of taboo kisses from my stepbrother sends throngs of pulses to my clit.

"I'm launching my own clothing line. Your mom loaned me money to get started, but I need a serious investment to cover me for a few years. I'll be taken more seriously if I'm not backed solely with family money. I found an investor, but then I heard him saying he thinks the clothes are ugly and really just wanted a stake in my plus-size line for publicity purposes. So I turned him down."

"Jesus," Charles mutters. "I didn't even know you

44

were a designer. Good for you. Principles are in short supply these days." There was a lot he didn't know, but I don't hold it against him. We were never close. Yet, something feels electric between us all of a sudden. "Jordan *is* a lawyer. Talk to him. Maybe you have some kind of case against this guy. Slander, or something. If he can't help you, he'll find someone who can."

"Thank you. It's a little sensitive." I take a breath. "I was sleeping with the jerk." I don't name James Pace because I'm already embarrassed enough. The guy's a playboy billionaire and I bet it looks like he took advantage of me.

"Oh." Charles' body goes still as his eyes sweep over me.

"That's the gist. Since I'm in a bind, I called your mother to ask if she would consider loaning me more money to keep going while I find another investor. And, well, she pounced."

He barks a sexy laugh. "She's good at that."

"I'm glad she did. I literally had nowhere to go." I choke up and hide my eyes welling with tears as it all hits me at once. How close I came to being homeless.

"Stella, I'm sorry." He crouches in front of me. "But you always have a place to go now, all right? I'm telling you, right now, you come to me when you need something, especially money. My mother should have paid for your school. You're not paying her back another dime. You hear me?"

"My dad's care is expensive," I say softly, justifying his mother's reasons.

"She's got plenty of money. We use the same accountant. I'm the beneficiary of everything. I get statements."

I hadn't thought about Katherine's estate. Isn't my dad supposed to get something? Even if he is incapacitated. Then again, we didn't have any money when he married Katherine. But he worked for twelve years on movies. Where did *that* money go? Not to me.

"I'll figure something out when the month is over." I notice Gia looks sleepy, so I lift her up and begin patting her tiny back, waiting for a burp.

Charles stares at his daughter with a smile. "We usually get a little crazy here each year, but obviously, that's not happening this month. Plus, I have a deal to put together. A big one."

"What's the hold up?" Alex waltzes into the nursery.

"Go. We're fine here, Charles. Seriously. She looks ready to pass out. I'm gonna raid your refrigerator and probably take a swim. If I didn't come here today, I'd be sleeping on my assistant's sofa or in my car." I glance around, blinking. "I'd rather be here."

It takes a moment to realize how brightly I'm smiling from holding Gia who smells like lavender.

Charles smiles back and crosses the room to me and Gia. He plants a gentle kiss on his daughter's forehead. She smiles and coos, and my heart punches through my chest. I'm about to turn away, when Charles gently grips my arm and... Kisses my forehead too. "Thank you," he whispers all breathily. "I'll see you, later." He puts a hand on my shoulder and I feel him stiffen.

Glancing down, I see the swell of my boobs and I'm guessing Charles caught a peek as well. It stopped him in his tracks. What the hell?

Charles and Alex jog down the circular wooden staircase. From the window, I see Jordan leaning against his vintage cruiser.

He looks up like he knew I was checking him out. His stare captures me and I can't move. He grins at me. But it's not a friendly grin. It's...predatory.

I'm coming for you...

I shiver and wonder what is happening to me. I have irrational and disturbing sexual feelings for my stepbrother *and* both his wicked friends who I just met. I wonder if it's because I've not had an orgasm from sex in years.

I faked them all with James. Somehow my body knew better than I did.

"I hope you're a good sleeper, Gia, because I'll be using my vibrator to help *me* sleep." After I put a fresh diaper on her, I give her another kiss, loving the smell of her skin and the feel of her smooth cheeks.

Holding her with one hand, I open a drawer to hunt down a clean onesie, but an empty drawer stares back at me. Checking the next, my heart starts to pound. They're all empty. My free hand opens the triple-louver closet doors filled with shopping bags.

"I know what I'm doing tomorrow." I close the door with an exhale and dress Gia in a spare onesie from the diaper bag. The crazy-soft fabric feels like heaven against my skin and her eyes are already closed as I snap the last snap.

On a table next to the crib is a baby monitor, which I turn on, and scoop up the handheld radio.

Before closing the door, I check the outgoing volume so I know how to turn it down for when I use my vibrator later.

six

ALEX

I get us a high-top table in the bar area at the best Mexican food restaurant in all of Southern California. What should feel like electricity through my veins is a dull hum. Something's not right with me. I've felt off for months. Six to be exact.

My eyes flutter as I hate to conclude it's because Pierce stopped fucking me. What we had ran its course. I've been with a dozen or so women since then, but I always left them feeling unsatisfied.

I made it clear to Pierce, I don't do long-term relationships. With guys or women. I certainly don't want to be in a relationship with three people. It's hard enough keeping one person happy.

Jordan and Charles strut in a few minutes later. They stayed in the car to take a business call.

"Did you order a round yet?" Jordan asks with his million-dollar smile.

"Not yet."

"You guys drink, I'll drive back," Charles says, smoothing a hand down the tight black tee-shirt he changed into before we left. "I have to be sharp for Gia."

"You have a nanny," I remind him.

Charles looks up from his phone. "She's not staying the whole month."

"Why not?" Jordan asks sharply, giving away his immediate attachment to her.

I knew it. He's gonna try to make her his Sub.

"Did I hear her right? She's in financial trouble and needs a place to stay?" I say, signaling for the waitress.

"I'll get the full story tomorrow. I'll give her money to get a place of her own and whatever else she needs to get by. She's my sister."

"Stepsister," Jordan corrects him sardonically. "And even that seems in name only."

"How much older than her are you?" I ask Charles.

He shrugs. "Thirteen years, I think. I feel like a piece of garbage how she means nothing to me. I was in Harvard when my mother married her father. She was just a kid. And when I came home, she...stayed away from me."

"Then you won't object to me finding out if she's interested in some Sub training." Jordan gets right to business.

Charles doesn't respond, only narrows his eyes. He opens his mouth to speak, but stops when the waitress shows up in a red tube top and cut-off white shorts. She's got a perfect body.

And nothing stirs in me. *Again.*

Damn, what is wrong with me? I got more excited watching Stella with the baby.

The waitress stares at me so I give her our drink order. "We'll do three large margaritas with extra shots on the side."

"One *small* margarita and no extra shot for me," Charles interrupts. "I'm driving."

"Chips, guac, and salsa to start for the table." I keep going because she keeps looking at me. "Then for me, I'll do the taco trio, all fish. Black beans and plain rice."

"Barbacoa platter for me." Charles raises his hand.

Jordan studies the menu even though we've eaten here dozens of times and it's a one-pager.

"I'll get your drinks and your chips." The waitress looks anxious and leaves.

I take the menu from him. "Just get the chicken tacos, and we can swap."

"What are we, a couple?" Jordan mocks me.

"Considering you usually steal one of mine and then eye my mouth as I'm eating the other one…" I trail off when he turns white.

The waitress returns with our drinks and before she even puts them down, Jordan barks, "Steak burrito."

I don't eat red meat, so he's ordering that to piss me off.

She leaves and I dig a chip into the fresh guac. "Why are you on your phone, Charles? Checking your security feed? Spying on the nanny?"

"She's not a *nanny*," he snaps and puts his phone away. "She's…helping me. She's a fashion designer."

"That's cool." Jordan sips his drink. A few dashes of pink Himalayan rock salt stay on his upper lip until he licks them away with a sweeping tongue.

I'm fucking mesmerized and horrified at the same time. He's one of my best friends. And straight. He bangs just as many women as Charles, before Gia landed on his doorstep. The guy was going for a record with a different chick every night.

"Any word from Ana, Charles?" I ask.

"No." He brushes a hand over his face looking like he hasn't had a good night's sleep in a week.

"She *is* coming back, right?" Jordan asks.

"She said." Charles goes pale and utters, "What if she doesn't?"

"Then you have a beautiful daughter all to yourself."
I raise my glass.

Smiling, he clinks it. "Damn right."

"Are you gonna do a paternity test?" Jordan can't
help himself.

"I considered it. Then I figured out the time Ana
probably conceived. We were in Hawaii. Gia has to be
mine."

Jordan nods, the straw resting lazily on the side of
his mouth. "If you're sure."

"Stop it," Charles barks. "Look, we have to finish
the Tyler Pace proposal this month. We have mountains
of venue contracts to go through."

"It sounds like you *need* a nanny," I say again.

"Alex is right." Jordan squeezes my shoulder. "Did
you really think we'd just hunker down like *Three Men
and a Baby* this month and fumble through diaper
changes and bottle-making while putting together our
final bid?"

"She's an easy baby, Jordan. Sucks down formula
every few hours and then sleeps most of the day. I
thought we'd take turns." Charles shakes his head,
looking annoyed. "I guess I was fucking wrong."

Jordan blushes. "I'm sorry. I was shocked to hear the
whole baby-on-your-doorstep news too."

"So shocked that you took one concerned breath
while fucking your latest Sub into oblivion?"

"She ghosted me," Jordan says bitterly. "A few days
ago."

"Sorry to hear that." This shocks me. I knew he'd
end whatever contract he had with a woman before our
vacation. I just never imagined a woman would walk
out on him.

Charles probably didn't know this either because his head's been up his ass for a week. "Fine… Stella stays. I'll figure out what she needs to get back on her feet and help her."

"Fashion designer, huh?" I rub my chin. "Maybe you can hire her as a stylist? Make that a new tour package option."

Charles nods. "That's a great idea, but she wants to sell her own clothes. Not dress people in someone else's. She's designing a plus-size line."

Silence lingers in the air as we look at each other, wondering who will say the obvious. It's L.A., and body image here is cut-throat. Neither of us can deny how friendly she is and sweet with the baby. That makes her beautiful to me, considering the heartless souls we come across on a day to day.

"Cool on the fashion goals," I say, remembering what she wore and how she carried herself so nicely.

Beautifully, really. My groin throbs and I look down to see a chubby pressing against my zipper. *Really?*

"I hear it's a big market," Jordan says wryly, and I'm surprised it took him this long.

"*Watch* it," Charles warns with more bite in his tone than I've heard in a while.

"Poor choice of words," Jordan backtracks and sips his drink, blushing. "I mean, it's a strong niche. Good for her. And it's good she's plus-size too. It gives her credibility in the market. Customers will want to look as good as her."

"Nice save." I smirk at him and face Charles. "How close are you to landing the deal with Tyler Pace?" It's also to take the attention off Jordan. I feel protective of him for some reason.

"Close. I think." Charles dips his chip in the salsa. "Other promoters backed out because they don't think rock sells out stadiums anymore. That's our specialty."

"That and Tyler's brother is an asshole," Jordan rejoins the conversation. "He's listed as the primary financier."

"Who's his brother?" I ask, wondering if I heard of him, although finance and venture capitalism isn't my jam.

"*James* Pace," Charles answers and finishes the guac on us.

seven

CHARLES

Our meals come and for the first time in a week, I'm not wrecked with worry over Gia. I take a bite of my dinner without wanting to heave the whole thing back up. When the lightheadedness from being so hungry passes, I open my mouth to speak, but look at Alex, who's staring at me. "What?"

"What *are* we gonna do this month?" His plate of tacos is licked clean. "You know, for fun. We're usually balls-deep in women by now."

By now means the first night.

"Or someone's cock is balls-deep in you," Jordan adds, directing his comment to Alex.

Alex has been sleeping with guys since college. A kink he confessed one night when I caught him and a guy coming out of a bathroom stall. I thought he would come out as gay. Which didn't bother me. He said it's just something he craves once in a while. And considering how cut the guy is, he gets his fill of pretty good-looking men.

But Alex still bangs as many women as he can. "Are you offering to satisfy me since it's clear you and the CEO over here have a different focus this month?"

Jordan's right cheek twitches, but he doesn't say no. I grip the end of the table thinking he might say yes.

"Another round?" the waitress interrupts and shamelessly brushes her tits against Jordan's shoulder.

Why she goes for him out of the three of us, I'm not

sure. But I'm silently glad. As much as my body is screaming for release, the idea of taking someone to bed right now doesn't get me hard.

Tired. I'm just tired.

My body responded to Stella in a way I wasn't expecting. And that makes me feel like a sick fuck because she's my stepsister. And now my nanny. Only, Christ, that makes my cock throb harder. The double-dose off-limits, taboo nature of our new relationship has me thinking of nasty shit I shouldn't be entertaining.

Jordan smiles at the waitress. She's cute and young with shoulder-length brown hair. When she leaves, he's off his chair and next, his hand is on her ass as they head to the bathroom.

Alex lowers his head and mutters, "Asshole."

"Hey, listen to me. You do what you need to do this month." I'm suddenly glad I have Stella. Clearly, my friends aren't thrilled to have a baby around.

Alex flashes me a knowing grin. "Looks like we're stuck here for a while. Jordan keeps his car keys in his pants. You know that fucker can go for hours."

Yes, I know that because we usually share women. The guy's well over six-foot tall with a monster cock to match. When we double-penetrate a woman, I can feel that gigantic dick rubbing against mine.

My heart pounds at the image of Stella sandwiched between me and either Alex or Jordan. I get so hard, I'm nearly dizzy. "I doubt the waitress has *hours* to take a break." I finish my water, realizing I'm stone-cold sober, and dying to come.

Surprisingly, Jordan returns to the table without a hair out of place. He fucks women so hard they grab onto his thick black hair like it's a handle.

"Did she turn you down?" Alex asks in disbelief.

Not meeting anyone's eyes while counting the cash we left as a tip for the third time, he says, "Yeah. Let's go with that."

"Shit, did you get rough with her?" I grab him by the shirt collar. "I don't need that heat right now, Jordan. Keep it in your pants unless a woman is spread out for you and dripping, *verbally* begging to be fucked."

"She was begging, all right," he bitterly responds. "I couldn't…"

"What?" Alex's jaw drops.

"Fuck you. I'm forty. It happens. Grow up." He kicks his stool and storms off toward the door.

Wow, Alex mouths and follows him out.

*

Back at the house, Jordan doesn't say goodnight, just grabs a bottle of Grey Goose and disappears outside. I grunt, hoping he doesn't get drunk and drown in my pool.

As if Alex reads my mind, he heads that way too. "I'll look out for him."

That leaves me alone in my house. It feels so eerily unfamiliar. I associated this place with hard drinking and hard fucking for years. Now I have a baby upstairs and a woman sleeping in a bed that's not mine. Well, it's mine… Technically. Not the same thing.

Next, I'm climbing the stairs to check on Gia. Her room is quiet with a gentle glow from a nightlight on one wall. The smell is all powder and lilacs from an air freshener plugged in somewhere. I spent plenty of nights staring into her crib in my penthouse, feeling the weight of being a father.

Something I didn't have. My dad refused to marry

my mother when my grandfather laid an unfair pre-nup on him to sign. Dad took a settlement to go away instead and we never heard from him again.

By the time Mom married Stella's dad, my grandfather had passed, leaving my mother as the sole heir and free to live how she wanted. From what I saw, she loved Griffin. Until he got hurt and became a liability.

All those thoughts empty out of my head when I see Gia sleeping peacefully in her crib. With the moonlight pouring into the room, she looks angelic. Her chest, rising and falling with her little mouth is tipped open. Babies really are a miracle. This is a life I created and I'm responsible for her until…

My last breath.

Jesus, that would sober me up if I were drunk. I really need to hit the liquor cabinet. I can pass out without worrying Gia might cry out in the middle of the night.

That thought is quickly wiped away when I realize Stella isn't here to work 24/7. She's not Gia's mother. Christ, where is Ana? What the hell happened there? That thought has too many thorns to grasp and sting so I reach down to snag the baby monitor to find just one sitting in the cradle. Stella must have taken one with her to bed. Relieved, I figure one night I can relinquish control, but I notice Stella grabbed the wrong monitor.

An easy mistake. I scoop up the correct one and stalk quietly down the hall.

At her door, I listen and don't hear a sound. My hand closes around the knob and even though I know I shouldn't do what I'm about to, I open the door. I'm a father right now and I need that other monitor. I'll check that she's asleep, quietly walk in, and take it. What I hear stops me in my tracks.

Buzzing.

Moaning.

I release the door and step back. The thick carpet cushions my movement and blocks out the noise. Only, the monitor in my hand crackles to life after being activated by the sound of Stella's voice on the other end.

Uh oh...

I walk backward until I reach my room and close the door. With my forehead leaning on the back of it, I grip the monitor, telling myself to shut it off. I'm not sure my heart can take listening to what's going on in that room. In that bed.

Is she naked? I could go complete stalker creepy and check the security monitor in her bedroom. My hesitation to do that is a welcome relief that I haven't completely lost my mind.

Stella whimpers and the sound is so incredibly captivating, I don't need to see what's going on. I'd rather picture her in my mind.

See her the way I want to see her. With her gorgeous creamy thighs wide open for me as I slide right into her pussy.

"Oh yes, right there," Stella mewls.

My cock is painfully hard and I picture her beneath me. What the hell is wrong with me? I should turn this off right now. But I can't. I also can't stop my hand from reaching into my jeans. I'm not in my right mind at the moment with all kinds of impure thoughts firing through me.

Next, they're down around my thighs and I'm

pumping my cock to the sound of Stella fucking some imaginary man in her head. Her ex?

"Oh, dirty girl," I say into the monitor even though she can't hear. At least I fucking hope she can't hear me. "Who's making you so wet right now?"

"Mmmm. Yeah. Yeah. God, this is so good." She's yelping now. "Don't stop."

"Not in a million years," I whisper, pumping my cock. It's harder and bigger than I remember in a long time. Christ, I can barely get my hand around the thing. What the hell is happening to me?

"Charles," Stella whines, and I stop mid-stroke.

"What?"

"Right there, Charles. Lick me right there."

Me... She's picturing *me*. Oh, Christ... I'm on an edge like I've never known, a fire crawling up my spine.

"I'll lick you, dirty girl." I picture my tongue laving her pussy. "I love how you taste. So fucking sweet." I'm sprawled out on my bed, my hips gyrating while I fuck my hand.

"Charles, I'm coming," Stella moans.

I fall over the edge too and I get dizzy. My breath strangles from my lungs the way my climax strikes me with such voracity. Next, my hand is full of my cum. It's hot and thick with ropes of it sliding down the side. I've not come this hard in... Christ, maybe forever.

"Oh shit," Stella says, her voice completely different. All headiness is gone.

I look up, afraid she's standing in my doorway, staring at the mess I made of myself.

No, but I do hear footsteps. I wipe my hands on a towel I tossed on the floor before we went out and pull up my pants. Perhaps she heard Gia. My brain's gone completely off the rails at this point.

I step into the hall to see Gia's door open and hike that way.

Inside, Stella's wearing just a tee-shirt that drapes lazily off one shoulder. And nothing else. Nothing. Else. Her blonde hair is piled on her head in a messy bun.

In the days when I spent the night with a woman, I loved that look, versus perfect makeup and hair. When a woman looked like Stella, it meant I fucked her good.

"Shoot," she says, looking at the empty monitor cradle.

I stalk up behind her. "Looking for this?" The words come out of my mouth in a gritty tenor.

She whips around and I place a hand over her mouth so she doesn't shriek.

"Shhh. It's okay. It's just me." I drop my hand, but stay close to her.

Breathing heavily, she takes me in, her eyes looking different from earlier. "I grabbed the wrong monitor." It's clutched in her hand.

The correct one is clutched in mine so I show it to her and wait for the realization to spread over her face. Her eyes tell me everything, but we say nothing.

I speak after a beat of unbearable silence, controlling my breath. "I'll keep the monitor in my room at night. You don't work 24/7, Stella." Saying her names spikes my heartrate.

"Um, okay." She steps back, and stumbles, but I catch her. Christ, she's so soft. Her skin feels like velvet.

"You okay?" I keep our lips almost touching because

her sweet smell is fucking with my brain.

"Yeah." She doesn't move and our faces are so close, I smell peppermint mouthwash.

"Stella," I say her name again on a strained moan and hear the words *get in my fucking bed* come off my lips.

"Yeah?"

Gia stirs and releases a little cackle. We both look down, but my daughter is still asleep.

Stella pushes a hand through what's fallen out of her bun. Then pulls the tie completely out, her hair spilling in gorgeous waves across her shoulders. "By the way, none of her clothes were unpacked. They're in the closet. I'll unwrap everything tomorrow." She steps away and adorably tugs down the tee-shirt.

"I'll help you," flies from my mouth even though I know I have tons of work to do with this proposal.

She's bathed in moonbeams from a skylight above when she turns to me. "Okay. Good night, Charles."

My head spins, hearing her say my name in the same tenor as when she made herself come a few moments ago. Like it's sitting in her brain. This night will stay in mine for a long time.

God, I'm in so much trouble.

eight

ALEX

The door to the pool house is open and I find Jordan pulling open drawers in the guest room's dresser looking for the extra swim trunks Charles leaves in here.

Did he really not get it up with that gorgeous waitress? And why didn't I jump in to satisfy her either? Literally and figuratively. I love pussy. But I've never been *in* love and don't want to be.

I need to get laid. One way or another. I waited for this month thinking I could just keep my dick deep in pussy. Ironically, that got blown spectacularly out of the water because Charles fucked the shit out of a woman in Hawaii for a week straight and now has a baby as a result.

Jordan turns around and I'm standing there gawking at his ass. "What?"

"I was going to sleep here." I point to my luggage in the corner. "You're in my room."

He wipes his mouth. "Shit, sorry." With the gait of a panther, he saunters toward me. "Do you think she's asleep?"

"Who?" I lift my suitcase onto the bed and start to unpack.

"Stella."

I exhale. "Go in the house and find out."

He shakes his head. "I'm afraid of what I'll see."

"What do you mean?"

"Are you blind?"

"Jordan, just fucking spit it out." I storm into the open kitchen and yank out the filtered water pitcher I filled before we left for dinner. I drink around 100 ounces of water a day.

"Charles wants to fuck her."

"I didn't see that at all." I gulp at least ten ounces and then add, "I know you want to."

"I don't want to just fuck her. I want to train her. Stella seems pretty ripe to learn submissiveness." He licks his lips.

A thought hits me. We've brought women here to the beach house before and took turns with them. It's one of the hottest things we do here. We can each fuck anyone we want all year long. This vacation is about debauchery. So why not…share Stella?

But I'm not sure I should suggest that. She's not a woman we'll wave goodbye to in the morning as the sun rises over the mountains. Stella is staying here for the month, even if Charles doesn't think so. To sleep with her, we'd have to…commit to her in some way. Something none of us are interested in.

Having a baby here changes everything about this vacation. Maybe we have to change too. It would be great to have a gorgeous woman around to just lay out and fuck anytime we want.

"Feel Stella out, see if she's up for some fun." I drink more water and refill the pitcher. "Just give her a day or two to adjust for fuck's sake."

Putting the pitcher back in the fridge, I catch Jordan sporting wood. I'm guessing it's because he's thinking of Stella.

"Yeah." Jordan hikes to the closet next to the

bathroom and yanks out a towel. "I'm gonna swim. You coming?"

Not yet.

"No. I want to get up early and do laps." I work out close to three hours a day. Four sometimes when I'm here because I have the extra time. Charles and Jordan are in great shape, but they usually sleep in.

"Okay, good night." Jordan claps me on the shoulder and heads out. A whiff of salty air from the outside is replaced by his scent.

I close the door, then go to the window, ready to draw the drapes. But my arms freeze when I see Jordan toss aside those swim trunks he wrecked my bedroom to find and step out of his shorts.

Something stirs me and I brush it off, thinking it's because I need to get laid.

Charles is messed up.

Jordan wants to train Stella.

One baby. One woman. Three men. Thirty days.

This should be interesting.

nine

STELLA

I wake up just as the dawn breaks over the mountains. The room Charles gave me is in the front of the house, no ocean view for me. It's better than a room next to the house manager behind the kitchen with a view of trash cans.

All of this hits my brain and I bolt up in bed, crystalizing where the hell I am. Pushing the covers away, I listen for the sound of a crying baby. Nothing.

I heard Charles say she sleeps all night. Slipping a short robe across my shoulders, I pad into the hallway. Closed six-panel doors keep the hallway chilly and I regret not throwing on something warmer. The short satin nightgown I put on after my run-in with Charles last night feels cold against my skin. Mostly my tits.

God, I hope he didn't hear me masturbating and calling out his name through the baby monitor. While I think it's creepy he would listen, I also find it hot as fuck. What is wrong with me?

I ease Gia's door open. The room isn't pitch black, but dark enough with a soft glow from the nightlight. As I draw closer to the crib, a delicate giggle hits my ears. Gia lies on her back and stares at the mobile. She's smiling and kicking her legs.

"Good morning, peanut." I reach in and touch her skin. Not too warm, not too cold.

Today, I'll go through all those bags and find her pajamas.

As I lift Gia into my arms, I realize my mistake. I should have gone downstairs and made a bottle first. Now that I have her in my arms, there's no way I'm mixing the bottle the way I saw Katherine do it with one hand.

Gia is also too small for a high chair.

Then the smell hits me and I feel how full her diaper is. I bring her to the changing table where Katherine set up a tower of diapers and wipes on one side. Tubes of lotions and powders sit on the other side. After removing the diaper, the powerful odor of poop makes my eyes water.

"Whoa," I say, whisking the diaper away. "You must be a chill baby to sit in this for hours."

I keep her legs in the air with one hand and gather wipes with the other. A tall garbage can sits to my left. Thanks to a foot pedal, it opens and I dump the diaper. Then I use wipe after wipe until her butt is clean.

I slide a fresh diaper on and wait to ask Charles about the lotion and powder protocol. From what I know about babies, their diapers get changed every few hours. With Gia's skin looking smooth and clear, I figure she can go a few hours with just a clean diaper.

She has her fingers in her mouth and drool on her chin, ignoring my manhandling of her. I changed a friend's baby once at this age and the kid nearly launched off the table, he was so wild. That was before he peed all over me.

I lift Gia so I can put her back in the crib and go make her breakfast, when the door opens. A tousled, shirtless Charles waltzes in wearing sweats and holding a bottle.

I swear, it's the fucking sexiest thing I've ever seen.

"Hey, I changed her," I whisper.

"Thanks, she usually wants to eat around this time." He approaches me slowly and I see him debating whether or not to just hand me the bottle or stay to feed his daughter himself.

The only thing sexier than seeing him *with* the bottle would be to watch him feed his daughter shirtless like that.

I'm used to taking charge and orchestrating the outcomes I want, so I say, "Can you feed her while I fish out another outfit from the diaper bag?"

He doesn't blink an eye and takes her from me, our bodies colliding. My skimpy baby doll nightie shows miles of cleavage. I glance down and my nipples are also hard from being chilly. And seeing Charles shirtless. Again.

He lifts Gia onto his shoulder, but his eyes are on my body. Men can't help it, I get it. Turns out, I *love* his eyes on me.

He sits in the white-brushed, wood rocking chair and coos to his daughter with a kiss on her forehead. "Morning, princess."

My chest pounds at how sweet he is with her.

I should put something else on, but fuck it. Breaking my stare at him, I take out the spare clothes in the diaper bag.

With the outfit laid out on the changing table, I open the sliding closet doors. "I'll empty these after her bottle."

Charles nods. "I told my mother to get a mat. After she's done eating and all burped, I put her down on a play mat."

"Tummy time," I say softly and catch Charles

grinning. "What's her day like?" I ask with my arms crossed.

"Feed, burp, change, hang out, nap. Feed, burp, change, hang out, nap. Feed, burp—"

"I get it." I hold up my hand, stopping him with a soft laugh. "Sounds easy enough."

Taking care of a baby clearly is about routine. I make a mental note of what was in the diaper bag, and that I should replace it. Not that I think we'll be going anywhere. Infants aren't really good in public.

I wonder if Charles and his friends *could* have taken care of Gia alone. But I don't voice that because I need the money and a place to live.

Glancing around the room, I say, "I'll have the nursery all put together today."

"Thank you, Stella." He's got Gia on his shoulder again and he's rubbing her back followed by targeted pats.

One, two, three, and Gia burps.

"How much do you need to get your line in production?" he asks.

I hesitate to answer even though I recall the madness of yesterday and him saying he would help me. "Basic costs to get one line produced is about fifty grand. But my investment package includes two years of growth. Hiring additional designers and the production costs for two more lines. I have a great woman working for me who really dug into the business end. I want to keep her and pay her well. She graduated with honors from FIDM too. A big designer will poach her from me." I turn around and begin organizing the bags layered in the closet.

"Stella, that can wait." Charles stands up, and to my

surprise, dresses Gia himself. "Keep talking."

"I want to stay the lead designer. I want people to see me and trust that I know how clothes feel on someone...my size." I wait to see his reaction.

"Did you design the outfit you had on yesterday?" Charles doesn't look at me, but smiles brightly at his daughter.

"I did. I wear all my own clothes."

"And what did your investor promise you again?"

"Three hundred grand," I say softly.

Right there, I know the number is irrelevant to him.

My issues don't mean much watching him having a moment with his daughter. I had a great relationship with my father both before and after my mom died. But I'd been too young to understand the sacrifice and the choices a single dad has to make, the mountains they have to move to make a child feel loved.

Charles will be a great father. Gia is lucky. That's the story I want to hear and not my own sad dilemma.

"I know a few venture capitalists and can get you in front of them." He's holding Gia again, rubbing her back. "And you're welcome to stay here as long as you need."

"Thank you so much, Charles." Those words comfort me immensely as far as staying in this gorgeous beach house.

"And you're not giving another dime to my mother," he says sharply. "Tell me what your tuition costs and I'll write you a check."

I shake my head. "That's okay. I'm good with the deal we made. And it feels like a win/win since you needed me. I appreciate she gave me the money at all."

Charles frowns. "She didn't *give* you anything if you

had to pay it back."

"Semantics." I shrug. "But thank you again. My production window with a Kansas factory closes at the end of the month. So yeah, if you can introduce me to a VC, that would be great."

"If not, I'll give you the money myself." His voice is strong, possessive.

Pushing a hand through my hair, I say, "I'd rather not be fully invested from family. It will send a signal that my line is a vanity project and I won't be taken seriously."

Nodding, Charles hands me the baby and strokes my cheek. "I love your fire and ambition. We'll make this work for you, I promise." He walks out of the room, his back muscles flexing, his round ass so visible in those damn sweats.

I put Gia in the crib so I can take a shower. My body is thrumming with lust and need. I don't know how I'm gonna make it through the month without Charles catching me masturbating and saying his name.

ten

ALEX

Sweat trickles down my cheek when I reach my sixtieth push-up. It's not the number of reps, but the sun's heat already burning my back. I sink into the wet sand, and it cools me off. I love beach workouts, but the twenty-five-minute drive it would take to reach the coast from my townhouse in Culver City during weekday traffic isn't worth it.

It's better to change up my workout routine anyway. Muscle confusion is key, something I learned from Pierce who has a degree in Kinesiology. I bite my lip, remembering those workouts we did on the beach in Santa Monica and then the ones in his apartment and shower.

Why am I struggling with the loss of that relationship when I fucked dozens and dozens of women since? Why hasn't a woman touched my soul the way he did? I've been denying that I had developed feelings for Pierce. I knew he didn't have feelings for me. Sex with guys was just a kink for him, although he committed to Cooper, so maybe it *was* me.

I snap up to my full height of around six-three and consider a swim in the ocean when my brain detects two figures jogging toward me. Nice figures. The number of beautiful women with perfect tits and bodies is nearly nauseating if I'm being honest. Like a row of gorgeous rose bushes. After the third or fourth, you start to yawn because it's all the same. I once walked in on a casting call for a director I trained and I thought I stepped into a cloning lab. How the fuck do they pick?

Glad it wasn't my job.

I love my job, actually, running a private gym and training on the side. When Charles started his own tour promotion firm and it grew to one hundred people in less than a year, he asked me to consider running the company gym. I was able to keep my top clients. Here in Los Angeles, most people use a personal trainer.

I don't recognize these women coming toward me, but I wait for my body to react. Nothing. Something is up with me. Their eyes graze my bare chest covered in tatts, but they keep jogging and I couldn't care less. Charles' house sits about two hundred feet from the shore and the steps to get up there are a workout in and of themselves.

When I reach the top and punch in the gate code, Jordan and Charles are sitting at one of the tables near the pool. They're holding mugs of coffee and by the serious looks on their faces, I wonder what the hell they're talking about.

Usually, the morning after our first night, they'd look exhausted, but smiling from all the fucking. Heck, some mornings we don't even bother putting on clothes. We get out of bed and walk around nude. This vacation couldn't be any more different. Charles is shirtless in a pair of sweats and Jordan's wearing a blue tee-shirt with tan docker shorts.

"Hey," I say to them.

"Hey, you. Where you been? I'm starving." Jordan cracks a smile at me.

I stop walking. "Am I the personal chef around here?"

Jordan puts down his mug. "What the hell is up *your* ass?"

"I think it's what's *not* up his ass," Charles snidely mutters into his coffee.

Holy shit. They really think I'm mooning over Pierce. Do my best friends know me better than I know myself? Still, I bark back, "You don't know what you're talking about."

I take a few breaths and realize I don't want to fight with them. They care about me even if they have a funny way of showing it. "How's Gia?" I ask Charles.

"Good." Nodding, he says, "Stella has her."

"Are you keeping her as a nanny?" I ask, ignoring that Jordan wants food.

"I should, right? She needs a job. A place to live."

"Did she tell you what happened with her clothing line?" Jordan asks, sitting back, the tee-shirt stretching across his pecs.

"She said she overheard her investor badmouthing her and the line."

"Badmouthing how?" Jordan snaps back up in the seat, looking very protective all of a sudden. Maybe more than Charles.

Charles makes a fist. "He called her clothes ugly and only wants to invest in her line because it's plus-size. Wanted the PR for being inclusive, I guess."

"Guy sounds like an asshole," Jordan huffs.

"She was sleeping with the asshole too." Charles picks up his mug and snarls into his coffee.

"Who was it?" Jordan keeps going.

"I didn't want to press for more details. It's not like it matters." Charles shrugs.

The conversation about Stella and her fashion line

stalls, so I start another one. "Have you heard from Ana?" I ask.

"No." Charles' face darkens. "But when she does come around, I'm definitely asking for custody. I'm not letting my daughter grow up without knowing her father."

"Then you'll need a full-time nanny," I say. "Why not throw money at Stella for that?"

"No one that young wants to be a career nanny." Jordan's probably fucked several of them and knows their hopes and dreams.

"He's right." Charles agrees with Jordan. "Once I figure out what the hell is going on with Ana, I'll make permanent arrangements for Gia to live with me and I'll get help."

"Or you can get a wife," Jordan says with a teasing grin.

Teasing because we know Charles is a confirmed bachelor.

I look up and see Stella standing there holding Gia. I'm not sure how much she heard, but I'm guessing she caught the tail end. After my eyes leave Gia, who's smiling in a blue and white striped onesie, I take in Stella. Her blonde hair glistens in the sun and the red print sundress with thin straps is low-cut. Maybe too-low cut for a trio of ravenous men who've been denied pussy.

Her curves are a welcome change. It's not just her pretty face and warm smile or holding a baby who lights up in her arms. It's that I-don't-give-a-fuck confidence she radiates. Very bold in this town. But it makes her shine and stand out, and next, my cock is stirring.

I could see myself settling down with someone like her. I've got the best shot. Charles is her stepbrother and Jordan only fucks Subs. I don't have the same hang-ups. How would she feel about me fucking men on the side?

"Morning, want breakfast?" I ask Stella, walking toward her and giving Jordan the finger behind my back.

Her eyes meet mine and something stirs inside me. Something grounded and real. Pure and true. "I was gonna see if I can get you guys something to eat."

"You're not the cook here, Stella." Charles stands and takes the baby from her.

I halt, watching them. That look she gave me is now on him and I see them having a moment.

What the fuck?

Charles smiles stupidly, holding his daughter and a teething ring. He takes a seat and when I look back at Stella, her eyes return to me. That feeling spreads through my chest again.

"Come on." I smile at her. "I usually take care of breakfast."

"Two eggs, rye toast, and cut strawberries," Jordan says, putting his feet on an empty chair while watching TikTok videos on his phone.

I don't argue or I'll look like a dick in front of Stella. I would have made us breakfast anyway. I just don't like guys ordering me around. Except in bed. Smiling at Stella, I say, "What do you want, Charles?"

"Same." He bounces Gia, who's reaching for the ring.

"After breakfast, I'd like to rearrange Gia's room. Can you guys help me?" Stella stands there with a hand on her hip.

"What's wrong with how it's set up now?" Charles swings around to look at her.

"I think her changing table should be closer to the door and the crib in front of the window. The wall unit is completely blocking the outlets. It's several pieces so I'd like to spread them apart. It will make the room look bigger."

Jordan tilts his head back. "Then we'll move it around." He tosses her a wink. "Whatever you need."

Their eyes lock and I know he's picturing her on her knees. The first step in his Sub training. He usually ends a contract before we come here for the month, and he can't resist getting dominant with whatever woman he chooses to fuck. The guy loves getting his dick sucked by a woman kneeling in front of him.

I prefer to lean across a woman and fuck her mouth. Charles just likes his dick in a pussy. The guy can go for a while, I've watched him.

I steer Stella back into the house by the waist until she walks ahead of me. Her butt moves deliciously in the dress. God, I'd love to grab it and fuck her from behind. Her pussy and then her ass.

In the kitchen, she stands there lost. In fairness, it's huge. "Willow, Charles' house manager, stocks up the food to get us started. Then we shop as needed."

"I'll take care of that, just keep a list," Stella says, staring into the refrigerator.

"Charles said you're not our maid. You're helping him with Gia."

With an expression I can't place, she says, "I'll want to get out once in a while."

"Right." I shake my head, not realizing that.

Usually, we're out every night, the three of us. Then bring women back here and have fuck-parties in the pool. That's not happening.

"How about shopping will be something you and I do together?" I watch how she reacts.

"Sure," she says casually, but her eyes linger on me.

"What?"

She blinks, and sounding almost annoyed, says, "Seriously, how do you get a stomach like that?"

I look down at my washboard abs. "If that's some kind of come on, you need to work on your delivery."

She blushes adorably. "I wouldn't dare come on to you."

"Dare?"

"Look, I like my body the way it is. I've tried losing weight. I don't know if I have a slow metabolism or something, but I have to starve myself to lose anything. I've just accepted this is who I am."

"Good for you. Your confidence is very uplifting." I move to the refrigerator and take out the 18-pack of eggs, then the jumbo container of strawberries. "I want to help people who want help. I don't judge those who don't want help."

"That's cool." She takes the strawberries. "I'll slice these."

I get her the cutting board and hand her a knife. "That doesn't explain what you meant by you wouldn't dare come on to me."

Shrugging, she says, "I have a knack for understanding human behavior. I have to know what will catch someone's eye. I have to know what makes people tick."

"I'm a trainer and I'm usually in workout clothes,

but I like getting dressed up." I begin breaking and whisking a dozen eggs in a bowl to make one large cheesy skillet. I'm not cooking four individual meals. I'll be here for an hour. "Still doesn't explain what you meant."

I want to draw out of her what she thinks of me in that regard. Even though I'm not sure why. As much as I'd like to fuck her, I know that's not a good idea. She's living here. I wouldn't fuck her then go out and fuck another woman the following night. That's just rude.

"I assume that takes a lot of work, abs like that." She waves the knife at me. "A real commitment. It's not just doing a few sit-ups. It's diet too, right?"

"Most of general fitness is diet. Bodybuilding is equal diet *and* weight training. And by diet, I don't mean starving yourself. It means eating certain foods in certain quantities at certain times of the day. So yeah, it's a commitment."

"So why would *you* want someone who doesn't have that same commitment? Don't you see people who just want to sleep in and grab a donut for breakfast as lazy?"

I laugh. "Hey, I love donuts. I don't fault anyone for one donut. A dozen a day maybe. Too much sugar and fatty foods are just bad for your health. That's not judgment, that's medical science."

"That's very cool of you."

"I think I'm an open-minded guy." I remember the comment about the boyfriend pretending to be supportive. After I put the eggs on the stove, I turn to her and say, "Touch me."

"What?"

Getting closer, I say with a playful drawl, "Touch me."

"I don't think I should." She's adorably coy.

"Why not?"

Slicing the strawberries, she mumbles, "I may not want to stop."

"So?"

She exhales. "Fine."

"Put down the knife first please."

She drops it on the cutting board, and next, her hands are on me. It's a delicate touch that starts just under my pecs. Immediately, my blood starts to move under my skin faster. "You're so warm."

"All this muscle keeps my body temperature up."

"And smooth." Her fingers follow the grooves in my abs, stopping in between. I'm sensitive as fuck there and growing painfully hard. "Do you wax?"

"Usually for this vacation."

Not looking at me, her hands explore further. "I know you guys go wild here this month. I follow Charles on Instagram."

"He posts what goes on here?"

"He's a playboy with an image to protect."

Christ, I have to go check his profile to see if there are any lewd photos of me. "He sure is a playboy." I say this with evil intent because I don't want her with him. But I see the looks they give each other. Forbidden lust between step-siblings is powerful.

My earlier caution crashes back into me. I can't fuck her unless I plan to fuck only her for a month. My cock twitches at the image of having this beautiful lush female in my bed every night in the pool house. God, what a good move that was. I can take her all night long. Even though I like my best friends watching me. Hearing me. I'm pretty vocal.

Stella's hands inch lower and I bite my tongue to keep from telling her if she wants to touch my cock, she can. I have no idea what her plans are after this month. Ana *will* pick Gia up. What mother abandons a baby? Charles will no longer need a full-time nanny. I doubt he'll get full custody. I also doubt Stella will give up her fashion design dream to be a nanny.

My mind wanders back to Pierce who committed to both a woman *and* a guy. He's never looked happier or more satisfied.

Then again, he shares his woman with *two* other men. One of whom he's fucking. That sounds like a recipe for disaster.

Or it could be total heaven…

eleven

CHARLES

Rage soars through me, seeing Stella fondle Alex's show-off abs in my kitchen. Only, I'm not sure why. What's happening to me? We share women all the time and I love it.

This is different. She's my... *Sister* comes to mind, but that reeks of phony, convenient hesitation. On one hand, she means nothing to me. Hasn't meant anything to me forever. She's my mother's husband's daughter who I've never lived with and barely know. I'm also ridiculously older than her. Which means I should know better.

But something about her has me on an edge I can't explain.

"Ahem," I clear my throat and watch Stella jump back.

She blushes when she faces me. "Hey. Gia all right?"

"Yeah." I give the baby a bounce in my arms. "I have some work to do in my office, I can put her down on the mat in there, or you can take her."

"Work?" Alex protests, shaking the skillet in the center of my stove.

The sizzling noise and that sudden smell of cooked eggs reminds me how starving I am. "I told you, we have that proposal to submit."

"Proposal for what?" Stella looks up from slicing strawberries and I worry she'll cut herself.

"A tour deal." I don't name-drop Tyler Pace because

81

we signed all kinds of non-disclosures.

When Stella drops the strawberries into a glass bowl and lingers to stare at Alex again, I pull a dick move. "Stella, can you change Gia upstairs?"

Alex picks up on the tone of my voice and shakes his head. "She's helping me. And we were talking before you came in here."

"She filled up her diaper already?" Stella glides smoothly toward me, her eyes on Gia out of concern, and I feel like an asshole.

"I think so."

"We're eating in a minute." Alex pops slices of rye bread in the toaster oven, and then from the pantry, takes out a fresh jar of locally made jam because the guy thinks butter is evil.

"I'll be down with her in a minute." Stella scoops Gia out of my arms with a smile. "Did you do potty already?"

The way she sweet talks my baby kicks me in the gut. She'll make a great mother someday. Gia's smiling face in Stella's arms makes me unsteady on my feet. I doubt Ana *won't* come back for her daughter, but I plan to be part of my child's life. I don't want to be an absent father. No way.

Coparenting means this may be the official end of our summer fuck-fest. For some reason, relief washes over me thinking that. Gia's just an infant, and it would be great to give her a childhood filled with memories of summers at daddy's beach house each year.

Without all the fucking that goes on.

Alex is plating the eggs across four dishes when he looks up at me. "Don't say it."

"Say what?" I cross my arms, realizing I'm just as

bare-chested and broad as Alex, yet Stella hadn't asked to touch me. Jealousy burns through me and I hate that. I don't want to feel that way with my best friend. We share…everything.

Shit. Would I share Stella with him? Would she be up for that?

"You're gonna tell me to stay away from Stella."

"We should all stay away from her. She's working for me. She's not a fuck toy."

"Who's not a fuck toy and where are my eggs?" Jordan saunters in.

"He's telling me to stay away from Stella." Alex garnishes the plates with a few strawberries and then turns around to pull the toast slices out.

"Are you saying that as her boss because you want to fuck her yourself, or because she's your stepsister?" Jordan bites a piece of toast and rolls his eyes because it doesn't have any butter on it. "*And* you want to fuck her?"

"Can you keep your voice down? This place has cathedral ceilings and sound travels, asshole." I pull a plate toward me. Damn, it smells good. Alex cooks food just the way I like it.

He pushes a jar of apricot jam at me knowing I like that too. "You didn't answer his question."

"Both." I stab at the eggs, wondering if he'll throw that frying pan at me if I asked for ketchup.

"Both, you're the boss and you want to fuck her, or both, you're her stepbrother and want to fuck her?" Jordan the lawyer cross-examines me.

Alex chuckles and bites into his eggs. "Good leading question, counselor. Now he has to admit he wants to fuck her."

It would be useless to spend all month denying how I feel when surely every action and sentence from my mouth will prove otherwise. "So what if I want to fuck her? I'm not going to. And neither will either of you." What should be curses thrown at me, is silence. I look up and see jaws dropped. "What?"

"Damn, I didn't think you'd fold and admit that so easily." Alex shakes his head and keeps eating.

"I need to get laid this month," Jordan announces. "Either I'm leaving so I can be near my club every night and find a new Sub, or I bring home beach bunnies and fuck them in the pool."

"Good Christ," I mutter.

"Or you let me train Stella." Jordan makes a sandwich out of the eggs and the rye toast then dunks the whole thing into a glob of jam. "I'll share her with you. Both of you. I love watching my Subs suck dick while I fuck their asses."

I just hope Stella doesn't hear this and packs her bags.

Alex smiles wickedly. "This I want to watch."

"Just give me a few days to test her out. See how…compliant she is." Jordan speaks like he's trying out a new workout band at the gym. "It's all about consent."

I roll my eyes, staring at my plate.

"It's been less than twenty-four hours, but she seems very feisty. Hard to break." Jordan breaks women pretty well.

"What if she doesn't want any of this?" I ask.

"The way she touched me just now…" Alex nods confidently. "She wants me at least. And probably for just a fling. Which is great."

"Then you'll go back to pining over Pierce?" Jordan needles him.

"Fuck you." Alex throws a piece of toast he never would have eaten because the guy also thinks carbs come from the devil.

With my world upside down because of this project and Gia dropped in my lap, I realize my best friend has been going through something. I've never seen him upset over a woman and thought his guy-fucking was just a kink. I suddenly feel like shit.

"Jordan, lay off. Alex, what's up?" I turn to him. "Do you want to talk about this thing with Pierce?"

His face reddens and his jaw quivers like he's ready to lay some heavy shit on me. But a scent of mint and gardenias floats past me. I see through Alex's eyes, Stella has returned with Gia.

"No," he abruptly says and takes off into the yard.

twelve

JORDAN

After breakfast, we head upstairs to rearrange Gia's nursery. Charles and I move the crib, while Alex, who's technically the strongest, pushes the wall units apart to expose the outlets.

After Stella puts Gia in a bouncy seat, she digs several bags of clothes out of the closet. I can see she's an overachiever by the way she brings all of them out at once.

"Let me help you there." I take a few bags from her and when our skin touches, it's electric.

Fuck me. I don't want to feel anything like this. Then I'll make stupid decisions.

"I think Gia will grow out of much of this before she gets to wear any of it." Her eyes lift to mine and she gasps, finally taking me in.

"Katherine goes overboard," I say, sifting through the clothes in her arms.

Stella scoffs, "Not with me. I got the opposite from her."

Charles goes still.

"Shit, Charles, I'm sorry." She inhales sharply. "Your mom wanted my dad and not me. At least that's how she made me feel."

He shakes his head like he's trying to process that, but the guy's a mess right now. His heart is being picked apart by Gia even if he doesn't know it, leaving him vulnerable to falling in love. The interest in Stella he confessed to earlier isn't surprising.

My heart dancing in my chest all of a sudden *is* surprising. Along with a dose of protectiveness that isn't like my usual possessive nature. Hearing how Katherine mistreated Stella infuriates me.

Stella drops to the carpet and makes piles of clothes while Charles and Alex check out her ass. I resist an eye roll, imagining them trying to charm her in a house where she knows if she wasn't here, they'd be boning women on the dining room table.

I watch her carefully for signs that she'd be open to Sub training. Even if it's just for fun. For the month we're here.

The usual way I assess whether or not a woman would be a great Sub is to simply tell her to get on her knees and suck my cock. Of course, that won't work with Stella taking care of a baby. Only, I've relied on my blunt-force Dom commands for so long, I don't think I can be charming anymore.

Charles kneels in front of Gia, playing 'got your nose' and I catch Stella looking at him like she wants to cry.

Alex yanks tags out of all the drawers and next, *those two* are staring at each other. When Stella goes to stand, Alex is there helping her and I feel their connection.

I agree with Charles' assessment, she probably only *wants* Alex right now. He's fucking handsome as hell with a body that even makes me stare. I wonder who he'll start fucking to satisfy that kink. Or, shit… If it was more than that, he might go and get a boyfriend. Explore that side of himself further.

Good for him, only…

Fuck, that makes me jealous as hell and I don't understand where those feelings are coming from. I've never been with a guy. Never had an interest. I'm not against it in any way. My best friend sucks dick, how could I be? Plus, there are a few masters at the club with adorable twink Subs.

I can't breathe all of a sudden and I'm not sure who or what I'm jealous of. How the simple act of extending Alex's hand to help her might land her in his bed tonight.

Next, she's putting clothes in the drawers as Alex holds them so she doesn't have to bend down. Which also means he's an idiot. Okay, chivalry is more effective sometimes.

But so is good sex, damn it. When I go down on a Sub and make her come, I get her addicted to it so she'll beg for more. Crawl on the floor for it. Subs don't do that *just* because they want to be good Subs. They want my dick to make them mindless. If I get a Sub into that zone, she won't even pee unless I tell her to.

With a baby in the house and my best friends hovering though, I'm not sure who or what to be.

An overwhelming desire to get in my car and leave has my hands itching for my keys.

Charles breaks the awkward silence we're all working through. "How *is* your dad, Stella?"

She bites her lip, accentuating how lush and full the lower one is. "I haven't been there recently, to be honest." Her long neck turns a delightful shade of pink, the color I want to see on her ass when I spank it. "Maybe in a day or two I'll take a ride down there. I'll bring Gia, if you're okay with that."

"Sure."

"I'll go with you," Alex says and smirks at me.

I narrow my eyes at him and stand up holding several pairs of tiny yellow socks. "Do you want these and the onesies in that changing station?"

It has drawers on the side and I recall from my sister's kids, she keeps socks, undershirts, and pajamas in the changing station.

"That sounds like a good idea." Stella strolls toward me.

I catch Alex as well. They're both in my frame of vision and my brain is having trouble focusing, like I want…

Like I want them both.

And not in the usual way Alex and I share a woman.

No… It would be Stella and me sharing.

Alex.

I'm hard and holy fucking shit…

We put the clothes away except for a rascally pair of yellow socks that may or may not have accidentally fallen from my hands. Stella bends down to retrieve them, but when she goes to stand up, I'm hovering over her.

"Hang on, Stella." As if my words and my stare signal her brain that pleasure is the reward, she freezes. "Lean back." I gently push her butt down till it hits the back of her heels. "Just like that," I whisper. When she tries to look at me, I say, "No. Not until I tell you."

With her eyes lowered, I glance at Charles and Alex. The gobsmacked expressions on their faces are priceless. Alex stares from her to me, that same look of confusion coursing through me a few minutes earlier.

My hand brushes the top of Stella's head and her soft

hair pricks at something soft in me. Something foreign. I stroke the glistening locks, and mutter, "Good girl." Then, with a sweep of my fingers under her chin, I lock eyes with her. "You kneel very nicely for me."

"Thank you," she utters under her breath and she blushes so fucking wonderfully.

I want to correct her and say, *'Thank you, sir,'* but she's not ready for that.

It's like hypnosis, I don't want to break the spell I cast on Stella. Even Gia is quiet and stops bouncing in her pink and yellow contraption.

That's right, little baby, let me take care of the woman who will take care of you this month.

With Stella's hands free, I'm tempted to put them on my cock, but I have to take this slow. Instead, I bring those beautiful pale hands to my mouth. "Just breathe, Stella, and listen to my voice. Consider my words. Right now, I'm thinking of all the ways I want to take you." I slip one of her fingers into my mouth. "Shall I keep going?"

After a pregnant pause, she whispers, "Go on." But it's a strangled reply, like her spirit fighting to be in control is screaming at the top of its lungs in her brain.

"You dropped to your knees just the way I like it. Do you like...obeying me?"

"I..." Her eyes are glassy. "I do."

"Good girl. That's smart. Girls who obey me get rewarded."

"How..." Her voice goes deep, like I've hit a nerve she doesn't know she has. "How do they get rewarded?"

"I promise you, you'll find out soon enough." I kiss her hand again and leave the nursery, smirking at

Charles, but Alex's look stops me in my tracks.

It's deadly. It's hurt. It's…want.

Walking to my room to deal with this massive hard-on, I'm left pondering…

Does Alex want to be trained too?

thirteen

STELLA

I was seconds away from pulling Jordan's cock out of those shorts to start sucking him off, when he just left.

I shake myself out of this sex spell he put me under, grab Gia, and practically run out of the nursery.

"Stella," Charles calls out to me in the hallway. "I'm sorry if Jordan—"

"It's fine. Gia needs to eat. I'll finish putting everything away. You go do…" I give Charles a once over, shocked to see him so erect too. "Whatever you need to do. You have a proposal to work on, right?"

He tilts his head to the side. "Yeah. You sure you're okay?"

"Perfect." I don't wait to see his expression. Instead, I spin around and carry Gia downstairs, holding the railing as I go.

I had no idea what the hell happened to me back there. How Jordan's voice riveted me. It was straight out of *Fifty Shades*. For a moment, I sink into that fantasy because all women want a Christian Grey. I just didn't think it was real.

Jordan's commanding voice was very real. It flipped a switch in me. God, I was wet. The power in his tone screamed confidence. A man doesn't get that way without delivering mind-blowing orgasms. I faked it with James and right now, I need to come so badly.

All that talk of obeying and setting me on my knees

means Jordan must be a Dom. And sounds like he wants me to be his Sub. I know those relationships are highly sexual, but are they also temporary? I like the idea of playing with him for a month. He's gorgeous, smart, and has that right amount of arrogance that spills into his sexuality. If I play with him, will that get in the way of me taking care of Gia?

In the D/s relationship, the Dom comes first. No one will come before this baby. It's only been one day, but I easily make the bottle of formula for Gia with one hand, holding her steadily in the other.

I can't deny my attraction to Alex too, though, and that's what has my mind twisted like a pretzel. Even Charles looks hungry for me all of a sudden. I've seen what goes on here. I've gawked at pictures of them with *one woman* in the hot tub that hinted they like to share. I'm not sure I can give myself to three different men like that. Right?

I roll my eyes, thinking of all the women I've seen in those photos. Young, skinny playthings they probably used over and over. Now they're stuck with *me*.

No, they get *you.*

My confidence breaks the grave surface, resurrecting from the shame of how James betrayed me. Used me to fix his reputation. And called me fat behind my back!

I deserve a little worshipping.

The guys stroll into the kitchen and I don't make eye contact with Jordan, but I'm not sure how long I can ignore him. Or how the talk of a reward intrigued the hell out of me. Even if it were a little straight to the point in a jarring kind of way.

What the hell happened to romance?

At least Alex flirts with me. Is sweet to me. Even

Charles' eyes look tortured, but seductive when we stare.

"Stella?" Charles' voice turns me around and I smile at him, burping Gia. "We're gonna head out for a few hours."

We… Them. Not me. Right, I'm the nanny. Not their friend.

"Sure. I have some work to do as well when Gia goes down for her nap."

"What kind of work?" Charles looks perplexed.

"I have to check in with my assistant. Make contingency investment plans."

"Oh, right." Charles gets close to me and strokes Gia's arm. "I'm sorry I wasn't around for so long. No more. I'll do what I can. I respect you for not wanting to take family money. I feel the same way. I built my company solely on my own."

I wonder if being a father kicked in a caring mode he lacked for years. "Thank you." I reach up and hug him, holding Gia gently wedged between us.

His arms wind around my waist, his skin scorching the exposed section of my back. He's so warm. The hold tightens briefly before he lets go. He leans in to kiss Gia's forehead and then does the same to me.

It's shocking and erotic at the same time.

"You sure you'll be okay here alone?" He shoves his hands in his pockets.

"Absolutely. I have plenty to keep me busy. All day. I won't have time for anything else." With that, I send a look to Jordan whose stare is evident behind the expensive shades.

He nods, accepting my refusal to kneel anymore today. I have a lot to think about.

The guys leave and it's like air deflating from a balloon. They take all the energy in this house with them. I return to the nursery and change Gia's diaper. I gently lay her back in the crib where she coos for a few moments and then drifts off.

While putting the rest of her clothes away, I get Bernadette on the phone.

"Hey, it's me."

"Where are you?" She knew I moved out yesterday and I'd left off that I would call her if I needed to sleep on her couch.

"Malibu. I called Katherine yesterday and she told me to meet her here. Then my stepbrother shows up with a four-month-old. Katherine agreed to waive some of the money we owe her if I agreed to be his nanny for the month. At least I have a place to sleep."

"Really? That's great, but it doesn't help get our clothes in production. We need a new investor." She's a business person and is probably struggling to accept that I walked away from the three hundred grand out of pride.

"I know. Let's go back to the list of candidates who expressed interest after the showcase."

"Okay." She sounds flustered because we thought we were done with that stage.

"Not today. It's Saturday. Your day off."

Bernadette is quiet and then asks, "How is it, staying there with your brother?" She knows not only about my stalking him, but my irrational desires for him as well.

How?

One word.

Wine…

But I cringe, hearing her call Charles my *brother*,

95

considering the dirty thoughts I have about him. "Stepbrother. *Stepbrother*. Step. Step. Step."

"That was an emphatic correction," she chuckles. "And he has a baby all of a sudden?"

I give her the rundown of that part of the story and Bernie gasps. "And how is the baby?"

"Perfect. She's a perfect baby." Which has me wondering why her mother didn't just hire her own nanny and bring her on the assignment to Alaska.

Unless... I hold on to the crib. Did Gia's mom not plan on returning? Poor baby. Looking down at her as that sinks in, I feel grounded like never before. This is where I belong. In some capacity.

Gia may need a new mom. I'm not sure I can be *that* for her. But I'm also her aunt. Katherine never made any attempt to parent me, or be loving to me. I won't repeat that.

"So how is that Malibu sex house up close and personal? Are you stepping around the guys banging women on the floor?" Bernadette got a colorful explanation from me in the past about what goes on here.

"Not even close. Charles said something about a proposal he's working on. His company's GC is here too." I can't say Jordan's name yet. "And a personal trainer who I think runs the gym in his office."

"Are they hot too?"

I close my eyes. "Unbelievably."

"Enjoy the view for a month," Bernadette chirps.

"Bernie, I'm attracted to each of them." I brace for the condemnation.

"You're raw and on the rebound. It's normal. They're called transitional men for a reason. And in your case, it looks like you can have more than one."

"What makes you think that?"

"Nature. They're three virile men and you're a gorgeous, sexy woman living under the same roof. Have fun."

Fun… "Don't those flings have consequences?"

"Other than STDs and accidental pregnancies, none I can think of."

Oh, God, all Charles needs is to knock up another woman. I blow out a breath and say, "The lawyer made me an offer."

"An offer?"

"I think he's one of those Doms."

"Really?" Her enthusiasm meter ticks off the charts.

"He just looked at me with hypnotic eyes. Told me to kneel and I did!"

"Whoa! Then what?"

"He called me a good girl and said something about good girls getting rewards. I nearly came in my panties, just listening."

"I hope you put the baby down before you let him fuck you," Bernie jokes.

"Are you kidding? How can I let someone boss me around for his own pleasure?"

"That's not what the Dom/Sub relationship is about."

"How do you know?"

"I watched *Fifty Shades*!"

"That's not real life. And from what I remember in the book, Christian was an asshole about it." I also remember something about having to stick to a diet. Makes me want to sit in the yard with a six-pack of beer and a bag of chips when they come home.

"Not everyone's relationship is exactly the same.

Think about what you would want out of it and bargain. You're a great negotiator." Her confidence is uplifting.

My breath stops and I let it out, realizing getting involved with these guys is a mistake. One, two, or all, despite being attracted to all three.

Sleeping with James, a man who wanted to invest in my business was a mistake and it cost me everything. I have to get my loins in check. Charles sounded very serious about helping me. I did so much to elevate myself with no help. Accepting a hand up from him is nothing to be ashamed about.

That means I can't sleep with his friends.

Or him.

I'm his sister and his daughter's nanny after all.

*

Over the past few days, Gia kept me busier than I expected. But I loved it. I play with her in the pool, splash around with her at the beach, and we take walks down to the eclectic shops along Pacific Coast Highway. I found a great coffee shop where I can sit with her in a stroller and people-watch. I often get design ideas by seeing fashion disasters.

I've even been sketching baby clothes. But that's just for fun.

The guys left early for a day trip to Catalina. Alex made me a plate of cut strawberries and carb-free pancakes, which were shockingly delicious. Of course, that could have been because of the butter and syrup I added after he left.

I get back to the house and it feels so empty without the three hulking men who don't seem to want to wear shirts. Gia fell asleep on the walk back so I lift her out of the stroller and lay her in the crib. She seems so happy in this nursery. Such a shame that it's only temporary. It's beautiful.

I received several texts from him, checking on Gia. The latest one says that he, Alex, and Jordan will be home late. Alex sent a text too, suggesting a few different things for dinner. I ended up making a box of macaroni and cheese.

Gia is long asleep when the headlights shine against the trees that hang over the garage. I'm sitting on the edge of the pool, my feet in the water, the baby monitor on a table nearby—the correct one—while I read a book when I hear the back sliding glass door open.

Alex strolls outside alone.

Charles more than likely went straight to the nursery to check on his daughter and maybe Jordan is hoping I'm waiting for him somewhere on my knees. I've barely looked him in the eye, but when I did, the heat there unsettled me.

I chuckle low and to myself, but Alex catches it. "Something funny?" His voice is light. He seems tipsy, but not sloppy-drunk.

"How was Catalina?" I close my book and lean back, my legs softly lapping against the water.

"Great. You should come with us next time. It was a spur-of-the-moment trip. But Charles couldn't stop saying, Gia and Stella should be here. Stella would love this, Stella would love that."

My pulse thunders in my throat, thinking he'd spent an entire day on one of the most beautiful channel islands off the west coast and thought about me the entire time. Thinking it through, I say, "Was he drunk?"

"Ha! Charles doesn't get drunk." Alex stumbles to the door to the pool house.

"Have a good night." My voice makes him stop.

"Did you have a good night?" he asks me.

"I did. It was nice and quiet."

The light catches Alex's face and he looks so stunning it hurts. He's wearing a white short-sleeve button-down shirt and tan dockers. His bulging biceps are testing the sleeves. I should stand up right now, stroll over to him, and kiss him. I bet he'd let me and bring me into that pool house and do what James couldn't do.

He smirks, but then drops the grin. A shadow appears and I think it's Charles. I hope it's him. No, it's Jordan in a swimsuit with a towel slung over his shoulder. Swimsuit is generous. It's not a speedo, but it's tight and short, sitting low on his hips and showing off enough to make my mouth water.

Alex gives Jordan a salute and disappears inside the pool house. Has Jordan laid some kind of claim on me?

I lift my feet out of the pool, ashamed I couldn't do it smoother. "I'll let you have a swim."

"Stella, please don't go," he says with a kinder voice than the Dom intonation he used on me a few days ago.

I still get to my feet. "It's late."

"I'm sorry if I got inappropriate with you the other day." He crosses his arms across a broad chest and I don't think it's an accident we're having this conversation while he's dressed like that. Or *not* dressed.

I swam earlier while Gia was napping and after taking off the wet bathing suit, I just threw on a black cover-up that skimmed my knees. I'm wearing only a thong underneath because it makes me feel sexy. I let my hair dry naturally, loving the beach waves from the salt pool and the brine in the air from the ocean below. "It's fine."

He stares for a moment. "I do want to swim, but I'd like you to stay."

"And do what?"

"Watch me." His directness stills me.

"Watch you do what?"

"Convince you."

"Convince me of what?"

"That you want me." He winks and drops his towel on a chaise.

I say nothing, and sure enough, I stay and watch him dive into the deep end.

Because he's right. I want him.

fourteen

JORDAN

I don't have to glance at the side of the pool. I know Stella is there. Watching me. I had her pegged right all along. She's submissive when it comes to the bedroom. Women who succeed in business make the best Subs because they keep a firm grip on their lives in every other manner. They need to let go. When it comes to sex, they want to be controlled.

That's where I come in.

After lifting out of the pool on the opposite side, I stride to the chaise I dropped my towel on, but decide not to dry off. I use my body when I have to and this is one of those times. Stella not only needs to want me, I need her to crave me.

Our eyes lock as I approach her. When she presses her hands on the concrete to stand, I hoof it faster and get there to help her up.

First and foremost, Doms worship their Subs. That means helping them out of chairs and cars, soaping them up in showers, toweling off, slicking up with lotion, and dusting with powder. I once blew a woman's hair dry because she'd hurt her wrist at a Tai Chi class.

I want to be that and more for Stella.

"Thank you," she says softly.

But I keep my hands on her arms, the hold loose, but very much there. Her eyes drift that way and I use my other hand to guide her chin. "Eyes on me, Stella."

"I have some questions." She holds my gaze and it moves me in a way I don't think I've felt before. In fact, the first rule for the Sub is to stay kneeling and looking down until she has permission to make eye contact with me.

I got things backward with Stella, but she's not a trained Sub. It's been a while since I had someone so raw, so fresh, and I worry my Sub-training skills are rusty.

But this teaching, assuming she agrees, will not be my usual lessons. There are two other men living with us who also need to be fulfilled. Sharing usually doesn't happen until the Dom and the Sub have explored every aspect of their own relationship, depending on the needs and wants of both partners.

My only concern is, I'm not sure how Stella feels about what I did to her the other day and what she knows or *thinks* she knows about the BDSM lifestyle.

"Ask your questions, Stella." I break our stare and the air around me feels different.

"Why did you need me to kneel?" Her question isn't unexpected.

"Why *did* you kneel?" I steer her to one of the patio tables and pull out the chair for her. "Sit."

"Are you going to answer all of my questions with your questions?" Her wavy hair glistens in the moonlight combined with the amber lights strung across the pool.

"There." I put my hand on her head. "You're feisty and strong. That's why I made you kneel."

"I thought men liked feisty and strong in a woman."

"Feisty in bed, yes. Hell, yes." I lift her eyes to me, smile, and then lower her chin again. "Strong-willed is

103

good in business. In the bedroom with a Dominant, it's…dangerous for the dynamic. For a relationship to work."

"You want a relationship with me?"

"I want *this* kind of relationship with you, Stella." I lift her chin again.

"BDSM?"

"You're familiar with the lifestyle?"

"I sure am," she sasses me.

"The stronger you come off with me, Stella, when we're in our roles, the more I will need to break you."

"Break me…"

"Break you down."

"That doesn't sound like fun."

"No pain, no gain." I hate that cliché, but it fits. "If you're open to the relationship, it's necessary to level you out to your baser needs. Because when you've cleared your mind of all the muck that messes with your head and prevents you from having an orgasm, you'll thank me." I squeeze her shoulder and sit across from her. "I'm getting ahead of myself. Let me explain to you what being my Submissive is all about."

"Yes, please explain." There's a hint of condescension in her tone as she crosses her legs.

I debate how to tell her that training begins with at least an hour of her kneeling in silence until I tell her to speak or move. This could be difficult considering she's here to tend to a baby, and I'd never interfere with that. I can however demand she not touch herself for hours while wearing a butt plug.

Only then do I realize she's in a partially sheer cover-up and the gentle sway of her breasts suggests she's not wearing a bra. Heck, she may not be wearing panties either. I tuck that thought up in my head. I'll make sure she stays braless and commando in the house this month. That shouldn't interfere with taking care of Gia.

Thank God, she's an infant.

"As a Dominant, it's my job to care for my Submissive. In every way possible. If we're in a closed-proximity situation like this…" I glance back at the house. "It's up to me to see to your every need. Safety. Meals. Hygiene."

"Hygiene," she rebukes sharply. "You think I'm dirty?"

I quirk a smile at her. "I think you can be very dirty. Filthy. Take my cock deep inside you and drive me fucking out of my mind. But I meant, it will be up to me to get your showers and baths going."

"Sounds like you're a dad and I'm a five-year-old."

"You can call me daddy if you want." I'm exactly fifteen years older than her. But when she pales at that one, I clarify. "It's called caring for you."

"And why would you go through all that work when you can just have a normal relationship with someone and fuck like bunnies when the mood hits?"

"First of all, it's an insult to say a BDSM relationship is not normal."

She waves her hand, blushing. "That's not what I intended. Sorry."

"Not good enough." I have my opening to give her a taste of the punishment aspect. "Stand up."

Her face twists and I think she'll defy me. If she does, this won't work and I'll be crushed. So, when she presses down on the chair's arm and stands, my heart pounds and my cock hardens. These damn swim trunks are tight and she'll know. But I don't care.

"Good girl. That's what you'll hear when you please me. But part of this relationship, Stella, includes punishment when you defy me."

"Let me guess, you're gonna spank me."

"Yes. And if I were in my business suit, it would be with my belt."

"Yeah, I'm not liking this."

"Because you haven't seen the pleasure side of it. That part has to be earned, Stella." I stalk closer to her and her body reacts. She's probably five-seven, five-eight. But I'm close to six-four and despite her being curvy, I'm broad and jacked up. She's tiny to me. "Hands on the table."

"What?"

"Every question gets you one more spank." I know she needs to be convinced. I step back and remove my cock from my swim trunks. "You can walk away, but then you don't get my cock. Do you have any idea how good I can make you feel with this?"

Her eyes are locked on my dick and it pulses in my hands. God, I want it in her mouth.

"Hands. On. The. Table."

To my surprise, she leans over and grips the edge. I shove my cock back reluctantly and ease her hands into a flattened position. Her floral scent drives me wild.

I push her wavy, blonde hair off her shoulder and whisper in her ear, "Good girl. Now let me do this. You'll thank me, I promise."

I lay a gentle kiss on the back of her neck, and she shivers at my touch. My throat is tight as I lift her dress.

She gasps and flinches, but says nothing.

"Tell me to stop…"

When she just breathes and pushes that gorgeous behind into my groin, I finger the lace thong that disappears into her ass. "This is your first rule, kitten. No bra. No panties." I slide that thong right off.

Her ass is round, smooth, and cool to the touch. I graze my hand over her skin. "Gorgeous, Stella. I'm an ass man." Gripping the cheeks and spreading them, I lose my breath, seeing that tiny puckered hole. "And I'll fuck this ass really good too. First things, first." I lay a whack and the sound of my hand hitting skin is louder than I thought.

Stella yelps. "That hurt."

"It's supposed to." But I rub where I smacked her, pinching and kneading the enflamed skin. "What you need to focus on is that this kind of punishment is followed by my pleasuring you."

I don't want to scare her off, and given how defiant she is, I'll be doing this a lot, so I pace myself. I give her two more smacks, followed by massaging the skin. With her cheeks spread, I gently lick her hole.

Stella flinches around my tongue, but groans. "Oh God."

"Not God, kitten. Me." I run my hand up her leg and breathe heavily, feeling so much smooth skin until I reach her pussy. "See, you're wet."

"You just licked my ass," she whispers.

"And you apparently like it."

"Maybe."

Minx. "Sit down." I hold the chair for her and when her ass is in that seat, I'm transfixed. "God, you're gorgeous. Your eyes shine and your mouth drives me nuts. I want to see you bite that lip from the strain on your pussy as I push my cock inside you."

Her eyes flutter, taking in my words. My offer. I can see her picturing me fucking her behind her eyes. She's needy for pleasure, I can smell it.

"Do you like getting fucked from behind? Because that ass you're trying to hide from us is ripe for me to grab. I want a handful while I pound your pussy."

"Maybe," she whispers, fighting me.

"I'll know you want me because you'll be begging. Dripping for me. Clawing at my chest." I see her squirming, her hips pitching slightly. "Now spread those fucking luscious legs for me and show me your wet cunt."

She bites her lower lip. Her calves tighten as those gorgeous, painted toes turn out and her legs open.

"Lift your dress. Show me your pussy." When she does, I grow even harder. Christ, she's perfect.

Waxed and plump.

I lower to a crouch and graze my finger right across the slit.

Stella grips the chair's arms. "God."

"That's just my finger, kitten. And one feather-light touch. This is what I'm telling you. I'm here to pleasure you." My finger runs the length of her drenched slit and her head falls back. "Look at me. Watch my hand." I dip one finger inside and I nearly lose my balance feeling how tight she is. How hot and wet. "Are you on birth control, kitten?"

"Yes." She breathes.

"I'll want to take you bare. And come inside you. Again and again."

"I'm clean," she moans, her hips writhing.

"We'll address all that in our contract."

"Contract?"

"Yes. A Dom and a Sub need to sign a contract. Don't worry, I'll make you come tonight without it. Hard and good." With that, I lower my head and devour her pussy with my mouth.

The taste of her blows me away. My tongue pushes through her folds and it's even tighter than I thought. God, she'll hold my cock so snuggly. Her bulbous clit throbs and I suck on it, my entire mouth engulfing her pussy. She's so damn wet and creamy on my lips.

Stella pulls my hair. "Don't stop. I'm already close."

Withholding an orgasm is part of the training, but we didn't sign the agreement, so I suck on her clit some more to make her explode in my mouth. She gushes on my tongue and stifles a scream. Her pussy convulses around my tongue and I'm not sure I can handle how she'll strangle my cock.

I kiss her thighs and then, working my way up her body to hover above her lips, I say, "Good?"

"I don't think I've ever orgasmed like that."

"Ha. There's so much more where that came from. My turn." I stand up and lower my swim trunks, my cock swinging and needing to come. I want her on her knees, but the cement will scrape her skin. I'm tall enough and with her sitting, her lips line up perfectly with my cock when I stand next to her. "Suck my cock, Stella."

Her cheeks are flushed and her chest is heaving, but she grips my cock with more force than I was prepared for. I don't know why she'd be shy about it. Just that touch tells me she's not the novice I expected.

"Hold on." I stop her, taking control of this. "Lick the tip. Swirl your tongue around the head. Suck in the pre-cum."

"Mmmm," she groans and takes me fully into her mouth.

Everything goes hazy behind my eyes. Everything else shuts off and I just feel my cock sliding so deep in her mouth until I hit the back of her throat. Fuck, I may have chosen the wrong girl to play with. She can easily turn the tables on me and get me to kneel for her, it's so fucking good.

Amazing. For a guy who gets his dick sucked a lot, that's saying *a lot*. Jesus fucking Christ, her mouth is erotically warm and wet and she knows what the fuck she's doing. She licks and sucks in a sublime rhythm and every part of me is on fire.

Her hands smooth around my hips and she grips my ass the way I did hers. Spreading my cheeks so wide the ocean breeze tickles my asshole. Fuck, my cock pulses. She moans around my shaft and this fucking blow job is wrecking me. Chiseling away at me, bit by bit. It's just the sound of the waves below that remind where the fuck I am.

"Holy shit, Stella, my kitten. Look at you with my cock in your mouth. After five fucking days. You bad girl."

She moans again and opens those amazing blue eyes at me. Right there, my world shatters.

My balls tighten and my cock throbs like a heart beating. "I'm gonna come," I rasp and take hold of my cock to keep it in her mouth. "Swallow me. Relax your throat." I spurt my cum across her tongue and then slip my cock out to thoroughly coat her lips. "Don't you dare move, kitten," I warn, in case she thinks of pulling away. Then I slide my still pulsing cock past her cum-soaked lips and as far down her throat as I can go. Next,

I vigorously thrust my cock and empty down her throat.

I step back, my body shaking more than I expected. My brain levels out and my heart thunders inside my chest. That may have been the best blow job I've ever had.

"Good girl, kitten. But you're in trouble."

"What?" She wipes her mouth, but I stop her, doing it instead. "Why?"

"Me, I take care of you. You're in trouble because sucking my dick that good means I'll have it in your mouth. A lot."

fifteen

STELLA

I'm not sure what echoes in my head louder. Jordan's voice or the blood pounding in my ears from such an amazing orgasm.

After putting his semi-hard cock back in his swimsuit, he leans his head into me again and says, "Good girl. Let's pick this up tomorrow and talk about the contract."

"Wait," I say and brush my hands across his shoulders.

"Yes?" He's broad with warm skin even though a chill from the ocean has swept across the pool deck.

Jesus, I hadn't come from oral in the longest time. And his dick? I could barely fit it in my mouth. But I made him come pretty quickly, which has me wondering, is he just full of shit and hasn't been laid in a while, or was I that good?

"Don't I get a kiss goodnight?" I ask with a smile.

His face contorts for a moment. "I don't usually kiss my Subs. The relationship isn't about love."

"You just kissed the shit out of my pussy."

"That's different."

"Why?"

"Kisses on the mouth send a different signal." He crosses his arms.

"Will that be in the contract?" I stand to confront him. "No kissing?"

"It's a hard limit for me, Stella." He calls me Stella

and not kitten and I feel a little crushed, like the magic we had a moment ago is not only gone, it was an illusion.

"What's a hard limit?"

"Something I'll never do."

"Oh." That stuns me. I thought I understood the dynamic of a Dom and a Sub. Right, he's a control freak. Gets off on it.

"If we sign a contract, you're free to negotiate your own hard limits."

I'm about to nod, but something catches my attention. "Negotiate them?"

"Yes, it's a contract. We have to agree."

I'm not sure I want the kissing part, but I can't help but be a brat. "What if I don't agree to kissing being your hard limit?" In fact, I might make that the hill I die on especially if I know it's something that will force him to feel something.

Licking his lips in an evil taunt, he says, "I would need a lot in return to take kissing off my hard-limits list."

This has me thinking. "What are your other hard limits?"

"That's it."

"One?" I step back and laugh. "Sounds like you have a massive hang-up. I'm not sure I even want to get involved with you. In fact, I'm sure Alex will kiss me just fine."

His cheek twitches. Men are too easy. "You want access to Alex as part of our contract?"

"Maybe." I'll eventually admit I was kidding. Or am I? "He probably doesn't want me that way."

"You're so very wrong." Jordan studies me and his

eyes land on my breasts.

"I'm guessing we'll never know."

"Do you doubt you're desirable to him?" Jordan stands over me. "That insults me."

"How?"

"That I would find a woman desirable that he doesn't."

I'm not sure I get his logic, but the passion in his eyes takes me back. "Okay." I shrug.

"Not good enough. Take off that cover-up."

"Why?"

"I want to see your body."

"Is this an audition? What does my body matter, you've seen and apparently enjoyed the only part—"

"Stop!" He towers over me with a look of anger on his face. "A Sub *does not* degrade herself to her Dom. You've insulted me once."

"I didn't—"

"Yes, you did. Don't lie on top of it." He steps back. "Cover-up. Gone. Now."

Maybe the kissing isn't so important. My brain has been going a million miles an hour for weeks. If this man can satisfy me, it might help calm me down and I'll make the right decision as far as my life.

"Just so you know, this isn't me giving up on the kissing." I lift the cover-up and my brain processes every second my body is visible. I'm not perfect by L.A. standards. I'm curvy and round. That also gives me full breasts, which I like. Heck, I love my boobs. "Happy?" I hold the cover-up with the tips of my fingers.

"No," he deadpans.

I snatch it back and cover myself, horrified.

"Stop." He grabs it in his hands and next, I'm standing there completely naked. Charles can come walking out any second. Alex, too.

"You're too pale. That's what I meant." Jordan eyes me up and down again. "God, you're *fucking* gorgeous."

"Now, you stop. You don't have to blow smoke up my ass." Just lick and suck it. "I care more about what people think of my personality and how I'm a hard worker than what they think of my body." Even if that attitude doesn't fly largely here in L.A.

"You want kissing, huh?" Jordan rounds me like a drill sergeant, but doesn't touch me.

The chill sweeping in from the ocean intensifies and my nipples are rock-hard now.

A sudden warmth spreads across my back from Jordan, and next, his body presses against me. I feel nothing but skin. He must have removed his swim trunks. A very hard cock spears my lower back, the tip wet. At least now we're both naked.

I've come this far. "Yes. I want kissing."

"And you're willing to forgo any hard limits?" His hands come around and cup my breasts. "Like anal sex?"

I haven't checked online for a full list of hard limits. I bet it gets dicey. "Anal is fine. Just nothing with pain."

"Oh, my cock in your ass will hurt." He breathes in my ear. "Just for a moment before the burning turns to intense pleasure as I move in and out. You'll love it. I promise."

I shudder at his descriptive promise and my pussy throbs all over again. "Okay. But nothing sharp.

115

Or…fire. Or…"

"Those are not the limits I engage in." His lips trail up my neck. They're so wet and soft. His body comes around I think he's going to kiss me, but he licks one nipple and then the next. I lose track of his hands until a finger slides into my folds and my legs buckle.

He lays me out on a chaise, and with my legs spread, he's rubbing my clit while sucking on a nipple.

I throw my head back, ignoring the fact that my pussy is on display and right in line with the windows in Alex's pool house. The idea that he's watching forms in my head and I explode in Jordan's hand.

"Good girl," he whispers. "But when we're under contract, I will be making you wait to come. And there will always be a turn for me."

I stretch my jaw, thinking I have to blow him again. He just straddles me and with his knees bent, he takes my breasts in his hands. "Lick my cock, Stella."

I don't have much of a choice since my hands are behind me, holding me into a seated position. He uses his hands to guide his cock up and down my tongue. "God, your mouth is so sexy. I'm gonna love fucking it every chance I get."

Next, he slips his cock between my boobs. It's really a goddamn perfect piece of male machinery. It's freaking huge because he's tall, but it's not overly thick. It bends like a beautiful banana and as his hips flex, it pops up and out of my cleavage. It's all wet now, full of precum. "I'm gonna fuck you so raw, Stella. Jesus, I hope you're this tight." He thrusts some more, that dramatic cut V pushing against my face.

I lean forward to lick his skin.

"That's right, baby. Taste me. Taste every inch of

me. When I'm your Dom, you have all of me. I'm yours." His head dips back and groans some more as creamy spurts bubble from the tip of his cock.

I hold my boobs so they drip down the sides like ice cream on a hot day.

"Fuck. *Fuuuck…*" Jordan bites out, jerking his cock to empty on my chest.

Breathing heavily, he stares at me, and then at my lips. He wants to kiss me, but he has to go back and make a list of every lewd thing in the world a man can do to a woman in exchange for kissing me. Except, maybe that list won't be as long as I think.

I look around, knowing there aren't any napkins or tissues handy. Might as well wipe his cum with my dress. I have nowhere else to dab it, but I prefer not to walk through the house to my bedroom with a pearl necklace.

"Stop." Jordan holds my chin and then takes my hand.

"I can clean it—"

"Stop!" Jordan snaps again. "Me. I take care of you." He's talking like we already agreed I would be his Sub. Or maybe this is a trial run. Maybe he has no idea how to be with a woman otherwise. He leads me to the hot tub, and says, "Get in."

Given my body temperature is dropping, the warm water is welcome. The minute it touches my skin, my heart starts to pound. I go to submerge, but Jordan stops me by holding my breasts.

He gently laps water across my chest and the swells of each breast, cleaning me. "Good girl. You did so good tonight. We're gonna have fun this month, Stella."

"Can I stay here in the tub for a little while?" drops

from my mouth and I blink in astonishment. I just asked him if I can stay here.

I can do whatever I want. He doesn't own me. Yet, it feels good to ask. And even better, getting his nod of approval. "Sure. Let's soak for a while."

I submerge myself, but my tits bob in front of me. Under the surface of the water, my body looks magical and sexy. "You said I look pale?"

"Yes. I want you out here every day getting color."

"Not *all day*, I'm here to take care of a baby."

He doesn't respond, just looks away like I killed the mood. "Charles is my best friend, of course, Giana comes first."

"Thank you, Master." I shake my head, in one night he's worn me down.

"Sir, is more appropriate."

"Sir." I tease him.

"Is this a private party?" Alex's voice makes me jump.

Holy shit, I'm stark naked in a not-so-foamy hot tub and Alex is right there, wearing only a towel. I wonder if he's nude underneath.

"Not at all," Jordan says.

Alex looks down at me. "This is okay, Stella?" He drops the towel.

Yep. Naked.

"So okay," I mutter, watching him get in.

Only, I can't stay in this thing for long. It's too much. I'm still wound up. All these bubbles and the saltwater are stirring me up again. I know I can stand up and sit on Jordan's dick. Ride him until we both come. While Alex watches. Or maybe he'd join in.

I stare at Jordan, wondering if he'd share me.

118

Something tells me he's very possessive.

Damn, that gets me even hotter. I'm extra curious now about this contract I have to sign. Both Alex and Jordan are smiling at me. And damn, I feel fucking sexy as hell.

My cover-up is on the other side of the pool. I bet if I asked Alex to get it, he'd hop out and grab it for me. Bring it back with his dick swinging like it was nothing. That's what the old Stella would do.

James fucking me over was a wake-up call. I'd been hoping the sex with him would get better. I cornered myself and now I am...

Free.

God, that feels great.

Free to do whatever the hell I want. And whoever the hell I want. Charles sneaks into my mind and I don't understand why even with these two alphas looking ready to devour me, I picture Charles kissing me. I guess the crush I had on him growing up never really went away.

My body is fully charged up now. "This has been fun, fellas. The nanny needs her beauty sleep to take care of our precious little girl. Have a good night."

With that, I lift out without bothering to cover myself. Alex's jaw drops, and his hand sneaks under the water.

Jordan winks at me. "Tomorrow morning, Charles' office."

I stand there completely nude, feeling more amazing than I ever felt in my life. The salt in the hot tub makes my skin shimmer and feel so damn soft. Trying to be as poised as possible, I lift my leg to get out, knowing I'm flashing my pussy at Alex, but I don't care.

Strutting and shifting my hips back and forth, I get to the chaise and grab my cover-up, not looking back. I know they're gawking at me.

And I love it.

With the cover-up against my dripping-wet body, I'm lost in a euphoria I've never known. Steps away from the sliding glass doors to the kitchen, I give a glance back and, sure enough, they're still watching me.

This was the greatest night of my life.

Until I slam into a wall of muscle and fall on my ass.

The cover-up releases from my hand and a whipping wind takes it up, up, and away. There I am, naked, sitting spread eagle with my stepbrother staring at my pussy.

Throb, throb, throb....

Sixteen

CHARLES

This has got to be a dream. Stella is on the ground in front of me. Completely naked with her legs spread. She's breathing heavily from our collision and I wonder if I hit her in the head because she makes no attempt to cover herself. Or close her damn legs.

I'm a man, so of course, I look.

Christ, that's one gorgeous, bare pussy. Plump lips and a cute triangle of hair above. I take in the rest of her, she's wet with the kind of glisten to her skin the water softener in the hot tub gives your body. Her breasts are just fucking delicious. Bouncy, but firm with hard nipples.

My cock hardens immediately and I hope this is a dream. Because then I can fuck her, feel what it's like to be inside her once and for all without any consequences. Damn, I would take her so hard.

Figuring this *is* a dream, I undo the string holding up my sleep pants.

"Charles?" she shrieks.

I'm startled back to reality while my sleep pants are sliding down my ass. I grab them, and tie them back up, bumping into my now raging hard-on. It happens fast enough that I'm not sure she notices.

"Christ, what happened? I'm sorry." Ignoring her nakedness, I reach down and lift her up.

Yep, her skin has that softness and the gentle fragrance of lavender from the hot tub. My eyes shoot that way and see Alex and Jordan perched on their crossed arms smiling at me.

The three of them were naked in my hot tub. I'm not sure if I'm pissed that they didn't invite me or that they were taking advantage of my sister.

Shit... Stepsister.

"I bumped into you." Stella stands there, attempting to cover her body.

My brain snaps so I lift off my tee-shirt and then hand it to her. "Do I want to know what's going on?"

"Probably not." She holds the tee-shirt in front of her body, but the way it just hangs there, I still see everything.

God, those curves look amazing on her. "Were they bothering you?" My voice drops an octave.

"No. Not at all." She brushes her hand through her hair. It's wavy and untamed for a change.

I like her better this way. "I just checked on Gia. She's sleeping."

Nanny, she's also my nanny this month. That should be more of a barrier to doing anything with her. My two best friends are open-season as far as Stella is concerned. They aren't her stepbrother. She isn't their nanny. Mine. She's my nanny.

A wild fantasy that she'll come back to my penthouse with me after this month and look after Gia permanently tears through my pounding chest. Although, I have no idea how long Gia will be with me. I know I want some kind of regular custody. Would Stella be a part-time nanny? I can't imagine she'd give up everything just to watch Gia a couple of days a week.

But then we could...

Christ, I'm so hard now I have to cover myself. "Were you going to bed?"

"Yeah." She breathes and our eyes just lock.

Fuck, what's happening?

I want to kick Jordan and Alex out of the house, but I need my GC to help me with venue contracts. With the office shut down for the month and everyone else working from home or also on vacation, Alex would have nothing to do.

"Okay. Good night." Ignoring that she's still naked, I lean in and kiss her on the cheek.

She's quivering, but warm and smells so damn good. "Good night, Charles."

The way she says my name sounds so damn sexy.

I fight the urge not to turn around and look at her bare ass, but I lose.

I'm not sure how long I'm gonna last before I do something really stupid. Her classic hourglass figure and round ass drive me so crazy. I see myself just pinning her down and fucking her from behind until we both pass out.

With my eyes still glued on her, she turns around and catches me staring. I'm about to feel like the biggest pervert ever. But she…

Smiles and turns the corner to the living room.

Fucking, fuck. She liked me looking at her. What the hell do I do with that?

I have no idea.

seventeen

STELLA

I'm absolutely mortified.

Not for what I did with Jordan. But for Charles to catch me naked in his yard. I'm here to take care of his daughter. Not fuck his friends.

The feral look in his eyes, though, sent a stake through my heart. Then again, I was a naked woman spreading my legs, showing him my pussy. Any man would be affected by that.

Still, I have to apologize. Make sure he's not mad at me. Clothed this time, so he can concentrate and tell me how he really feels about what happened.

Dressed in a tee-shirt and a pair of shorts, I step out into the hall and meet a wall of quiet. But that's normal. With Gia sleeping in one of the bedrooms, everyone tiptoes through the halls, terrified of waking her up.

I note the time, knowing I'll only get a few hours of sleep at this point. I'm mad at myself, but I can't go to bed without talking to Charles.

The window facing the backyard is next to his bedroom. Glancing that way, I see Jordan is back in the pool, but the lights in the pool house are dark.

Charles' master suite faces the ocean, Gia's room too. On the other side of the landing are my bedroom and Jordan's. At the door to Charles' bedroom, I notice it's ajar. I don't know if he sleeps with it like that, perhaps to listen for noises in the hallway that might disturb Gia. He and I have been trading the monitor back and forth.

Tapping on the door, I see his light is on, and I whisper, "Charles?"

After waiting a few seconds, I peek and see his massive king-size bed is unmade. The swirl of sheets looks quite erotic. Looking around further, I wonder if he's in the loft above the bedroom, but that area is dark.

Then I hear the water running.

He's in the shower.

At this time of night?

Or... Is he running the shower for the steam? Is Gia sick, all while I was sunk too deep in my embarrassment to hear her? That has me moving and pushing the door open gently so as to not startle Charles, but I want him to see my concern for his daughter.

I immediately realize that I'm wrong. The body behind the steamed-up glass halts me in place. I see he didn't bother with a frosted panel. If he just got into that shower and someone walked in, a housekeeper perhaps would see... Would see the most gorgeous body.

Even wrapped in steam, Charles is perfect. He's not rippling with muscles like Alex. He's not towering tall like Jordan. He's six, six-one maybe, with golden-blond, rumpled hair that gets curly when it's wet like now.

I'm staring at him naked like a peeping Tom when I hear the noise.

Groaning.

Oh shit, he's...jerking off.

My eyes sharpen and I see a meaty hand around his cock. From the range of motion, he's long. That outline I caught in the sleep pants suggests he's thick too. My pussy immediately clenches because what I'm witnessing is truly erotic. A thump startles me as Charles' other hand slams against the glass. The pumping increases and the moans heighten.

"God, yeah. Yeah, take it. Take my cock." He's fantasizing about someone. I wonder who? Ana maybe. "Christ, yeah. I'm gonna come, Stella."

Hearing my name slip from his lips shocks me. Charles is picturing *me*. Holy. Shit.

"Yeah, baby. Ride my cock. You look fucking gorgeous riding me with that bad, curvy body," he groans, and then it's all inaudible moaning.

I'm frozen, processing what this means. Bad, curvy body? Does he want me for me? Or just because I'm here in the house and this is his month to fuck anything that moves? He doesn't look at me like I'm a piece of meat. In fact, he looks at me like I'm…precious. Like he cares about me all of a sudden. Like he sees me for the first time. And most important, like we're equals.

When the water stops, I amble backward to get the hell out of there. I don't want to force this conversation. Nothing can happen between Charles and me. We're…related. In a way. And I'm his nanny. I work for him. In a way. His mother is forgiving part of my debt and he said he'll help me find a new VC.

I can't fuck him. Then I'll never know if his help is because he believes in me, or he just wants some more ass.

I also just fooled around with Jordan. That means I'm his for this month, right?

Stepping back to my bedroom, I can't help but feel that I belong to all three of these guys. A smile tips my lips, liking that. No…loving that.

eighteen

JORDAN

I tag along with Alex to a 10K near Faith L.A. hospital on Friday afternoon. He's not running the race, but said he'd give a hand to his trainer friends who put up a hydration booth. That's how fucking bored we are during the day. We're standing around waiting for sweaty people who need a drink.

Stella is on a non-stop rinse-repeat cycle with the baby throughout the daylight hours. She's up early and naps when Gia goes down. It's been three days since we fooled around by the pool and I've only gotten polite smiles from her. Can she seriously be thinking of turning down my offer?

Charles kicked me out of his office to help with the contracts because he said I was starting to growl.

I think today is going to be awful, but when I see Alex come to life as a trainer and really support the people running, it uplifts me. When runners stop with cramps, Alex helps stretch their calves and hamstrings.

He's my best friend and I know he's committed to fitness. Plus, he's a genius at what he does. Seeing him in action and how other people respond makes me so damn proud that he's mine.

The wording in my thoughts stops me on a dime. He's…mine. Whoa? What does that mean?

The race takes about four hours and now it's just a few people here and there trudging along, looking like they're ready to die. We're not even set up at the halfway point.

Alex claps me on the shoulder. "Thanks for doing this with me."

"You're welcome. But I didn't do anything." In fact, I feel quite useless.

"I saw you cheering people on." A devilish smile reaches his amber eyes. He hasn't stopped smiling all day and I'm glad we did this.

"Hard not to." I lift weights, but running is a different fitness ballgame altogether.

"They have another team now so we can leave." Alex pushes his hands in his pockets and shrugs. He takes off his baseball cap and shakes out a mop of light brown hair that shines in the sunlight. Something I've seen hundreds of times, but today it sends a jolt of electricity through me.

What. The. Fuck. Is. Going. On?

Stunned, I stroll behind him on a walking path parallel to the running course in order to reach the street where I parked. A hotdog cart sits near the entrance and I feel stupid for not grabbing a water back there. I'm parched from my throat turning bone dry.

"Want a water?" I point to the cart.

"Nah, I'm good." Alex waits for me near the entrance to the park and checks his phone.

As I'm walking to meet him after buying a water, I see it happen in slow motion.

Pierce approaches Alex. And the guy with him sporting shoulder-length blond hair, I assume, is Cooper.

Alex looks up and I hate that he's standing there alone. He mentioned Cooper is a running coach and it makes sense he'd be at the race. But why couldn't they see Alex surrounded by adoring runners back at the booth? No, they caught him alone.

Fuck.

I jog up that way.

Alex acknowledges me and I wedge myself into their huddle. Everyone's smiling, so I'm sure it's been a pleasant exchange.

But Jesus, I can feel the energy between Pierce and Cooper. Alex made it clear that he screws guys for fun, but the way their parting is affecting Alex, Pierce might have meant more to him. I wonder if Alex ever told him or showed him how he felt. Pierce had the capacity to go deeper in his relationships with men all while committing to a woman too.

"This is Jordan," Alex says, pointing to me. "This is Pierce and Cooper."

"Nice to meet you." Pierce grins at me.

He thinks we're together.

Cooper shakes my hand. He's a good-looking guy. Tall and lean. Not as tall as Pierce, who I'm guessing is six-four, like me. But Jesus, this guy is a beast with tattoos everywhere.

"This is the month for your Malibu vacation, right?" Pierce says to Alex, pinching his chin. "Banging everything you can get your hands on?"

Alex scoffs. "Not this time."

Before I let him explain about the baby and the nanny, I put my arm around him. "His hands are all over me now." I pull Alex in and next, I'm kissing my best friend.

I had no idea how it would feel. His lips are so damn soft. It takes him a minute to figure out what I'm doing, and he's either going along for the ride or he's caught up.

Me? I am *floored*. I haven't kissed anyone in years. Heck, I used kissing as a veto tool with Stella and here I am…my mouth is devouring Alex. I can't help but drag a finger through his course stubble and it lights me the fuck up.

I only stop because Pierce and Cooper are still standing there.

Pierce beams and pats Alex on the arm. "I'll let you get to it."

"Nice meeting you." Cooper struts away with a devilish, "Have fun."

"What the fuck was that?" Alex steps back, wiping his mouth, looking as shaken up as me.

"I don't know." I exhale, feeling something spread through my body I can't explain. "I've seen you with other guys and I admit, I've been curious."

"I'm your little lab experiment?" The hurt in his voice guts me. He's raw from seeing Pierce, and my plan to prop him up may have backfired.

What started out as fake turned into something so real, so fast, I don't know how to handle it. I force my aloof mode back on and punch his shoulder, gently. "You are a good kisser."

"Yeah, okay," he says and walks ahead of me.

I follow him to my car feeling a massive hard-on with every step and I don't know who I want to fuck first to make it go away. Stella or Alex.

Or both…

nineteen

ALEX

My heart is pounding from that kiss in the park earlier today and it's messing me up. What should have been a slight jolt from seeing Pierce and Cooper got eclipsed when my best friend rammed his tongue in my mouth, and I felt like I got struck by lightning.

We get back to the house to find Charles and Stella in the pool with Gia. Jordan doesn't say much to me, but sneaks me looks that suggest his head is messed up too.

Charles orders in dinner and Stella disappears with Gia for her evening routine, which seems to get longer and longer each night. If I didn't know any better, Charles and Stella are already fucking and just don't want us to know.

"I'm gonna check out the game," I say, rocking on my heels, wondering if Jordan has the nerve to be alone with me in the pool house after that kiss.

He stares at his phone and only lifts his head for a brief smile.

I huff a quick breath, figuring I misread what happened in the park. Of course, he wanted to make it seem like I found a new fuck buddy so Pierce wouldn't think I was pathetic. If he did, at least Jordan's tongue in my mouth blew that out of the water.

After several painfully slow innings, I consider taking a walk on the beach with a beer to stare at the moon. I get up and look out the window to see Jordan strutting toward the pool.

I consider going out and taking my walk, but he drops his swim trunks. The sight of his ass sends electricity through me. The smooth, round cheeks that flex with every step make me think of how much the guy loves sex. The way his ass moves when he fucks always stirs something inside me. That kiss blew a hole in my armor, and I'm stunned to realize I have a thing for my best friend.

Which is a problem because Jordan may have kissed me like he loves dick, but I know he doesn't. As far as I know, he's never done anything with another man.

Now, after I've tasted his lips, I can't stop thinking about him. And what would have been a simple shrug at seeing him dive into the pool naked now has me so fucking turned on looking at his long, lean frame under smooth skin. His physique is sculpted whereas I'm all veiny at this point, my muscles are so cut.

But Jordan doesn't dive into the pool. He walks around it naked. Pretty bold considering Stella can stroll out at any moment. Or maybe that's what he's hoping. He hasn't made her his Sub yet. From what I know about his contracts, they're exclusive, exploding my idea that we'd share her.

I shut the living room lights and pull closed the sheer drapery panel with diamond-shaped stitching. Standing in the window, but behind the panel, I reach into my shorts and fist my hard cock. My knees buckle at the contact.

Christ, I'm gonna masturbate watching my best friend. Jordan climbs up on the diving board, his big dick swinging, and I swear I've never wanted a cock in my mouth so bad.

In truth, if Stella was out there, wiggling her ass, I'd probably be doing the same thing. And if the two of them were getting it on? Him fucking her ass, as I know he likes... Jesus, just thinking that makes me nearly lose my shit.

Jordan jumps several times before swan-diving into the water in one perfect line. Without even stroking myself too hard, my balls vibrate, and I'm already coming all over my fist. It's hot. It's creamy. It's dirty. After getting my breath back, I keep stroking, realizing I'm not getting soft anytime soon.

Jordan gets out and holy fuck, his body glistens with pool water. He pushes his thick ebony hair out of his eyes. He looks like a god. I wonder if he knows I'm watching, which I doubt he does because he's not focused on me. I suspect he's thinking about Stella because he's facing the house. And holy shit, he's touching himself.

Christ, I'm jealous. But maybe I'm wrong. We just get so filthy here. But now we have a baby and a woman with us. That shit's not appropriate. I button my shorts to go outside and remind him. But he walks toward the hot tub with his cock now fully erect.

Great, he's going to jack off in the hot, foamy water. Will he think of fucking Stella in there? Will he think of me? Fucking her from behind or in her ass, while she sucks on his cock?

Christ, that's what I'm thinking about.

I couldn't have made up a more interesting twist to this week.

twenty

JORDAN

Stella passed out shortly after dinner. Gia was fussy all day, and Charles sent a warning glare to leave her alone.

God, I want to fuck her, but I'm also charged up over kissing Alex. The two emotions war in my head, leaving me feeling upended.

I walk out to the pool hoping Alex will come out and join me for a swim. I realized his announcement about watching the game was a passive invitation and I blew it. The lights are on in the pool house. I'm so tempted to go inside and just kiss him again. See where it goes, but something holds me back.

We always swim naked here and Stella's seen and sucked me off. No reason to be shy now. It's one of the most gorgeous nights that I can remember. Stars are so bright here at the oceanfront and I feel like I can reach up and touch them as I float on my back in the pool. The water is damn silky since Charles changed it to a saltwater filtration. Despite it being in the middle of the summer, the crisp breeze off the ocean keeps my skin cooler than I prefer.

The hum of the hot tub a few feet away calls out to me. I roll over and the water hitting my dick again feels exhilarating. After swimming to the edge, I lift out the side in a smooth move. Nothing like Alex. The fucking show-off lifts out into one beautiful handstand.

Stella's face hits my brain and I grow painfully hard.

My dick swinging in front of me, I pick up the pace and lower into the hot tub. The warm, bubbly water feels amazing against my skin.

I sit on the edge and lean back. In less than a minute, my hand closes around my cock. My eyes are closed, and the same silkiness of the pool is twice as effective here in the hot tub. My dick feels like it's been dipped in lube. The kind of slick feel of a bare pussy I love.

Electricity crackles around me and I'm stroking myself good now.

Behind my eyes, I see Stella's beautiful face. In my mind, she's standing there in a black lace camisole. Her panties are see-through with red satin laces up the front.

Stella's smile has inviting lips to sink my dick into. I flip over, my knees on the smooth cement step. I crank my hips, fucking my hand right at the water level. In my mind, it's her mouth. It's warm. It's wet. It's soft. So fucking soft. My thumb swirls over the crown of my dick.

Want a hand? Stella's voice in my head rockets through me.

"No. Stay there," I order in my Dom voice to no one. "Watch me." I sit up so my cock is fully on display and not submerged. "You like, kitten?"

Meow.

"Fuck, come lick my cock, kitten."

I feel her swallowing me so damn deep like she did the other night. How wet and hot her mouth felt isn't ever leaving my memory. Her tongue feels so smooth, but everything turns grainy in my mind. The tongue is longer and swifter in its movements. The sucking feels harder too. I'm still jerking off, but in my mind, I'm holding a face, fucking a mouth. But the cheeks are coarse with stubble.

Oh fuck…

No, this isn't happening. In my mind, I'm fucking Alex's face. Where is all of this coming from? Even crazier, I shift until one of the jets is lined up with my asshole. The water pressure feels impossibly good. My mind lights up and it's Stella licking my ass.

Something I fucking love.

"Yeah, kitten, lick me there."

The assault on my erogenous zones is too much and I'm ready to blow. In my mind, I'm not alone in this hot tub. Alex is on his knees in front of me and Stella is behind me. I turn around and squeeze my dick harder, imagining sinking into her tight cunt.

As Alex takes over licking my hole.

My leg muscles explode as I roughly fuck my hand, the water splashing all over the place.

"Come for me, kitten." She does in my mind because I always make women climax on my cock.

I spill into the hot tub, hard with a rush I wasn't expecting. I see stars behind my eyes and every cell lights up like kerosene on a campfire.

My knees give out and I'm breathless. I wait for the Sub who kept me enthralled for a few weeks to appear in my memory. No. Stella's face flashes through me.

"Are you done?" A gruff male voice sounds behind me.

That's quite real. It's one thing to be caught fucking a woman. Catching me whacking off and talking to invisible people servicing me is embarrassing. Clearing my throat, I twist and sit on the end of the hot tub.

Charles is standing there, his arms across a bare chest. Another time, he'd be naked too with a cock dripping from fucking a woman in the living room.

Not even close. He's wearing a pair of sweat shorts I've seen him sleep in.

"Yeah, I'm done. You want to give the water a go?" I chuckle and slide back into the warm foam.

"No. I'll let the filter clean out your cum first."

Thinking I've lost my mind, I try to push out some crude remark to hit on Charles because for all I know, this might turn into a month-long gay orgy.

I rake my eyes across his broad chest.

And...

Nothing.

Which means I don't want any dick.

I want *Alex's* dick.

twenty-one

CHARLES

It's been a long day. Jordan and Alex have been acting strange since yesterday. I meet Stella upstairs giving Gia a bath. They're adorable together.

The water is running and Stella is leaning over the side. She wears these cut-off terrycloth shorts that I don't think are part of her collection. If they are, she's a genius because just enough butt cheek and pussy lips stick out.

Tuesday night in my shower, I came so hard just picturing her fucking my cock that I had to hold on and damn near broke the shower panel.

The door creaks and she turns around, catching me staring. She stares back at my bare chest and the swim trunks I put on because I'm ready to do some laps to help me sleep.

"Stella?" I call out because she looks like she zoned out. "The water is high enough."

"Jeez." She reaches over to shut the faucet off.

But my feet move and next our hands are tangled, turning off the water together.

"Sorry." Shaking her head, she adds, "You're looking pretty tan, there."

"Thanks." I distracted her to the point Gia might have been submerged. Of course, she would have cried out. Still, the effect I have on Stella isn't good.

She's here to take care of my daughter, but it's not a 24/7 job. I'm Gia's father. I have to be sharp too.

As every day goes by, all I think is I want to fuck Stella. My goddamn stepsister.

She finishes bathing Gia while I pretend to futz with a clogged showerhead as an excuse to stick around and watch her. She lifts my daughter out of the tub and says, "I want to know where your mother bought these towels." Swaddling Gia, she adds, "They feel like velvet. Absorbent too."

"Those are my towels, actually. Feel free to pilfer them." I nudge her shoulder and my eyes lock on her mouth.

Gia cries out and Stella snaps back. Next, she's walking my daughter into the nursery, giving me an amazing view of her ass.

This isn't going to end well for me.

I lean into the nursery, and say, "I'll come kiss her good night in a little while."

"Take your time." Stella thrusts her up in the air and Gia coos happily, sticking fingers in her mouth.

The scene is so heartbreakingly beautiful and I know I can't have Stella as a full-time nanny, but I want to see this every night. I just don't know how to make that happen.

Frustrated, I head out to the pool and plan to inform Jordan that he can't have Stella. She's fucking mine.

He and Alex are sitting at a patio table playing cards, tumblers of some gold liquid in front of each of them. Whiskey or scotch, I'm not sure.

"Beat you again. Your money smells delish." Alex slaps down the cards that beat Jordan's hand and whisks what looks like a few twenties from the center.

"I swear you have to be cheating." Jordan tries to steal the money back, but their arms intertwine.

They're caught in a stare and holy fuck, they look like they're about to kiss.

Shocked, I bark, "What the hell is going on with you two?"

They break away and I see them blushing.

Jordan shakes the ice in his glass, and says, "By that wood you're sporting, I would ask you the same thing?"

"Let me sum it up, I saw Stella naked and her bare pussy a few days ago and I can't seem to unsee it when I look at her. You should be worried if I wasn't hard as a rock."

"Is it? Hard as a rock?" Alex mocks me.

"Yes." I take a seat, the swim forgotten.

"We're all hard," Jordan grumbles. "There's a gorgeous woman walking around. One willing to sit naked in the hot tub with us." He lowers his hand under the table.

It's come to this. Jerking off together because we're so fucking strung out and in need of sex.

"Truth or dare?" I say low and darkly. Plus, I didn't bring down any money to play poker.

"It would be more fun if Stella was still here," Alex says, sitting across from me. "But okay."

"You two are gonna regret this," Jordan says. "Who goes first?"

This is gonna get ugly.

Or very dirty. "It's my fucking house. I go first. Jordan," I snap because I'm sure Stella being naked in the hot tub with them was his doing the other night.

"Ha, truth," Jordan says proudly.

Smart... He wouldn't take my dare right now. "Did you fuck, Stella?"

"Nope." He wouldn't lie to me. Plus, he knows I

have cameras. "Alex."

Alex narrows his eyes on Jordan. "Truth."

"When we saw Pierce yesterday, did you still want to fuck him?"

"You saw Pierce yesterday?" I ask Alex, who nods.

"Did you want to fuck him?" Jordan asks again, rubbing his knuckles anxiously.

"No," Alex playfully sneers and looks at me. "Charles."

"Truth," I say because clearly, we don't trust each other with the dare option right now.

"Were you pissed when Ana showed up with Gia after never telling you she was pregnant?"

Before I can answer, Jordan whacks Alex across the chest. "Don't ask him that. And as your lawyer, *don't* answer that."

Still, the question rocks me. Of course, I was pissed. She was pregnant, telling God-knows-who I was the father and clearly, I wasn't around, making me look like a douchebag. I'm thirty-eight years old, I should have settled down by now, I know that. Something always held me back with anyone I dated. Instead, I stopped dating. Buried myself with work and my business, and just fucked around. That became my new excuse. Too busy for a relationship. The longest I ever spent with a woman was that week in Hawaii with Ana. And by the end, I couldn't wait to be alone again.

There was nothing wrong with her. She was lovely. Fucked me great. I just itched to be by myself. I'm set in my ways. Yet with Stella, I wake up every day dying to see her and anxious for what the day will bring.

"Have another question for me?" I ask Alex, smiling.

"Fine. Do you still want to fuck Stella?"

These are my best friends. If I can't be honest with them, who the hell can I open up to? I slide by on a technicality. "I saw her pussy. I haven't been laid in two weeks. Of course, I want to fuck her."

"Even though she's your stepsister?" Alex smirks.

"It's not your turn," I answer him. "Jordan."

He purses his lips. "Truth."

Christ, we'll be here all night until something interesting happens. "Have you ever been with a guy?"

Alex goes still next to me. I can't help myself, so I'll help him if he needs an opening to start fucking Jordan. It's there, I see it. Something in the looks they give each other. Holy hell, what did I miss yesterday?

Finally, Jordan answers, "No. Charles."

Here we go. "Truth."

"Have you ever been with a guy?"

"No." I glance at Alex. "Sorry. No offense."

"None taken," Alex answers with a shrug. "You just said you haven't. That doesn't mean you wouldn't. You don't know what you're missing."

"Tell us." I *am* curious.

"Don't answer that." Jordan points. "It wasn't a question in the game."

"Fine." I give up. "I believe it was my turn. Alex."

He dips his head back. "Truth."

"Can you tell me what you like so much about sleeping with a man?" As far as I know, he was a bottom with Pierce. Regardless of which way Alex may have swung with other guys, I've seen Pierce. Ex-Marine. Crazy tall. Pure muscle. Tatts everywhere.

"And don't say it's just sex," Jordan adds, sliding back in the chair, and I wonder if he'll stroke himself while Alex lets us in on a part of his life that he's kept very private.

"It is just sex. It's just another way to get off. Why do you think the girls you fuck in the ass come so hard?" He looks from me to Jordan. "It feels fucking fantastic."

Jordan stares at him like he doesn't know what to say.

"Did it feel differently with Pierce?" I ask him.

"Wait for your next turn," Jordan huffs like he doesn't want to hear Alex talk about Pierce.

"My house, my rules," I bark. "What the hell is the matter with you? Our friend is going through something."

"No!" Alex hurls his glass into the pool. Great. "I'm not *going through something*. Yeah, I liked the guy, all right. But I never stopped liking women."

"You're bi, Alex. It's okay." I hold my hands up.

"He never liked a guy this much before," Jordan adds like he's had some insight into what Alex has been doing. "I think it's cool. Something different to talk about."

Alex scoffs a laugh. "Whose turn is it?"

"Mine, I think," I say, even though I have no idea. When no one corrects me, I say, "Alex."

We stare at each other. In that moment, I see into his soul and shudder when he nods.

"Dare," he mutters softly.

Smirking, I say, "I dare you to suck Jordan's dick."

twenty-two

JORDAN

My entire body hardens. We're playing a game and we're wired from not having sex.

"Time out," I say, even though I'm aching to come by something other than my goddamn hand and a hot tub jet. "What purpose does this serve?"

"Always the fucking lawyer," Charles mocks me.

"You asked for it, Chuck," I sit back. "Tomorrow, I'm drawing up a Sub contract with Stella. I'm gonna train her."

"Really?" Alex says and the pain in his voice has me confused. Is it because of me, or her?

Does it have to be that way? Something tells me Charles would never cross that line. It killed him to admit he wants to fuck Stella. He'll probably go limp before his dick touches her pussy.

But Alex... He wants her. I know the guy. This thing with Pierce just put him squarely in the bi category. Before, he was just fucking around and getting off from having his dick sucked by a dude, or fucking one. Or getting fucked.

"She agreed?" Charles sounds angry. "I'll ask her to be sure."

"Go ahead. She didn't see the terms yet. But get this..." I stall from Alex being dared to suck my dick because I'm not sure I can handle it. "She basically gave away all her hard-limit vetoes."

"I'm not sure I like this," Charles sneers. "Aren't

things like fire play on the hard-limits list?"

"And animals?" Alex adds, shuffling the cards, looking anxious about the open dare.

"What the hell kind of websites are you two looking at?" I shake my head. "My hard limits are all for pleasure. Just a little rough."

"Speaking of rough," Charles says. "I believe I have a dare on the table."

The dare isn't really for Alex. It's for me. Would I let him suck my dick? If we do a devil's three-way with Stella, I could imagine Alex getting handsy with me. Part of me wants to show up Charles. He thinks I'll storm off and look like an asshole.

I call his bluff instead. I push back on my chair. "Yeah, Alex. Charles dared you to suck my cock."

His face changes, seeing me unzipping my shorts. He stands in that sexy tank top, his muscles glistening with the kind of night sweat the ocean gives off in the middle of July. "You sure?"

Holding my dick, I bark, "I'm hard, aren't I? Might as well get a good night's sleep." I give a rough stroke up and over the head, which is so damn swollen and reaching purple in color. "Stella sucked me off. Now it's your turn."

Charles rubs his closed eyes, but says nothing.

"Hey, Daddy," I snap at him.

"Yeah?" He opens his eyes.

"You gonna watch this? You dared him."

"Guess so."

"This wasn't the vacation we had planned huh?" Alex's humor always gets me. He's standing over me looking down at my dick. "Last chance to back out."

"No way. I can take it if you can."

145

"And this doesn't affect our friendship?" Alex takes his tank off and puts it on the concrete to protect his knees. Damn, I should have done that. "If you start acting all weird on me, I'll—"

Something hits me. My mouth lands on his because I don't want to hear the end of that sentence. His kiss feels nothing short of a wild explosion. His firm lips hint at how he'll take me into his mouth. The stubble on his jaw runs against my cheek, never letting me think for a minute it's a woman kissing me.

Alex turns into someone I never met. He's gonna suck my dick, but he's in control of this kiss. If this were a dance, he'd be leading. His tongue swirls with my mine, and now, I feel like a Submissive. My asshole jerks to life, and I'm not sure whose tongue I want there. Heck, I might even want a butt plug.

Or… Christ. Alex's cock.

My dick throbs and I push him off my mouth. "Suck my cock already."

He bites his lower lip and drops to his knees.

"Holy shit," Charles mutters. "Do you want me to leave?"

"No way," I answer.

Alex kisses my fucking naked stomach and I imagine the view Charles has.

When warm lips close around my cock, I jump. It's nothing like I expected. Stella's mouth on me felt like rubbing a piece of soft cotton on my skin. Or a rose petal. Alex's mouth feels like a fucking vacuum cleaner hose around my dick.

And Christ, his stubble scraping against my skin feels intoxicating. I lift my leg and perch it on Alex's abandoned chair while I hold his head, easing it on and off my cock. Because I know Alex can take it rough, I push until I hit the back of his throat. Christ, it slides right down.

Alex's hands grip my hips with bruising strength. My head is tipped back and I'm lost to an ecstasy I've never known or could even dream of. It's not any better than Stella, just fucking different. Raw. Taboo.

"Suck me," I slur. "That is so damn good."

"I knew it," Alex breathes against my stomach and then swallows me again.

Christ, it's so amazing. I want to come so bad, but I hold off, knowing that will make it better.

What the hell are we doing? This is my best friend. He's sucking so hard now and I want him to swallow my cum. All of it. Every drop. I can't take it and feel something snap.

"I'm gonna come. Be rough with me," I mutter. "Your stubble. I wanna feel it when I blow." I want to know a dude is doing this. My balls contract and my cock jerks. Alex groans like he feels it too. "Suck me down. Take it," I say with my jaw clenched tight.

I open my eyes to stare at Charles, who made me do this. But he's…gone.

What the?

Alex milks me of every drop and to my surprise, he stands up to begin jerking off at me. I think he wants me to suck him off and I'm not sure I won't. Only he groans and hot cum lands on my cheek.

"That's right, bitch. I'm coming all over you." Alex sounds like a different person.

He licks all the cum off my face, kisses me, and…

Goes back into the pool house and slams the door.

twenty-three

CHARLES

I crawl into bed and cringe that it's nearly two a.m. Gia will be stirring in a few hours. I trust Stella will be there.

That scene outside was way too intense to stay until Jordan climaxed. I felt so confused watching Alex's head bob up and down in Jordan's lap, sucking him off. And I've been masturbating every day in the shower thinking about fucking Stella. What the hell is wrong with me?

What the hell is happening with *all* of us? We've been here a week and we're already fooling around with each other.

It reminds me of that joke I heard about being stuck on an island with Ryan Gosling. How many days until a dude will fuck or be fucked by Ryan Gosling? I remember the answer being something like fifty-eight days. We didn't even make eight.

I have no issues with those two boning each other, but I don't want anything to affect our friendships. Right now, the people closest to me are my life, the ones who will get me through this thing with Ana and Gia.

And Stella too. Hopefully.

*

I wake up Monday morning to Gia crying. I push off the bed and grab my cock just to make sure I'm dressed. Most times here I wouldn't care. But my brain is hardwired to remember that Stella is in the house. Probably because I can't stop thinking about her.

Inside Gia's nursery, I realize I didn't hear crying, it was laughter. Stella is there changing her. The vision stills me, Stella smiling down at Gia. She's kicking her legs out and slapping her hands. She's laughing because Stella is blowing raspberries on her stomach.

It happens in slow motion. Gia turns her head to me and...smiles. Then screeches a laugh, reaching out for me.

"Who's that?" Stella coos at her and glances over her shoulder. "Is that Dada?"

Our eyes lock and a spark fires off in my heart. It's not something I've ever felt before. It's deeper and more visceral. And has very little to do with sex. Stella is standing there in a gray tee-shirt and gym shorts. Okay, they're short. And tight, the outline of her round ass is so evident I get hard, but it's not just physical.

Maybe it's because she's caring for my child.

I felt that love-for-Gia zing immediately when Ana put her in my arms. I didn't need to see the paperwork she left for me. Just looking into her eyes, I knew Gia was mine. It felt as if I was there in the hospital and a nurse handed her to me. I fell in love instantly. Something I thought impossible.

Now my heart is open and I'm vulnerable to things I've never felt before. I'm still a prick at work. I have to be. But Stella is my... My what? Some would strictly see her as my sister because our parents are married. Stepsiblings, at least. But we never lived together. She was a shy, young girl sitting at the other end of the table at holiday gatherings looking sullen and not making eye contact with anyone.

I was twenty-one with zero mental ability to connect to an eight-year-old. My mother didn't push her on me, so I didn't bother. I went about my life as if she didn't exist. By the time she became an adult, I was neck deep in my business. And pussy.

Damn, I lived a selfish and reckless life. The child begging me to hold her is the result of that.

"Hey, Charles." Stella smiles at me with no hint of awkwardness in her voice at all.

Like I never saw her pussy. I've been waiting for it to get in the way and it hasn't.

Maybe it makes sense. Maybe she and I make sense.

I'm about to go to her, when someone bumps me from behind.

"What's all the racket, baby?" Jordan struts in wearing a pair of jeans and nothing else.

"Hey," Stella says to him, but keeps her eyes on me.

Jordan takes my daughter in his arms while Stella balls up a diaper and drops it in the trash. But Gia wails, still reaching for me.

"She wants her daddy, Jordan." Stella lays a wicked smile on me.

"Here's Daddy." Jordan hands her to me. "You can get her breakfast, I want to talk to Stella."

"I'll get her breakfast," Stella jumps in. "Isn't that why I'm here?" She breezes past me with a gentle whiff of lavender I find so damn sexy.

When she leaves, Jordan narrows his eyes on me. "Do you have a problem with what I did to Alex Saturday night? It was your dare. And man, you've barely looked me in the eye since."

And I realize he's right. "No, of course, I don't have an issue with it." My smile turns into a glare. "Just don't lead Alex on if you're not interested in taking anything further. Even to keep playing around. And *don't* be lewd in front of my daughter. Or Stella."

"About Stella…"

"Are you still considering doing this training thing with her?" I ground out, hiding my anger about it.

"Yeah." Jordan eyes me. "Don't worry. I plan to give her plenty of space to take care of Gia."

"Does it have to be Stella?" I close the door to the nursery. "This vacation isn't going the way we planned. You don't have to stay. Go home. Go to your club. Find a new Submissive there. Spend as much time as you want. Just be here when I need you."

"Tell me why you don't want me with Stella."

"Because she's here to watch my daughter. She can't do that tied up."

Jordan smirks. "I'll make allowances for her duties here."

I roll my eyes. Why can't I just say I don't want him fucking her? "Has she given any indication that she really wants this? You better not have pressured her."

Jordan thinks about that and looks away. "A woman realizing she's a Submissive usually takes persuasion, Charles. That's part of it. Girls are raised to be good. Not crawling up to a man to suck a dick, or lick cum off the floor. Plenty of women love the lifestyle, but it takes convincing to prove it to them. And lots of training to break down their mental barriers."

"I want to see this contract before you give it to her."

Jordan smirks. "I'm the lawyer, not you."

"She's my…" I struggle to answer that because I'm so confused at this point. "She's living under my roof. She's my responsibility. I see it or you don't give it to her."

"Fine."

I'm particularly interested in how long this contract will be for. I have so many reservations about acting on this lust I feel for Stella because I can't get her out of my thoughts. I need time to straighten my feelings out. Jordan isn't looking for a full-time Submissive, or a relationship.

I need to get through this month. When Ana comes back and she and I have worked out a permanent custody arrangement, I'll be in a better position to think about keeping Stella in my life for good.

But in what capacity?

twenty-four

STELLA

My heart exploded seeing Gia react to her father. And fussed when Jordan wanted to hold her. Was that a red flag?

She's taking her bottle faster than usual and I wonder if she's reached a stage for more. I check the container of formula, but it goes by weight. I lift her, trying to figure it out.

Alex strolls into the kitchen with mussed-up hair, jogging shorts, and a loose tank top. His body is sweaty and ear buds sit in his ears. He smiles at me and then waves to Gia, wiggling his fingers.

He sings to her, a song playing in his ear I suppose. He has a nice voice.

"Hey, Alex?"

He pulls a bud out. "Yeah."

"How much do you think Gia weighs?"

She's fussing and wiggling in my arms because she's hungry. I just don't know how much extra to mix up.

"How would I know?"

"You lift weights. You can't guess what a dumbbell weighs if you didn't see the label?"

He thinks about that and takes Gia, transferring her to one hand. "Fifteen pounds," he says confidently.

"Wow. You're sure?"

He's got her cradled in both arms. "I'd bet good money on it."

I figure out the difference in formula to make, but

stop. "What if that's not correct?"

"There's a scale in the pool house," he tells me.

"She can't sit up. I doubt laying her on the thing will be accurate."

"Nuh-uh." He shakes his head. "We weigh you first. Then weigh you and her. It's subtraction."

I go still. I'm not ashamed of my body, but I haven't been on a scale in years. And while Alex weighs a lot more than me because he's pure muscle, I'm sure he knows what someone my height *should* weigh. How could he not judge me?

Swallowing, I say, "I'd rather not get on the scale. How about you?"

Shrugging, he leaves with the baby, nuzzling her. I'm constantly floored by these giant men going gaga over a baby.

I get my thoughts in order and consider that I have to face Jordan about this Sub contract once and for all. I'm not against messing around with the man for a few weeks, but why the paperwork? Why does it have to be so formal?

I wanted to get serious with James, but the rug got pulled out from under me. I'm not sure I'm ready for anything serious. No matter what, my career comes first. I have a fashion line to get into production.

As much as I want to spend the day commiserating with Bernadette, the promise I made to myself to see my dad nags at me. And I hate that I feel that way. He hasn't recognized me in years. Or anyone.

The facility Katherine put him in is top-notch. I was stunned at how new and clean and professional the place was. Pristine, really.

Alex struts back in. "Fifteen-point-two. I'm

slipping."

"Thanks." I mix more formula based on the new weight and take Gia back.

"Can I?" Alex reaches for the bottle.

"Sure." I smile, but now my hands feel empty. "Did you eat breakfast?"

"Not yet. I'll make some eggs or a protein shake in a few minutes." He sits at the breakfast table in front of a set of eight windows with white wood blinds and cream-colored rattan shades. All perfectly lined up.

"Does Charles have someone who cleans when you guys are here?"

"Yeah. Every other week usually. If they think we're pigging up the place too much, they'll come each week. Hide your vibrator because they thoroughly clean the bedrooms."

I spit out my water. "I don't have a…" I end with a guilty throat clearing.

"Guys find it hot when a girl has a toy."

"Good to know." I pour some coffee, needing something stronger than water.

He lays a kiss on Gia's nose and hands her back to me. "Do you like sourdough bread? I can make you some toast."

"Sure." I love sourdough bread actually, but don't want to jump up and down since I'm holding the baby. Remembering that Charles and Jordan need to work on his touring deal, I say to Alex, "If you don't have any plans today, do you want to take a ride with me to see my dad?"

He stares at me. "I'd be honored, Stella."

I consider what I need to pack for Gia when Charles and Jordan come in. Charles is showered, given how his

155

hair is slicked back. His dark-colored docker shorts look elegant with his boat shoes and white golf shirt. I start to wonder if he's got plans to go out.

"Charles?" I call out to him.

He takes a second to make eye contact with a tight smile and then it widens for Gia. "Yeah?"

"One... Gia must have put on a few pounds since you... Since she's been staying with you. She needs the amount of formula for fifteen pounds now."

"Oh, okay. Great. Thanks for noticing that. What else?"

I take a breath, and say, "If it's still okay, I'd like to go see my dad. I'll bring her."

His face darkens. "No." Shaking his head, he strokes her arm. "She can stay here. I can manage."

Guilt pangs me. "But I'm being paid to take care of her. I can wait until next week."

We never discussed my days off. Especially since I got hit with this out of nowhere.

"No. It's fine. When did you see him last?"

My face heats up, saying this out loud. "Six months."

"Really?" Charles sounds shocked.

"He had a traumatic brain injury. He's not...lucid. I assume his wife has been monitoring his care."

Charles just blinks like he's not sure. It makes me want to go even more.

After the toast Alex makes for me, I shower with Gia in a bouncy seat watching me, and then I return her to Charles' office.

"You look nice," Jordan says, standing to greet me, referring to the yellow coat dress that seems appropriate for a head injury facility an hour south of Malibu.

"Thank you." I smile at him and he goes back to the leather sofa under the window with papers scattered on a coffee table.

Charles looks up from his laptop in dark glasses and he's even more handsome. "Jordan, grab the pack 'n play from the kitchen."

Without argument, he stands and struts out. He's in his jeans still, but put on a short sleeve button-down shirt. It's summer in L.A., but the ocean breezes keep everything around us cool.

"She's all changed and I made up two bottles. They're in the fridge." I bounce her and wait for Jordan to come back with the pack 'n play. "Are you sure you don't want me to take her?"

Charles checks his watch, a Tag Heuer monstrosity. "She should nap for a few hours. When she wakes up, we'll take a break. I'm gonna grill tonight for dinner. Willow has a shopping order being delivered soon."

"Sounds great."

Jordan comes back and puts the pack 'n play next to the desk. He goes to take the baby from me, but I shake my head. "I got it."

I lay her on her stomach and after cooing, she grabs a toy and shoves it in her mouth.

"I'll see you later. Just call if you need anything." I bend down to kiss Gia and when I stand up, Charles and Jordan stare at me like they want kisses goodbye too.

Better to do nothing than something inappropriate, so I skip out of the office like I'm not conflicted as hell.

"Hey…" Jordan follows me outside.

I close my eyes and turn around. "Hi."

"You okay?"

"About?"

He creeps up toward me and backs me into the wall. "I keep hoping you'll come to my bed at night."

"We didn't sign our contract."

He twirls my hair. "Didn't stop you from coming in my mouth."

Just remembering how I exploded has me heated. "It didn't. And you came in my mouth."

"What are we doing here, Stella? I want you, you want me. Why are we playing this game?"

I bark a laugh. "Isn't that the whole BDSM purpose? To role play?"

"I'm not *playing* a Dominant. I am one. And I've claimed you, Stella. You're mine. Contract or not."

The feeling of being claimed so viscerally hardens my nipples, but I'm also attracted to Alex and Charles. My stepbrother and I are working through some tension that is mentally blocking me.

They've shared women before so why do *I* have to choose? Of course, I'm not sure I can handle all three of these masculine bomb threats.

"Ready, Stella?" Alex turns the corner and sees Jordan pinning me to the wall.

"Are you ready, Stella?" Jordan purrs at me and then lays a look that's even more seductive at Alex. "I want you ready for me. Tonight."

"Only with a contract."

"Fine." He takes out his phone and asks for my email address. "I'll send it to you and you can read while you're on the road."

"I'm driving."

"I'll drive, Stella." Alex smiles, holding a cooler bag filled with fruit and water for the trip.

Now I'm gonna have to read a hard-limits contract

while sucking on strawberries. Alex might crash. "You keep the contract on your phone?"

"It's in the cloud."

"For when the mood strikes and you want to…" I stop and step back. "Fine, send it to me."

I can't believe I'm considering this.

Then again, tonight I could feel that cock of his deep inside me. I know I'll come so hard around him. That's assuming he lets me come.

That's a definite hard limit for me. I come when I say.

Me.

twenty-five

ALEX

"Where are we going?" I clip the driver's seatbelt in Stella's Ford Edge.

An air freshener that smells like vanilla hangs from the rearview and from what I can tell right away, the car is spotless.

"The facility is in Santa Monica," Stella answers, adjusting the side-view mirror.

I freeze, hearing that. For some reason, Santa Monica triggers me because of Pierce. I shake that away. Seeing him with Cooper, as jarring as it was, helped me move on. That and Jordan's kiss. Not to mention him letting me suck his dick.

We drive a few miles, and Stella says, "Take a left here to reach the freeway."

"I'd rather stay on PCH, if it's all the same to you." Pacific Coast Highway is truly one of the prettiest roads when you want to clear your head.

"You sure?" Stella grazes my hand, hanging lazily on the gearshift as she adjusts the GPS from her phone in the cupholder. Something shocks me and I close my eyes for a second absorbing her touch.

Swallowing, I say, "Yeah, I know Santa Monica."

"Do you have any clients down there? I feel like it's a real Zen enclave."

I laugh, thinking of Pierce. Definitely Zen. Something tells me I can open up to her.

Clearing my throat, I say, "I only have a handful of

private clients right now. Charles being one of them. I mostly run the gym in his office building." The silence stills between us like she knows I have more to say and probably expects me to mention an ex-girlfriend.

I rarely open up to women right away about how I love to fuck men. The connection to Stella feels deeper. She's related to Charles, one of my best friends. I don't know why she was absent all this time, but something tells me that will change. I saw the way she bonded with Gia.

Seeing her with a baby stirs something in me. How loving she is really turns me on.

It's easy to answer her question about how I know Santa Monica so well. "I used to fuck a guy who lives in Santa Monica." I wait for her reaction, which is immediate.

"Oh." She smirks at me. "That's cool."

"That's cool?" Then again, I know she's an artist. They tend to be open-minded.

"Was he, like, your boyfriend?"

I exhale. "No. We just fucked. Honestly, I thought it only meant sex to him."

"What happened?"

Shrugging, I say, "Life got in the way. He got busy at a new cross-fit center. I started running the gym for Charles."

"He's a trainer too?"

"Yeah. Bodybuilding. Kinesiology specialist."

"Huh." Stella glances at me. "People manage to have relationships *and* jobs. Did he…meet someone else?"

I scoff, "A couple of people."

"A *couple* of people? You don't mean at the same time, do you?"

"I do actually. He started seeing a doctor that he and two other guys were training."

"A doctor needs *three* trainers?"

Shaking my head, I say, "I didn't get the whole story. But one of the guys on her training team swung that way too. So Pierce..." I realize I hadn't said his name to her yet. "They all ended up together."

"The three of them?" She sounds surprised, her voice pitching.

"Four of them."

"*Four*?"

"How's that for Zen?" I joke.

"I've been working too much. People do this? Have multiple relationships?"

"I think it's called polyamory. It's not the woman being in a relationship with three different guys. They're all committed to each other. Like a family."

"Hold on..." She turns toward me at a red light. "I thought I heard Lacey Wilde, you know the singer, was in a similar relationship with..." She snaps her fingers. "I can't remember their names. They're rock stars."

"Look it up on Google. There are no unanswered questions in life anymore." I smile at her and keep driving.

"Here it is." She reads the article in some online magazine about Lacey Wilde, a former rocker girl turned music executive living with and bound to Jaxson Steele, Nate Domenico, and Aidan Marx via a commitment ceremony. The latter being her ex-husband.

I chuckled. "I'd love to know how that went down."

"It says here she lives in Malibu too," Stella adds, now biting a fingernail.

162

"That would be *they*." I make a note to ask Charles because I'm so running in that direction the next time I jog on the beach.

"This guy Pierce… Was it just sex for you or did you have feelings for him?"

My body heats up unexpectedly and I fidget in the driver's seat. "I think I found out too late that I had real feelings for him. It bothered me when he ended it."

"Awww," she coos at me like I'm a wounded puppy.

"You think my heartbreak is cute?" I snap. Heartbroken. Am I heartbroken?

"No. I don't know why I said that." She rubs my arm. "You seem like such a nice guy, and I bet that Pierce man didn't realize what he had."

"Let me reset this conversation. I'm not a nice guy," I inform her.

Stella laughs, her hair blowing in the salty ocean breeze from the open window. "Don't worry, Alex. We want to fuck the good guys too. Especially ones who are nice to us while being hard-ass pricks to everyone else." Her comment stills me.

She fooled around with Jordan and he's hardly a nice guy.

Heck, so had I. Something he and I are ignoring. But we rarely Monday-Morning-Quarterback our dalliances on this vacation. I just never thought I'd be put into that category.

I want to bring the Pierce conversation to a close. "Anyway. He's happy and I'm happy for him."

"You're not happy?" She looks at me with concern in her eyes.

"I can be happier." I lay a grin on her.

Jordan didn't make her sign that contract yet. I can

still claim her. I like her. I love her curves. I respect a well-toned body. Cut women are definitely athletic in the sack. But I like a woman who's soft and sweet, one who giggles with shyness. One who wants me for me. No one wants to be a foregone conclusion. That surprise in a woman's eyes when you touch her because she doesn't think you would is fucking intoxicating.

I also love a woman with confidence, and Stella's is magnetic.

"It's just up here on the right," she says.

I signal to take a left and park in an underground garage. "When were you here last?" I ask her and take out my credit card to pay for the parking.

"Six months ago." She blushes. "I've been so busy getting this line together. This place wasn't around the corner from my apartment in Glendale. God, that makes me sound awful. He just sits there and stares into space. I stopped seeing the point. He's well cared for. That's all that matters. And you don't have to come in. It's jarring. I know."

"I can handle it, Stella." I squeeze her arm.

*

Only, she doesn't handle being told her father was moved two months ago to a place in Van Nuys. I walk her to the car with my arms around her waist. I have to settle her in the passenger seat. She's so upset and can barely speak.

We race up north, crawling in traffic because Van Nuys is a pain in the ass to get to via the side streets.

Stella shakes the entire time after looking up the new place on her phone. "There's nothing but these horrific reviews. There's even a law advertisement popping up that says they're representing clients who were abused."

I hold her hand. "Stella, this is *Katherine* we're talking about. She's filthy rich. Maybe a doctor she trusts told her to put your dad in a smaller place so he could get better attention. Sometimes people just bitch."

"Please drive faster."

I do and she practically jumps out when we arrive. I eat my words, seeing the shape of the place. It's a two-story garden apartment complex with people milling on the not-so-maintained front lawn unsupervised. This makes me angry. But what can I do?

Stella goes into one of the apartments with a *Check-In Here* sign. When she doesn't come right out, I go inside.

"What's the problem?" I put on a mean face because, let's face it, people tend to blow off women and not men.

"They won't let me see him," Stella says from the corner slapping at her phone. "I can't get a hold of Katherine. She gave strict rules about who sees him."

"And you're not on the list?"

"No."

"That's got to be a mistake. Hey!" I snap at the woman behind the desk. "This is his daughter. You can't keep her from her father." I wish Jordan was here to start spouting some California statutes about patient and family rights.

"I'm sorry. I can't get a hold of his wife." The woman is clearly shaken up. "You'll have to come back when you're cleared. I'm sorry. There's nothing I can do. The spouse's orders overrule children here."

All this suggests Stella's father is being kept in terrible conditions. I've been to a number of orthopedic outpatient facilities and physical training centers. When they're great, people gladly show you around.

We leave and as we're getting in the car, someone catches up to us. "Are you Griff Raven's daughter?"

Stella whips around. "Yes. I am. Please. Is he okay?"

"We haven't seen Mrs. Raven since he was transferred here."

Stella doesn't correct the woman. Katherine never took his name and still goes by Katherine Harlow. "I didn't know he was moved. I've been…busy with my business." She blushes again.

"She assumed her stepmother, his *wife*, did the right thing by her father." I reach into my pocket for my wallet. "How much do you want to let us see him?" The *us* comes out with emphasis—I feel invested because, shit, I like Stella.

"I don't want your money." The woman waves us off. "I just wanted to know that he still had a family. We're doing the best we can with what we got. Seriously, if you can move him out of here, I suggest you do." She leans in. "Make a turn at that stop sign and park around the corner in front of house number 111149. There's an easement to the right. It will take you to the back of the complex."

The steadiness in her voice means she's given these directions several times. And I have a feeling there's no standing order from Katherine. This disgusting place doesn't want to be exposed.

"I'll put a handkerchief outside the window and you can look inside. It's the best I can do."

"Thank you," Stella whines. "Is he okay?"

"He's medicated and yes, he's okay. But he needs better care. See you in a few minutes. I have to go."

I pull into the road and dread the long drive back to

Malibu because I know what we're about to see will make Stella completely lose her shit.

twenty-six

JORDAN

Charles quietly looks at my comments on the Tyler Pace legal team's decimation of our agreement. He sits at his desk while I'm perched on a chair in front of him. I'm dying to ask him what he thinks of me taking Stella on as a Sub for real.

But I don't.

I could have dragged her into this office and presented her with the contract on our first night here.

But I didn't. I respect she needs time. She'll know when she needs me.

I stare out the window and see a bright red flower bloom float by in the breeze, and I instantly think of how it will look in Stella's hair. It hits me like a bolt of lightning. Why I see *that*, and not a Sub kneeling before me. Just Stella and me. It's an earth-shattering, life-altering moment for me and I hold on to my chair because I may tumble out of it.

I'm falling for Stella. For real. Sure, I want to tie her up and roughly fuck her, but the other noise that comes with being a Dom, withholding orgasms and kneeling for hours, holds little interest to me. I just want to enjoy the hell out of her.

But I'm not alone in my feelings for her. I must face that my two best friends appear to have feelings for her as well. And she them.

Then there's Alex. How I can't seem to get what happened between us out of my mind. Not just that he blew me. Christ, that was probably the greatest blow job of my life, if you mix in how good he sucked me off and the feel of his stubble. Then throw in the way he kissed me. Something I thought would have wigged me out.

It didn't.

It felt fantastic.

So maybe, I'll initiate a three-way relationship with Alex *and* Stella.

Where does that leave Charles?

"Are you going to fucking answer that or not?" he barks at me.

Not only have I gotten out of my chair to stare out the window, my phone is ringing. "Shit, sorry." I pull it out of my pocket and recognize the number of a lawyer colleague I often work on celeb cases with.

Charles has been cool with that so long as it doesn't interfere with my work at Harlow Productions.

"Lou Arnez. How ya doing? What's up?" I say into the phone, keeping my voice down so Charles can finish reading.

"Jordan Sawyer. Coming up for air from all the pussy?"

I scrub my hand down my face. Too many people know about our wild month here. "Not this vacation. We're…taking it easy."

Charles rolls his eyes. Considering we're all ready to fuck Stella and I'm ready to nail my best friend, *taking it easy* is an understatement.

"Eh!" Lou scoffs. "Being cagey as always. I'm calling to see if Charles the-fuck-horse Harlow is bidding on the Tyler Pace tour?"

My ears start to ring as I consider my answer. We

signed a non-disclosure, which usually includes the existence of a contract. "Hang on." I mute my phone. "Charles, did Pace's people publish their short list anywhere?"

He looks up, wearing his dark glasses. "No. We're still under NDA. Why?"

"Not sure, yet." I unmute my phone. "Can't answer that."

"I'll take that as a yes since Charles is one of the biggest promoters. Fuck, I hoped you'd tell me no," he grumbles. "I could really use your help with a case for his brother James."

"James Pace." I whistle. "Since when do you represent him?"

"He goes through lawyers like I hear he goes through condom packages to fuck models in the ass." Lou creates one hell of a visual. "I can't ask you to help me with his case if your company is trying to work with his brother. Too close."

"I agree." I'm about to hang up when I ask, "What's the case about?"

"He's suing some fashion designer he had an investment arrangement with."

The hairs on the back of my neck stand up. "Fashion designer?" When I say that, Charles looks at me. "What happened?"

"If you're not on the case, I can't get into specifics."

"Then generalize. I'm curious. I might be able to recommend someone," I add, giving him justification to tell me more.

"It's a hush agreement. Apparently, she broke into his house and *allegedly* heard him say damning things about her. Something about her weight and the clothes she designs. He's denying it. But he's afraid she's a loose cannon. Has mental problems, apparently. He wants to keep her quiet."

"Who's the designer?" Although I already fucking know who. "Is he doing it under seal?"

"Nope. He wants to drag her through the mud. You'll find out eventually. Some newbie, Stella Raven."

My heart stops and the vein in my neck feels ready to burst. Someone is trying to hurt Stella. My Stella.

"How well does he know her to call her a loose cannon?" If she broke into his house... Shit, why does that turn me on?

Now Charles' eyes are peeled, and his jaw hangs open.

"This is between you and me because we go way back." Lou's voice gets low. "I overheard him talking on his phone to someone, saying he was banging her."

Jesus fucking Christ.

"Okay. Well, good luck with that." *Not.*

Now I'll have to defend Stella if she challenges this hush agreement or refuses to sign. She could get slapped with something civil.

Only, *fuuuck.*

I work for the promotion company bidding on his little brother's world tour. And holy mother of hell, Charles is her stepbrother. *His* mother invested in her business. It's a massive conflict of interest on all sides that will eliminate us.

Unless we...eliminate Stella from our lives.

Throwing the phone against the wall, I say, "Holy fucking shit, we have a problem."

twenty-seven

CHARLES

That visceral burn stings again, listening to Jordan tell me that James Pace is gunning for Stella.

I was sleeping with him.

Christ, *that's* who she was fucking. James Pace.

"When is she being served?" For a moment, I set aside the possessiveness I seem to have developed for Stella in the last week. Where that came from, I have no idea. But the Pace Brother complication rings louder in my ears.

I'm at the top of the short-list to get Tyler Pace's tour contract. No one outbids me. No one out-performs me. Except, his brother is suing my sister. My stepsister. The asshole wants to destroy Stella.

I hate that something kicks at me to pay Stella off, boot her out of Malibu, and take care of Gia myself. The vetting process in the final round of proposals with Pace's team may be the equivalent of a cavity search in a maximum-security prison.

Someone will figure out Stella is my nanny. And that she and I are related.

"Sounds like the case is ready to go and she'll be served soon." Jordan paces around my office. He falls into his own world when it comes to the law.

I begged him to work as my GC because he's one of the few people I trust. The bargain was a sweet salary, rockstar parking at the office where he could come and go as he pleases, and the freedom to still take outside cases because the guy loves showboating in court.

"You're not taking that case, right?" I won't allow Jordan to hurt Stella.

"You heard me tell him no."

"Just making sure." My neck feels like it's on fire and Jordan notices.

"What?"

"Stella needs a new investor for her company. I've been figuring out a way to help her out there."

"Oh shit…" He dumps his head in his hands.

"Exactly. I didn't think it will blow up our deal. Now if I do that, Tyler's team *will* find out about that. We have to submit financial disclosures. I can't have that liability on either my personal accounts or the business." My heart pounds, realizing when that Pace lawsuit goes public, no VC worth their salt will take a chance on Stella. No one wants to get in the crosshairs of James Pace.

Jordan narrows his eyes at me. "You can set up a shell company in the Bahamas."

My stomach heaves. "With what? I practically emptied my savings and mortgaged this place to keep us afloat after no one toured for two years."

"Oh…" Jordan seems to have forgotten how the bottom fell out of the touring business. "We can solve her money problem in a number of shady ways. That doesn't solve *our* problem. You're related to the woman Tyler Pace's brother is suing. And she's presently in your employ."

"Technically, it's my mother's employ."

"They won't see it that way."

Pinching my nose, I say, "You're the lawyer. Does a stepsibling relationship qualify for a relative conflict of interest?"

"Yes. Unless I can find a way around it. Legally, she may be your stepsister, but in practicality, if I can prove you have no relationship with her... Damn, our present living situation kills that." He purses his lips. "You've hired her as a nanny and she lives here. In your house. That alone supports a family relationship."

"But she doesn't live here permanently. It's only for this month."

"Didn't she get out of her lease in Glendale?"

"Yeah."

"And all her stuff is here?"

"Christ. It will look like she moved in permanently."

"Look, we need to get her out of here." Jordan picks his phone up from the floor. "It's been less than two weeks. I have plenty of money, I'll put her up in a hotel."

"You're my GC. Don't the same conflicts apply?"

"Fuck." He drops the phone again and pushes two hands through his hair. "Okay. Okay. Disclosure. I'll call Pace's attorney. Invite him to dinner. I'll swear in an affidavit that as soon as we discovered the conflict, we took care of it. As a licensed attorney, unless it can be proven otherwise, which it can't because we *did* just find out, my word on an affidavit is considered the truth."

"Fine." I'm cornered. Glancing at the house, I cringe at the decision to mortgage it in order to bail out my company instead of asking my mother for help. If we lose the Pace contract, I can't pay for this house. "What do I do about Stella?"

"Formally fire her. I have a termination notice we can use."

I feel sick to my stomach. "Do it."

A few minutes later, Alex screeches into the courtyard, sending gravel flying against my windows.

Oh dear God... Stella found out about the hush agreement and is ready to chew me out. "Did you text Alex what's going on?" I ask Jordan.

"Of course not."

Footsteps pound through the hall to my office and next, Stella is in the doorway, hysterically crying. A primal rush moves my feet and I take her into my arms.

"What's the matter?" I hold her against my chest as she sobs.

I hear Alex hoarsely whisper to Jordan, "That place her father is in is a nightmare."

twenty-eight

JORDAN

We listen patiently to Stella recalling the insanely horrific condition she found her father in, and fire runs through my veins seeing her so upset. I've never been affected like this.

"What the fuck happened?" I whisper to Alex.

He pulls me aside. "Katherine moved him. We got to the facility Stella visited last and found out he'd been sent to some low-quality adult home in a garden apartment complex in Van Nuys. We went there next." He shakes his head, telling me all I need to know about the place.

"Christ," I mutter, knowing Charles will flip.

"Stella, please calm down. I'll fix it." Charles pulls her off his chest and the stare that settles between them has me reaching out to Alex.

He's going to kiss her. Right here in front of us. But he doesn't. She's too upset, and Charles is too decent to take advantage of her.

I'm not as decent. Or rather I know what she needs. She needs to get out of her head and give in to pleasure. The other option would be alcohol, but she's still a nanny.

This new development means she isn't leaving us any time soon either.

"Charles, can you take care of Gia for the rest of the day?" I say, making everyone look my way.

"What?" Stella wipes her eyes and steps back,

distancing herself from Charles. "What's going on?"

"Of course, I can look after my own daughter," Charles says. "What does this have to do—"

"Stella, I want to train you right now. You need space in your mind. You need to be lavished and cherished."

"Hang on," Charles stops me.

"It's what's best for her." I eye him in the most fervent way. It's the same look I give him in the office that usually gains his trust.

Alex struts up to her and strokes her arms, making me wonder what the hell they talked about all day. "Stella? What do you want to do?"

She stares at Alex and then Charles. My heart pounds, thinking she's going to lift her dress and beg *him* to fuck her. I doubt he'll say no since she just kicked up his most protective instincts.

"Charles?" she whispers and my heart falls.

But I accept her choice.

"Yeah, Stella?"

"Is...is it okay if I... Train with Jordan?" She doesn't need his permission, and I don't think she's really asking him for it. Then again, she's living in his house, taking care of his child. Maybe that's all I'm seeing between them. Or maybe it's something else.

Charles keeps his face even. I know this man. He's fighting himself. His eyes stray to me, and I read him loud and clear. Twenty minutes ago, we were discussing writing her a check and sending her on her way.

To an expensive hotel under a fake name. Until we fix her real problem.

A problem she's not aware of. Yet.

Charles trusts my judgment, so I nod. He closes his eyes briefly, and says, "Whatever you want. Just—"

"I won't let anything keep me from Gia." She turns to me with red-rimmed eyes still clouded with tears. "Right?"

Keeping my grin to a minimum, I tamp down my excitement, and say, "Absolutely. We're here working on a deal."

She shakes her head. "Of course. Did you have a productive day? Did Gia distract you too much?"

How adorable. She's worried about our deal and the baby. Without even knowing she might lose access to Gia too, eventually, if I don't figure out what to do. I must heed my own advice and forget these details to fall into my role seamlessly.

"She was a dream," I say, knowing what she needs to hear. I reach my hand out to her. "Come here, Stella."

Charles and Alex congregate when she crosses the room and takes my hand. Before leaving, she halts and then turns back. "Oh shit. My father. Charles…"

He dips his chin. "I'll take care of it. Go…lose yourself. Forget for a few hours."

I close the door to Charles' office and push her against the wall. I take her mouth like I'll die if I don't kiss her. I don't kiss Subs, but there's no contract between Stella and me. No agreement on limits.

She wants…*needs* me to dominate her. Strangely, I don't want a Sub at the moment. I'm not thinking of the rules.

Like how it's so much easier when the woman signs up to be a Sub. And *literally* signs. Experienced Doms don't touch a Sub without a contract. Or at the very least, an explicit-as-shit verbal conversation about hard and soft limits as well the length of the relationship.

This night with Stella will be unbounded and unbridled. I might be in control, but the doors are wide open. Anything can happen. And fuck, that excites the hell out of me.

"Stella," I rasp, lust spiraling through me. "I want to give you what you need right now. *I* need you to trust me. You'll take what I give you and have faith that I'll know when you've had enough."

"Sounds good." She licks her lips and grabs my face.

But I pull back. "Are you sure?"

"Yes."

"I can be tough. Mean, even. I need you in the exact state I want you in so you can be thoroughly stripped down and only thinking of my cock inside you."

She visibly swallows, a hint of fear finally darkening her eyes. "Okay."

I shake my head. "The proper response is Yes, sir. Say it."

"Yes, sir." It's just above a whisper and fucking sexy as hell.

But it's too meek. "Louder."

Clearing her throat, she barks, "Yes, sir."

"Good girl. Now kneel, my lovely pet for the afternoon."

She gracefully drops to her knees.

I take out my cock. It's the best way to set the understanding that I'm in control. If Stella is my Sub, she's here to please me and needs to think of little else. That allows me to overwhelm her when I want to make her mindless.

179

twenty-nine

STELLA

I sink to my knees at Jordan's command, my pulse thundering at the 'lovely pet' comment.

My heart pounds at what might happen next. I had to get what I saw today out of my head. I need to be leveled out and calmed down or I'll call Katherine and say things I can never take back. Words so horrible, Charles will never speak to me again.

I exhale sharply and when I do, I almost don't recognize the man before me. His face rearranges into something lethal. His shoulders square more sharply than before and he even looks taller. His dark hair and green eyes are always a combination I find intensely attractive.

His square jaw and long nose make him look like a movie star. Seeing this other side of him, the Dom underneath, a man I'm not sure really showed up that night at the pool, rocks my sanity. There's an audible hum coming off his skin, like a machine warming up.

A machine that promises to fuck the bad thoughts right out of my head.

"Say your words," he growls.

"Yes, sir."

"Eyes down, Stella." He circles me with slow, measured steps. "We didn't sign a contract yet. Given the circumstances, we don't have time. We'll keep this session as basic as possible. For now, we'll rely on safewords. And we won't get fancy there either. *Red.*

That's what you'll say, and everything stops. No yellow to slow down. Not now. Do you understand?"

"Uh-huh," I say, looking up with a bone-dry throat.

"That's not the proper response." He peers down at me with a dark, virile expression. "And I didn't give you permission to look up. I don't want to punish you. Not today. But you need to acknowledge your basic understanding of what this is between us. Yes, sir, and No, sir when I ask a question, and *Red* when you need me to stop." He squeezes my shoulder. "Do you understand?"

Nodding, I say, "Yes, sir."

"Good girl. Stand up." His lips land on the back of my neck immediately. "You need to be fucked hard. I'll make it so good for you, I promise, kitten."

My ankles wobble and to my surprise, he helps me. "Thank you, sir."

He strokes my cheek. "You're welcome. Take off your clothes."

"All...all of them?" I blurt and then bite my lip. This is harder than I thought, the sheer mindless obeying. Even though it's exactly what I need. And what I want right now. "I mean—"

Jordan's fingers land on my lips. "I'll give you a pass for not responding the way I asked, but when I have to ask for something twice, that's where the punishment side of this arrangement comes into play. I particularly like that part, but those are for my more experienced Subs."

My more experienced subs. Jealously rages through me.

I force my brain to quiet down and just obey. I nod, and unbutton my coat dress. It's cut full in the breast

181

and pinched at the waist. My eyes stray to the door that I know isn't locked. Charles or Alex can walk in any time. For some reason, that thought has me stripping faster and my pussy getting wetter.

With my dress unbuttoned and sliding off my shoulders, I'm aware of the bra underneath. Definitely not chosen for an afternoon delight. It's one of those unlined numbers with a faint jacquard pattern. At least my black cotton thong is cut high and looks sexy.

A visible ripple crosses Jordan's lip in what I think is approval. Or lust. "Keep. Going," he deadpans.

I realize this is part of the training. Couples needing to wildly fuck strip themselves. My hormones are screaming, but Jordan's patience awes me. He's controlling me masterfully. Trying to, at least.

Breathing heavily, I unhook my bra and clutch the front before letting it fall.

"Problem?" Jordan smiles and I think he's playing with me. Baiting me. Wanting to punish me.

"No, sir." I smile and drop the bra, but I keep the thong on, knowing my defiance gets him off.

When his eyes trail up and down my body, I wait to see some level of disappointment on his face. No, his fiery gaze rakes over every inch of my skin and it's the most thrilling thing I've ever felt. He stalks around me and picks up my dress, noticing the label. "Your design?"

"Yes, sir."

"Don't take this the wrong way, when I saw you naked last weekend, all I could think was you're much curvier than I thought. Trust me, I'm hard as steel looking at you. You're a goddamn goddess. But your clothes, they're masterpieces. Women who don't have your confidence will want them." He brushes my face again. "Need them. We're going to make your line happen."

I have so many questions, but all I can say is, "Yes, sir."

Jordan steps back and the kindness leaves his eyes. "Thong off now. Lean against the desk and spread your legs."

I back up until the wood hits my ass where I slip off the thong and slowly spread my legs.

Jordan stares, that control so evident. Until he stalks toward me and hovers. I don't have to guess what he did earlier, he smells of the salt and brine that perfumes the entire house when the windows are open.

"It's going to get intense from here. I need you to stay with me. I'm gonna take you to a place you've never been. Do you want that?"

"Yes, sir." I clear my mind and realize I've been stalling even though I need this.

"Are you wet for me?" The deep tenor of his voice hits a nerve.

Before I can answer, he pushes against me, and I feel a very hard cock through his docker shorts.

"Yes, sir."

His lips brush against my earlobe. "Good girl. But I'll be checking for myself." Jordan lowers to one knee and taps the bent one. "Foot. Now."

Doing so will spread myself open for him. I think of Charles for some reason, remembering how he saw my pussy. And that sends a wicked shiver through me. I close my eyes and picture him watching as I lift my knee.

"Eyes open, Stella. On me. Watch my face as I enjoy

touching you." He brushes a thumb on the hood above my clit and even if I don't want to look down, I can't help it.

I whimper and bite my lip, more wound up than I thought I'd ever be, being controlled like this. Pleasure erupts and if I weren't gripping the edge of Charles' desk, I might have fallen down.

"Christ, you're so wet." Jordan licks his lips.

Memories of his mouth on my pussy send a shudder through me, a thump that will ignite an orgasm any second. "Yes, sir," I breathe, wishing I had permission to say more.

But it's the restraint that builds the climax inside me in a different way.

"Can I taste you?"

"Yes, sir. Please."

He growls at my adding the extra word. A second later, his tongue slides into my folds, plunging in and out of me. "Wider," he barks.

To give him more access to my pussy, I have to lift my leg and hold it with my hand. So I do.

"Nice," he purrs.

His wet tongue laves my entire sex. Over my clit again and again. Inside my pussy and then down toward my ass. His fingers trail up my thighs and two thick fingers enter me while he sucks on my clit.

It's as if my heart dropped a couple of feet lower and throbs in my clit. The thumping is in sync with the pounding of my chest, and deep in my womb.

"Fuck, so sweet. Come for me, right now, kitten."

Decadent bliss explodes throughout my body, and my legs buckle from the intensity. I'm lightheaded and I see spots in front of my eyes. No, those are stars.

Jordan grabs my waist and stands. With our bodies lined up again, he kisses me with his hands all in my hair. "I need to fuck you. I need to be inside you. Do you want that?"

"Yes, sir," I say between his wild, frantic kisses.

"I won't be gentle. I need to come too. A few times." Clothes rustle off his body. "We'll be here a while. Can I do that? Keep taking you, so I can come again and again?"

"Yes, sir." Nothing has ever sounded so heavenly to me.

"Turn around. Hands on the desk. Hold..." His voice goes shaky. "Hold on, kitten."

I do as he says, but he still gently lowers my head until my chest presses against the desk. He kisses my back, his lips soaking my spine notch by notch, leading to the dip that leads right to my...

Before the thought finishes, Jordan's tongue slips into my ass. "Fuck, so tight."

The pleasure is nearly unbearable. He's rubbing my clit while his tongue makes love to my ass. The air changes. The shadow on the wall in front of me lifts up like a dark promise. The head of a cock presses against my pussy. "Feel that?"

My breath leaves me, but I mutter, "Yes, sir."

"Do you want my cock?"

"God, yes, sir."

He chuckles darkly. "I'm not a god. I'm quite evil in the bedroom. I play dirty."

"I want it dirty. I need it."

"Oh yes, you do, kitten. You're so incredibly wet for me. Dripping. I've waited to fuck you for two weeks. Each night wanting you more and more."

185

"Then fuck me already." I break my promise to only answer in his sexually robotic affirmatives. "Please, sir."

"Bad girl."

A sharp whack lands on my bottom, the sting waking up the blood under my skin. Like all the blood has rushed to my pussy.

Jordan enters me in one hard thrust, but the slaps on my ass continue in a frantic rhythm with his pounding. He's so long that his withdrawals leave room for my ass to get slapped.

"Fuck, you're so bad. But you're *my* bad girl," he says while pounding and slapping.

My tensions build again, but I bear down. I wonder if I'll have to wait again to come. I heard women always have to wait until a Dom says so. Assuming the Sub is a woman. And the Dom is a man. What if... My body shivers, thinking about a male Dom fucking a male Sub.

Next, I'm clenching around his cock. "Jordan!" I yelp.

"Yes, kitten. Come all you want. Today is for you. And I have so much more cock for you." His hands close around my hips and the pounding turns utterly relentless. "Christ, you got me. Fuck, I'm coming, kitten."

He slams into me even harder than before. Kissing the back of my neck, he's chanting, "Good girl. Good girl. Letting me come inside you." His hold turns bruising strong when he releases me and pulls out. "On your knees."

"Yes, sir." I drop, facing him and expecting to get a face full of cum or a pearl necklace.

He's breathing heavily, holding his wet cock, his entire body just as slick. He's not completely hairless. His pecs are dusted with dark hair, and a line goes from his belly button straight down to a neatly trimmed mound over his cock.

"Suck me, kitten. Get me hard again. It won't take long." He's completely naked, spread, sliding his cock in and out of my mouth. "I promise."

thirty

STELLA

As promised, Jordan turns hard in a manner of seconds. God, I'm in trouble. He bends down and kisses me. "Good girl. Floor. On your back."

I gracefully scooch, and the feel of coarse carpet against my spine kicks my awareness into high gear.

Shit, this may hurt…

Jordan crawls on top of me and settles in between my thighs until his stiff cock teases my slit. "Wrap those gorgeous legs around me, kitten," he orders.

The moment I do, he enters me again, filling me so completely that I don't remember my name, let alone the day I've had.

"Do you feel me, kitten?" he growls. "This cunt was fucking built for me. My cock fits inside you perfectly."

He pulls out and wipes his wet cock against my stomach. "See how wet you are? How hot? This is gonna get intense. I'm gonna fuck you for a while." He enters me again and it's less primal and more…romantic. The way he holds me and kisses me makes me want to cry.

I scratch my nails down his back until I get to that perfectly round, hairless ass and grip the cheeks to feel every thrust. "Don't stop."

"Stop? I'm just getting started. I can go again and again. All night, kitten. This pussy is so tight, it's driving me crazy." Jordan pounds me over and over, and now my eyes are tearing from the endorphin overload. He found a button inside me. I plunge into my most intense orgasm yet that I forget to breathe.

"Jordan, yes. Yes. I'm coming!"

"You feel so fucking good coming around my cock, Stella." He uses my name like the game is over and this is now us.

I don't know how much time has gone by because Jordan doesn't stop kissing me. He rests his head against my chest so he can watch himself power through pump after pump until he finds his own release.

"God, you're amazing. I swear, I've never fucked someone this hard, this good." Jordan breathes into my neck as he unloads into me for the second time.

"This good?"

"Slow and erotic." He glances down at me and kisses me sweetly. "Kissing you while I come. It's like nothing I've ever felt before." His eyes turn feral and then the kisses get rough, even biting at my lower lip until I cry out. "Fuck, kitten, what are you doing to me?"

"The same as what you're doing to me."

"I want to take your ass. I'll make it good. I will be rough. I can't help it." He grins wickedly. "That's what aftercare is for."

Returning from the never-never-land state of euphoria from so many climaxes, I grip reality by the balls and notice Jordan is wearing a watch. "What time is it?"

"Time for me to fuck your ass." He grips my hip.

The thought tightens my nipples even more than they already are. "I… I want that."

"The answer then is Yes, sir. Or do you want another spanking because—"

For a moment, I think none of what we just shared for the past however the hell long we've been in here is real. Because it wasn't. He's a Dom. He's training me to be a Sub. Right. "Red!" I blurt and Jordan shockingly lifts off me.

"What's wrong?"

I sit up and feel the need to cover myself. But I don't. I stand just as naked as Jordan with my shoulders just as squared. He stares into my eyes, but I kind of like his eyes on my body. It gives me some kind of confirmation he actually likes me. As a…girlfriend.

"Jordan. Sir," I say and bow my head because if I want us to continue training, he's going to be my Dom the whole time. And I want that. "I suddenly want to be with Gia. I want to go check on her. I… I miss her."

Sure, people get sick or need mental health days, but rarely do you bang your boss's best friend in the next room while claiming to be too upset to work.

Jordan's body softens and the fierce, lethal Dom-lover slowly fades away. The somewhat-arrogant goof returns. Even the shape of his face changes into something less sharp. Finally smiling, he reaches his hand to me. "Of course. Let me dress you."

Piece by piece, he puts me back together, the smile reaching his eyes the whole time. Watching him dress, reality creeps back in about my father.

Jordan walks out of Charles' office, and I remind myself to apologize for us using that room. We were supposed to be signing a contract that never even got presented to me, we were too wound up.

I hear Charles murmuring to Gia in the nursery upstairs from a monitor laying around somewhere. I turn to Jordan and ask with my head bowed, "Can I talk to Charles alone, sir, please?"

"Yes, kitten." Jordan drops a kiss on my nose and saunters away toward the kitchen.

Alex. I nearly slap my face thinking about him. Thinking about the nice drive we had, how we talked and laughed. How I felt a spark between us. Underneath, I know these guys are just ravenous men whose bodies are conditioned to fuck everything in sight this month. All they have to feast on is me. But Alex is warm and funny.

I hope he maintained enough good humor listening to me cry out Jordan's name over and over.

I climb the stairs and before going into the nursery, I catch a glimpse of myself in the hallway mirror. I look good and fucked for sure, but no body parts are hanging out. Smoothing my hair, I step into the nursery.

Charles is a picture of devastating, masculine beauty sitting in the rocking chair holding Gia, who is laying on his chest facing outward, swatting at a toy in his one hand. He's only wearing dockers and a tee-shirt, but with one ankle over his knee; the rich businessman is always present.

"Hi. I can take care of her for the rest of the day," I say to Charles like I didn't just bang his best friend.

On his desk.

Or his expensive carpet.

He looks at me in a way he shouldn't. His smile looks forced, but I don't blame him. I have the strongest urge to kneel before him too. I shirked my duties most of the day and I owe him an apology.

"Oh, and I'm sorry."

"For what?" he asks, with a teasing grin.

"I didn't come here to screw your friends." I'm

191

about to correct myself to the singular because right now I don't see that number increasing, but Charles responds before I can backpedal.

"My friends came here to screw someone." His words hurt, but I don't think he meant them that way. He's letting me off the hook. Like it's part of my job somehow, and I'm not sure how that makes me feel.

I have the most irrational hesitation with Charles, like I don't want to boast about how good Jordan was. I want someone I can talk to. Having that person be Charles personifies how lonely I've been.

I have Bernie and she's wonderful. But it's not the same comfort level.

"I promise, whatever that was won't interfere again with my taking care of Gia."

"You plan to do it *again*?"

That hurts. He thinks I just needed to get laid. Maybe he knows something about Jordan I don't. Unsure of what to say, I shrug all sex kitteny. But then wipe the smile from my face. Because now shit's about to get real between us.

"I want to speak to your mother about my father's care. I tried calling her, but she's not picking up. She never picks up my calls. Well before the day I showed up here."

"I'll call her." He pats his clothes, but his phone is somewhere else. He's been taking care of Gia all day and doesn't care about his phone when she's around. I feel the same way.

"My father signed a power of attorney naming her his advocate." I catch my breath. "I can't make decisions. Nor can I pay for someplace better at the moment."

Charles pinches his nose, and it gives me the chance to hold Gia. I did truly miss her. She calms me, especially the way her head sits under my chin.

"Perhaps Jordan can figure out a loophole since she's not available." Charles stands. "But don't worry. Whatever we can do, I'll take care of it. Your father was good to my mother for many years."

"You mean he put up with her." I find my confidence, and Charles laughs.

"That's one way to put it." Meaning, he knows what his mother is.

We stare, and I naturally fall into his arms holding Gia. It's comfortable and sexy, the power he has to make my problems go away.

I leave the room with Gia to make her a bottle, and find Jordan in the kitchen talking to Alex, who doesn't look at me. We spent all morning together, and I feel like we bonded. That spark I felt got spectacularly obliterated when we arrived at the dump Katherine moved my father to.

Alex leaves with Jordan, and he smiles at me over his shoulder while I prepare Gia's bottle, feed her, and then burp her. After a loud one, she practically passes out in my arms. I bring her back to the nursery. Her diaper is clean, so I lay her in her crib. I see Alex and Jordan talking near the pool. Their body language is so cryptic.

I go back to my room and grab my phone to start looking up care options for my father, even though I'm no expert. So instead, I find the last number I had for a doctor. I leave a message for the man to call me back in hopes to get an update, or at the very least a referral to a better facility. Making clothes for women like me seems trivial compared to making a very sick man comfortable. I lose track of time and when there's a knock on my door, I think it will be Charles.

Jordan opens it, and says, "Hi, kitten. You okay?"

"Hi." I lean back and pin my knees together. "And what do *you* want?"

He kicks the door closed and lifts his tee-shirt off. "More of that sweet pussy. Right fucking now."

thirty-one

ALEX

With Jordan and Stella fucking like there's no tomorrow, I process everything. Including how I feel about the woman *and* man I want to fuck, having fun without me.

It hurts more than I thought it would.

But Stella needs what Jordan can give her right now.

Not a nice guy.

We want to fuck the good guys too…

I'm also so wired at this point. And as much as I want to be sliding my cock inside Stella to make her feel better, what I saw at that adult home sickened me too.

Where's a cock to make me *feel better?*

Charles catches me in the yard, his face stern. "What the fuck happened at that place with Stella's father?"

I give him the play-by-play up until we got behind the building.

By the look on my face, Charles says, "That bad?"

"The guy was naked. Just lying there." I leave off the bed sores.

"Jesus." He pushes a free hand into his hair. "I'm going to kill my mother."

"The place told Stella she wasn't on the list to see him. But we think the manager knows how deplorable it is and keeps people away unless they bust balls."

"You're a ball buster."

I snicker. "I didn't want Stella to be faced with

something awful, but I'm proud of how she busted balls to see him. Christ, it was disgusting. The nurse who came out and told us how to see him said he was okay, but really needs to be moved."

"I'll make sure that happens. What's the name of the new place?"

I show it to him on my phone. "I'll forward this to you."

"Thanks. I'll add it to the list of shit I need to clean up."

"What else needs fixing?"

He brings me closer to my pool house door. "Stella is being sued by the guy who promised her the investment money. James Pace."

"Pace? Is he related to—"

"You bet. Tyler Pace's brother."

"What is James Pace suing her for?"

"He's trying to buy her silence by making her take his investment money. She turned him down saying he fat-shamed her and her clothing line. He was having a private conversation in his own home, but she had a key to get in and overheard him. He wants to make sure his comments don't get out."

"If she doesn't take his money?"

"I heard he buys bots to crucify his enemies on social media."

"Christ." I go inside the pool house and Charles follows me.

"Thank you for taking care of Stella today," he says with emotion in his voice.

"You're welcome. It was my pleasure, really." From the fridge, I grab a beer and down it practically in one gulp. My nerves are fucking shot. "You should call your mother."

Charles nods and takes out his phone. "Michaela, can I talk to my mother?" He presses his eyes closed. "What the hell is she doing there?"

Oh, shit. That's not good if we can't reach his mom.

"How long has this trip been planned? I saw her ten days ago and she didn't say a word to me." He scrubs a hand down the back of his neck. "How can she be out of range? The yacht has WiFi." He blushes.

As if I didn't know Katherine has more money than God.

Charles holds his phone against his chest. "If she's with another guy, I'll kill her. I get it, her husband's been a vegetable for seven years. She's in a tough position. But still. How dare she take off knowing the kind of place her husband's in without giving me a heads up before dumping Stella on me?"

I get why she wouldn't mention it if she's screwing someone. But I keep my mouth shut.

"When is she coming back? *Two months!"* Charles barks into the phone. "When you talk to her, have her call me." He throws his phone on the kitchen island.

"Where is she exactly?" I ask him as if it matters at this point.

"Out of the country." He grabs a beer of his own. "For her sake, it better be a place without any extradition."

thirty-two

JORDAN

I don't remember the last time I fucked a woman I liked. Sure, I adore my Subs, as a Dom. Not as a man. I want to dominate Stella in the traditional sense, and she enjoys me ordering her around. but I don't feel like a Dom with her. And she doesn't feel like a Sub.

Damn, I like her. A lot.

I think she likes me too. The real me. I've been the real me for the past few hours. We've been fucking nonstop. Reality washes over me. I'm in this house with two other men. My best friends, and we normally share women.

Both Alex and Charles look at Stella in a way they don't look at anyone else. She smiles so deliciously in Charles' arms, and her laughter is magical when joking in the kitchen with Alex.

It doesn't seem right to keep her to myself.

I pull my wet cock from her drenched, cum-soaked pussy, even though I'm already hardening up again. This never happens to me. And I wonder if my heart has something to do with how my body responds to her. That thought terrifies me. I have no idea how to be a boyfriend. I would need some serious help and patience from the right woman.

Shaking from that soul-shattering revelation, I kiss her neck and trail down to her breasts. They're beautiful, swollen globes, full and firm. Her nipples are pink, the tips red and sore from my mouth.

"Stella," I whisper to her with a tension-filled groan.

"Jordan," she moans back to me.

I work my way back up and kiss her. Can't stop kissing her. Her. Only her. She smiles when she kisses and it's so damn adorable. "Are you sore, kitten? Can you fuck one more time?"

Stella is a gorgeous, flushed mess, but she reaches for my cock. "Yes, sir."

I nearly cringe because I'm not playing the game anymore. "It's just me, Stella. You don't have to say that." I swallow harshly, not wanting to lose my option to go full-on-Dom on her later. "For now."

"Okay. Did I do something wrong?"

I lift off her, but stroke her cheek. "Wrong? You've made me come like twelve times."

"Maybe you just come a lot." She playfully grins and stretches into her pillow, her curly blonde hair spilling all around her.

"God, you're gorgeous and so fuckable." I kiss her again and find I don't want to stop.

"So fuck me."

I clear my throat and think this is where being a Dom might come in handy. Standing, and giving her a hearty view of my body, I say, "Stella. On your knees, right now."

"Oooo, I'm in trouble," she mocks.

I'll punish her with my belt later when I'm not so fucking spent.

"No, you're not in trouble. I want you to catch your breath. I have something I want you to do." I pet her head and lean it against my bare thigh. "A favor."

"Yes, sir." She slips into the role so easily, it's intoxicating.

I keep her there, and the feel of her against me like this overwhelms me. It takes everything I have to let go.

I dive into the shorts and tee-shirt I had on and take my time so I can watch Stella kneel and gaze at the floor. She does it perfectly, her back arched in that graceful way that makes a Dom crazy.

I take an extra minute to admire her beauty. Every part of her, especially how she embraces her curves and looks so comfortable in her skin. How she wants other women to feel that way. Women are catty and just as competitive as men. A woman with less grace wouldn't share that magic she has. We *have* to fund her line, Charles and I.

"Stella, stand up please." I reach my hand out to help her. "Get dressed and come with me. Just a tee-shirt. No panties."

"Yes, sir." I let her keep saying that since she seems to get off on it.

I'm hoping she'll answer me as enthusiastically when I give her my next command.

The hallway is quiet. Stella looks down at my hand and loosens it. She's the nanny here, and Gia comes first. I get that. I respect that. I...love that about her.

The nursery is empty, so Stella peeks into Charles' bedroom. He's on top of his covers, asleep with Gia on his chest. The sight even gets me because he's smiling.

Stella goes into the bedroom and lifts Gia. My heart sinks, fearing my plan would have to wait. But she puts Gia in the bassinet near the bed. The baby never wakes up and my Stella, my kitten, adorably tiptoes back to me.

"I feel bad that I probably messed up her schedule. She should be eating now," Stella whispers. "Where are we going? Will it take long?"

"Depends."

"On…"

"You'll see." I squeeze her hand and lead her down the stairs, then out to the pool house.

I knock on Alex's door, and he answers after a few seconds. He's shirtless, wearing only tight boxer shorts. His eyes rake over Stella, and I wait for his reaction to her looking used and fucked. Deliciously so. All while I can't stop staring at the outline of his massive cock in those briefs. I've seen it dozens of times, but things have changed between us.

Right now, this is about Stella.

"Do you have a minute?" I ask my best friend.

"Sure." He turns to walk deeper into the room with his back muscles flexing. The boxer fabric clings *inside* his round ass, outlining it even more prominently.

It stirs something in me, and I have to get a handle on these feelings eventually. I'm falling for a woman *and* my best friend.

"What's up?" He turns around and my eyes linger on his cock.

Christ, my brain is going there, isn't it? I've watched gay men at my club. The male Subs get fucked, but the Doms suck their dick first. *And* after to make them come if getting railed in the ass doesn't do it. It usually does. Apparently, I've been paying too close attention.

But I guess all that unconscious awareness was worth it if it will help me understand what I would need to do to…take care of Alex.

Getting my heartrate in check, I kiss Stella's hand linked with mine. "Stella, kitten."

"Yes, sir?"

I blink and get into the role. "Kneel, please."

"What are you doing?" Alex snaps.

"You'll see," I tease him.

With Stella kneeling, I walk over to Alex. His eyes land on my bare, sweaty chest, and I swear I feel it. He loves fucking women as much as men. Maybe more. Pierce and that breakup, if you can call it that, threw him off. He's probably questioning who he really is. What he really wants.

I can give him a chance to have both.

I know I want both of them. In...*gulp*...every way. After this month when we go back to our lives, we'll figure it out.

"She's gorgeous, isn't she?" I breathe on Alex's neck.

"She sure is." He smells of soap and musk, and it tickles the back of my throat in a good way. Does his cock smell like that too? What does it taste like?

"Her pussy feels amazing around my cock." I watch for Alex's reaction, but a tick of his cheek is all I get. "Wet. Tight. Hot."

"Good for you," Alex nips.

"No. Good for *you*. If you want her too."

"Huh?" Stella looks up and I'm dying to see something negative in her bright blue eyes. I'd never force her. I've ordered Subs to fuck other men before, the ones who agreed to it in our contracts.

"Stella, do you want Alex?" I clarify. "Do you want to get naked for him, spread your legs, and feel his cock slide into your warm, wet cunt?" I glance back at Alex. "Sorry, I spilled several loads into her."

"Do you..." Stella hesitates. "Alex, do you want me?"

My hand brushes down his back and into that amazing curve right before his ass bows dramatically outward.

These two seem hesitant and I'm crushed, or maybe it's because I'm in the room. Fuck-all, I'm not leaving.

"Stella, do you remember your safeword?"

"Red."

"Good girl. Now suck Alex's dick for me. I want to watch. Go on," I breathe against Alex's neck. "Fuck her face."

"Are you sure, Stella?" he asks, but his fingers are already skimming the waistband of his boxers.

God, the thought of seeing his ass flex with his dick in her mouth has me hard as steel.

"Yes. I'm so sure. Do you want me like this? Kneeling?" she asks Alex, not me.

"Are you comfortable, baby?" Alex slides the boxers down and steps out of them.

"I sure am." She licks her lips.

The way he walks toward her completely nude, something I've seen dozens of times, has a shockingly different effect on me. Jealousy. He made me come so hard by sucking my dick the other night. Something we haven't talked about.

But seeing Alex getting ready to have his dick sucked by Stella is a sight I'll never forget. His long, muscular legs are so smooth and beautiful. He waxes his entire body. Any light brown hair peeking through looks faint against his tan skin.

"You want my cock, baby?" he asks her, holding it.

"So much," Stella purrs back. "Please."

"Oh, baby. I can't say no to that. Open up for me." The way he groans, I know he entered her mouth.

I'm right behind him, deciding if I want to see his dick sliding in and out of her or if I just want to watch his ass while he fucks her face. I stroke myself roughly over my shorts watching Alex's ass.

It's fucking perfect as far as asses go. Round and muscular. It lifts right from his thighs and the power of his thrusts when he's nailing a woman is amazing. God, he'll give Stella a good, hard fucking. I'm sure as shit staying to watch.

A groan slips from Alex's mouth, forcing me to move. Get a better look. The vision stills me. Her hand grips the base of his cock, twisting gently while she takes him deep into her throat.

"Are you okay, Stella?" I say to check on her and to make my presence known. This is a voyeuristic act as much as it is an exhibitionist one for them.

"Yes, sir."

"Good, girl. Suck that cock."

I circle them until I'm facing Alex, who looks at me with a flushed face. Smirking, he lowers his gaze to Stella. "That feels amazing, baby. Suck me. I've wanted your mouth around my cock the minute I saw you."

"I doubt that," she murmurs.

"It's true. You're beautiful and sexy. God, that feels so fucking good." He pistons his hips more dramatically, bending his legs like he's getting so damn deep.

"Come in her mouth. She'll get you hard again," I say with gravel in my voice. "Then, I want you to fuck her."

"Is that okay, baby? Can I come down your throat?"

She responds by gripping his ass and making him pump harder.

"Oh, Christ. Yeah. I'm coming. Fuuuck." Every muscle in his body flexes and a glistening sheen covers his cut and beautiful torso.

It's like I'm seeing Alex come for the first time and it's making me fucking crazy.

Stella's throat muscles work so beautifully as she swallows Alex's cum. I have the craziest urge to taste it too.

But he drops to his knees and kisses her before I even lift my foot to step in that direction. It hits me that I forced them to skip a step. She and I had some playful, romantic moments and I denied Alex and Stella their first kiss.

"You taste so fucking sweet, baby." His mouth covers hers, and they kiss like passionate lovers.

It's beautiful to watch. And so fucking hot.

"Lay back, baby, I want to taste this pussy full of cum," he says with lust in his voice as he kisses her neck.

"Are you sure?" she asks quietly, pressing her fingers into her folds.

"Of course. I swallow guys' cum, remember?" He smiles and my heart stops.

I hadn't realized he told her he likes to fuck men. Christ, that will make what I have planned next go even smoother.

He lays Stella out on the couch and spreads her thighs. "You're so fucking soft, baby." Grinning, he says, "In the best way. Smooth, like silk. Christ, you look so sore. You fucking maniac," he snaps angrily at me with a wickedness I never saw before. "How many times did you fuck her?"

"I lost count," I rasp to be a brat.

"Are you sore, baby?" He brushes her plump folds.

"A little. I need some tongue care."

"Tongue care it is." Alex buries his face in her pussy and his tongue goes to work.

The sound of her soft moans drives me up the wall. I'm full wood, watching them, afraid I'll blow in my shorts before he's inside her.

This is insane, I've never come this much in one damn day. In between licking, he fingers her and her hips buck.

"That's so good, Alex."

"Come in my mouth baby, so I can fuck you from behind."

Stella pants in successive beats, my eyes laser-focused on Alex's tongue circling her clit. I can see from a few feet away how swollen she is. It's the most gorgeous thing I've ever watched.

"Yeah, make her come, Alex." My voice makes him look at me.

His eyes focus on my cock, which is now hard in my hand as he licks his lips. "Oh, I will."

"Christ," I groan and my dick pulses. It takes all my will not to come all over my hand.

He slides two fingers into Stella's pussy and one into her ass. That motherfucker beat me to her ass. But Stella fucking loses it. Groaning and whining.

She kisses him and they go off on each other like lovers. "Want my cock?" he whispers.

"Fuck, yeah."

"Bare?"

"Even better. Take me bare. I want to be bad with you." Her words drive me crazy.

Alex kisses her again, wide mouthed and seductive.

"Turn around. I'm close, baby."

I never saw a woman whip around and stick her ass in the air so fast, but so beautifully, so wantonly. "You okay, kitten?"

"You have no idea, sir. *Fuck me*, Alex."

He slides his cock inside her and his lower back spasms. "Christ." He pumps in and out of her wildly.

"Pull her hair," I say.

"Shut the fuck up," Alex barks at me. "She's mine right now."

"No." I come up behind him, my breath on his neck. "She's ours."

He leans forward like that will deter me. All it does is stick his ass out more. He's a bottom in his bi relationships, which means if we go further, he and I, I'm fucking an ass. But that thought has me throbbing even harder. I'm tempted to just shove into him right now while he's fucking her. Make him lose his mind.

But he and I aren't ready for that. We haven't spoken about taking things further between us. Hell, I might have to give him a safeword too.

My fingers lay on Alex's waist while he's fucking Stella like there's no tomorrow. The more she moans, the harder he rams her.

"You love a hard cock deep in your pussy, don't you," he groans.

"God, you're so big. Don't stop," she squeals.

"I sure am big. Hold on, baby. Not stopping." He lifts one leg and really fucks her hard.

I get behind him and slide my hand down his back with a slow, torturous trail over every notch in his spine. "Fuck her. Fuck her with everything you have," I whisper in the back of his neck.

I want to add, *I can be your Pierce. We can have it all. With Stella.*

Shit, I have to let Charles fuck her too. If he has the balls to let go of whatever is stopping him from throwing Stella down on his bed and ramming the shit out of her.

I push Charles out of my mind as my finger lands right between the two dimples of Alex's lower back. "The safeword is red if you want me to stop," I whisper in his ear.

"No, don't," he whines, playing with me.

No and stop are thrown around for teasing in my world. Makes things hotter. The mind reaches higher depths of ecstasy when the sex is forbidden or taboo. Like fucking your best friend. Who's also a guy. Or fucking your best friend's little sister when she's also his nanny.

My fingers reach the cleft in his ass, and I wait for him to swat me away. This is a first for me and the exhilaration is unbelievable. I love anal sex. How different would it be if my finger or dick slid into a guy's ass?

Not a guy. *Alex.* My best friend.

My brain goes haywire as I breach the outer ring of his tight asshole. I don't know why it wouldn't feel this snug. God, I can tear this ass up. Make it mine.

Alex throws his head back and gasps when I slide my finger deep into his asshole. My teeth graze the back of this neck. "Tell me to stop."

"Christ, no. Don't stop. Stella, I'm gonna fucking come."

With my free hand, I yank my shorts down to jerk off. I can't help it. I'm knuckle-deep inside Alex's ass and fuck, I feel the contraction of his cock muscle. It's so damn strong. I imagine how it feels inside Stella and next, cum is shooting on his ass.

Stella cries out, "I'm coming. Fuck," she bites out her cute expletive.

The three of us heave and pant. I let go of my dripping cock and reach around to pull Stella in closer to Alex, which brings me closer to him.

It's our first taste of an MMF threesome. And fuck, it won't be our last.

thirty-three

CHARLES

I'm drained from listening to what happened to Stella when she went to see her dad.

And fucked in the head over it. I can't believe just hours before, Jordan and I were talking about sending her away. Squeezing my eyes shut, I realize I've been so conditioned to write Stella off.

I hate myself for it.

Or maybe it's because I just don't see her as my sister.

Now I see her as a woman too. A beautiful woman with a beautiful heart.

I'm totally appalled at my mother for what she did to her husband.

I must have dozed off. I wake up to a piercing wail that shatters my soul. I immediately clutch my chest, remembering I fell asleep with Gia on the bed with me. Only, she's not on my chest anymore. My heart pounds as I feel around for her.

Thinking she fell out of my arms and is now wailing on the floor makes me want to throw up. How do I explain to Ana what happened? Only…Gia isn't on the floor.

But she's still wailing.

What the fuck? Where is she?

My brain snaps awake, and I see her stirring in the bassinet a few feet from the bed. How did she get in there?

I'll check my cameras later and find out who came in and took her from me. Stella, no doubt. But fuck, she did the right thing.

I get to the bassinet and immediately see something is wrong. Gia's skin is red and when I touch her, she's burning up.

"Oh shit. No. No. No." I lift her into my arms and rock her. "Shhh. It's okay. It's okay, princess. Daddy's here. I got you. I'll make it better." I rush to the bathroom and fumble through wetting a washcloth with ice-cold water.

I don't know what else to do. Ana didn't give me any instructions if she got sick.

Fuck...

"Stella!" I yell, not knowing where the hell anyone is.

The lack of sound tells me I'm alone. Alone and my daughter is sick. Please dear God, let this be a bad dream.

With the cool washcloth nestled in the back of Gia's neck, I slip into my shoes and carefully walk downstairs. My security control room next to the front door has a live PC with all my cameras. Glancing at all the feeds' black and white ceiling views, I don't see movement in the house. Except there in the last corner...

Pool House

There's movement all right.

Alex is fucking Stella from behind and Jordan is stroking his ass. What. The. Hell?

Gia wails again. She's burning up. I have no idea what to do, and my nanny is being railed by my two best friends.

"Fuck this." I grab the keys to the car I leave here in Malibu and rush into the three-car garage off the side of the house. Two jet skis are parked behind one of the bay doors and Jordan's Charger is in the other spot.

I breathe in relief to see my mother installed a car seat in my Benz. I put Gia inside it, even though she's still screaming. "I'm trying, princess," I whine softly.

Tears build in my eyes, but I hold them in. I have to be strong. All of this hit me so fast. Right now, I'm not sure I can handle doing this alone. I feel so damn isolated.

With Gia strapped in, I gut-wrenchingly get into the front seat and drive her to the hospital. I simply don't know what else to do.

I get there and leave my car parked in front of the ER. They can tow it, I don't care.

Help! My daughter's sick!" I say, rushing inside.

Thank fuck, people care about a baby. Two nurses and a doctor storm into the waiting room.

"I'm Dr. Sinclair. What happened?" one of them asks me as another takes my daughter.

"I... I don't know. I woke up and she was crying." I know how that sounds since it's not even eight p.m. Sounds like I'm hungover from day-drinking. I had that beer with Alex around three p.m., and that was it. The nap hopefully burned it off.

"When did she eat last?"

"I fed her around six. Then I burped her, she was fine. I laid down on my bed and we fell asleep."

"Sleeping in a bed with a baby is dangerous, sir."

"Sir, your daughter's name?" a woman from the front desk asks me, holding a tablet.

"Giana Harlow."

"Do you have identification for her?"

I freeze, realizing her papers, the ones Ana left me, are home. I forgot to grab them. "All of her paperwork is home. I was worried. I'm a new father for fuck's sake."

"Sir, there's no need for foul language."

"You're right. I'm sorry." I push a shaking hand through my hair.

"Sir, did you smother your baby?" Dr. Sinclair asks me.

Christ. This may have been a mistake. "No. Of course not. In fact, my nanny came in and moved Gia to her bassinet. She wasn't sleeping with me when she got sick. When I fell asleep, she was fine."

"Where's your nanny now?"

"Busy. Off the clock. I ran out of the house. I was worried."

Dr. Sinclair turns and joins the other two people examining Gia.

"Do you have her insurance cards?" the admin asks me.

"No."

"Can you get your wife on the phone for this information?"

"I'm not married."

"Where's Gia's mother?"

"I don't know." I step away and feel the way they're looking at me.

"What's her date of birth?"

"I don't know." Fuck, why didn't I memorize that day? "She... Her mother dropped her off to me three weeks ago. I have her paperwork at the house."

"What do you mean, dropped her off? Did the

mother of this baby abandon—"

"Stop. No. She didn't abandon her daughter." But I'm not sure. If Ana did mean to abandon Gia, I will bury that because then they'll take her from me until I do a paternity test. That could take weeks. I can't… Christ, I'm going to be sick. I can't lose my daughter.

"Sir, we're gonna treat your daughter. But we have a policy that when a parent arrives with no identification for a baby, we call social services. It's for your daughter's protection. In the meantime, I suggest you find someone to get that paperwork here."

I rip the phone out of my pocket and cringe. The battery is dead. I'd ask to use their phone, only I don't know anyone's phone number by heart. The beach house landline was destroyed in the Luna fire years ago and I never bothered to activate a new one.

I am good and truly fucked.

thirty-four

STELLA

Coming down from my umpteenth orgasm, I realize I have a lot to make up for with Charles. I'm Gia's nanny and I've been MIA all day.

I have this burning urge to talk to him. But right now, I have two men on top of me. By the time I came in a rush from Alex fucking me, Jordan's hands were all over me too.

Alex kisses my neck. "How was that, baby?"

"Oh my God, I can't even form words." I take a breath and look for my tee-shirt. "Christ, is that the time? I really have to talk to Charles. I'm supposed to be helping him with Gia."

"Of course, kitten." Jordan kisses me too and helps me up.

I leave Alex standing there smiling and over my shoulder, I say, "We'll…talk."

"Sure thing, baby."

Dressed in just the tee-shirt still sans panties, I amble through the yard and into the house. I hope to see Charles in the kitchen with Gia so I can immediately take her from him. Tell him to take those two fuck-horses out for a drink so I can wrap my head around what happened.

And process the issue with my dad.

What a day.

I slept with two men on the same day.

A first.

215

With the kitchen empty, I climb the stairs. A different kind of silence greets me and it's…eerie.

Charles' bedroom door is wide open. I left him sleeping an hour ago, maybe it was two. "Charles?" I call out, ignoring what I must look or smell like.

He doesn't respond and he's not on his bed anymore. I tiptoe inside and see Gia's not in her bassinet either. The bathroom light is on and the water in one of the sinks is running cold water, but there's no one around.

"Charles?" I call out louder, turning the water off.

Gia must be awake if he took her out of the bassinet.

The hallway is still empty, and Gia's bedroom is dark from the shades still being drawn from her earlier nap. When I left the pool house, I caught a pink-tinged sunset that I would have loved to have plopped my ass down on the beach with a bottle of wine to watch.

"Charles," I yell out now.

"What's the matter?" Alex asks me from the stairs with Jordan behind him.

"Charles isn't here. Neither is Gia."

Jordan yanks out his phone and after a swipe, sticks it to his ear. "I'll call him."

Something feels off. I look up and see a camera. "Where's the main terminal for the security system?"

"Next to the door," Alex responds.

"Can we check them?"

"I never had to, but I'm sure I can figure it out." Alex takes my hand and brings me downstairs.

"Chuck. It's Jordan. Call me, man. Where are you?" He puts his phone down. "Straight to voicemail."

The main terminal shows at least twenty little boxes, but they're labeled. The one marked Pool House sends shivers down my spine, realizing what happened with

Jordan and Alex got captured on tape. I'm on video being fucked by Alex with Jordan...helping out.

"He definitely went out. His Benz is gone," Jordan says, coming back from the hallway that leads to the garage.

"Where would he take the baby at eight p.m.?" I ask.

"Hang on, let me go through the camera feeds for the last couple of hours." Jordan sits in the small chair in front of the monitor.

"Start with his bedroom. That's where I saw him last." I bite a fingernail, feeling a pit in my stomach.

"Here he is. He's sleeping. Let me speed it up."

We watch him wake up and rush to the bassinet and lift Gia out. There's no sound. But something is wrong. He looks so stressed. When he dashes into the bathroom with her, I remember the cold running water.

"Oh shit," I say. "She's sick. Gia's sick. She must have spiked a fever and he was trying to cool her off. I bet he took her to the hospital."

"I'll drive your car, baby," Alex says, gripping my hand.

"Gia's paperwork. Let me make sure he has it." I run into his office and my heart pounds, seeing the envelope on the corner of his desk. "Crap. He left it here. They're gonna ask him all kinds of embarrassing questions that he probably can't answer."

"Good thing I'm his lawyer," Jordan says, taking it from me, and we jog to my car idling with Alex in the driver's seat.

*

We arrive at the hospital a few minutes later, but Charles' calls are still going right to voicemail. "There's his Benz." Alex points. "Jesus, what do you think happened to Gia?"

"He was soaking her with cold water because she probably felt super warm." I slap the window. "Please let me out in front. He needs these papers."

Alex parks and I smile at him, feeling tingly. "Thanks." I grin at Jordan. "You too."

This is what it would feel like to have two boyfriends. I...like it.

Inside the waiting room, every seat is filled, but I go straight to the window. "Hi. I need help. My... My boss is here with his infant daughter." I wave the envelope. "I have the baby's paperwork."

"Name?"

"Giana Harlow. Her father is Charles. Charles Harlow. I know he's here. His car is outside."

The woman's eyebrows raise, and she reaches to take the envelope.

I don't know what's in there, so I pull it against my chest. "Is Gia okay? I want to see her. I want to see Charles. I'm the nanny." I glance down at my tee-shirt, thankful I had the mind to put shorts on during the chaos of looking for Gia. "I was off today."

She waits another beat and then rings a bell. The double doors open, and she says, "Bay 6."

"Thank you." I rush in and look for the numbers over a row of curtains. My heart lands in my throat, seeing a police officer standing outside Bay 6. "Hey," I yell and wave the envelope. "I have Gia's paperwork."

Charles comes out from behind the curtain and my heart sinks. He looks wrecked. I rush to him the way I did a few hours ago after finding my father in horrific conditions. But his arms don't open for me this time, and his face is angry.

"What happened?" I hand him the paperwork.

"She had a fever. I didn't know what to do." His voice is cold.

I see two people standing over a table and Gia's feet in the air. Moving that way, I say to the nurses, "Is she okay?"

"She will be. We have an IV going with antibiotics. Are you the nanny?"

"Yes."

"Has she been coughing?"

"Not at all. She's been a perfect baby." I glance over my shoulder and see Charles handing documents to the police officer. "Where's your phone, Charles?"

"Dead."

"Did they call Ana?"

"I don't know."

My stomach twists at the idea that Gia's mother would show up and take her away from Charles. From us. All because I wasn't there. I can't say I wouldn't have suggested the hospital without knowing how warm she was. I would have looked it up. There's baby Tylenol in the changing station. I remembered getting cool baths when I had a fever as a kid. I could have done the same for Gia in her plastic tub. This could have been avoided, but I wasn't there, and it's too late now.

"I'm sorry," I whisper to him because I was getting railed by his two friends in the pool house when Charles needed me.

He opens his mouth to speak, but glances over my shoulder. I turn to see what drew his attention, expecting a frantic woman to be running toward us. No, it's Alex and Jordan. "Hey," Charles coldly greets his friends.

It takes two to tango. Or three. If he's mad at me, I hope he's mad at them too, even if that's selfish.

"How Gia?" Alex asks.

"Her fever spiked and I…freaked."

"Why didn't you come find us?" I ask, even if that means he would have walked in on us all naked. "I would have helped you."

"You were *busy*." He glances at his friends. "All of you were."

My eyes slip closed. Christ, he did see us in the pool house. "Like I said, I'm sorry."

"It's fine," he says tightly.

I hate Charles being mad at me. It feels awful compared to how he held me and kissed my forehead when I got home from Van Nuys. He's upset right now, and we're in public. I'll talk to him when we get home.

Home. Living with Charles in Malibu feels like home to me.

"When can we take her home?" I ask the nurses.

They look at each other, and one says, "Her temperature is already down. We just need clearance from social services."

"He's Gia's *father*. He's on the *birth certificate*." My umph isn't for show. A fierce sense of possession consumes me.

The nurses only shrug. "That's not up to us."

"You're clear, sir." The police officer returns the envelope to Charles. "Have a good night, and I hope your daughter feels better."

"Thank you, officer." He puts Gia's papers on a waiting chair and stands over his daughter with his arms folded, keeping his back to me.

"We'll be in the waiting room," Jordan says.

"Do you want me to stay here with you, Charles?" I ask him softly.

Without looking at me, he blurts, "No. You can all leave."

thirty-five

CHARLES

I know I'm being an irrational prick. In one breath, I say I don't need a nanny, then get pissed when Stella isn't there for me.

Or was it seeing her with my two best friends that has my gut in knots?

It's forcing me to admit I want her too. Only, that's wrong.

Right?

I'm her stepbrother. Aren't there rules against that?

What in the world would my mother say?

A grin immediately teases my lips when I imagine the look on her face when I tell her I'm dating Stella. Perhaps I should make sure her will is up to date.

That reminds me to look into her estate planning, now that Griff is incapacitated. If he dies... Where does that leave Stella?

My heart aches when I think about her, and I don't understand why. How could someone have gotten under my skin like this so easily? I'm a fixer. I started working for a failing tour company out of college as the CFO. Within a year, they posted record profits.

Two years later, I started my own company. It made me rich, but the last two years with everything shut down, no income came in. With the market crashing, I can't sell the beach house right now. I *need* the Tyler Pace tour to survive.

Now my relationship with Stella, her being my sister

in the Paces' eyes, her living with me, working for me as my nanny, will ruin that. James will make sure of it.

"Here's Daddy," a pretty nurse with dark hair under a blue cap says, handing Gia to me.

She's awake and smiling.

"Hey, princess." I nearly break down, thinking about what could have been.

No way am I handing this baby back to Ana without some kind of joint custody. And that means my life has to change drastically.

For one, I'll need a permanent nanny. Preferably one I won't want to fuck. And two, no more screwing a different woman every night. Going back to my old life leaves a bitter taste in my mouth. Despite the jarring eruption Gia brought into my life, I truly love being with her.

I love *her* and not just because I have to since she's mine. She's got me wrapped around her tiny fingers.

"I assume you have a car seat?" the nurse asks me playfully and not in the demeaning way they talked to Stella.

"Yes." I ignore the implication that I might have strapped her in a seat belt on the drive over.

"Is your nanny still here?"

My eyes slip closed. "She's…my sister, really. Stepsister, who's helping me with Gia. She's not a nanny in the traditional sense. And no, I sent her home."

"Oh…" The woman perks up. "I'll help you get Gia into her car seat."

"I can do it." I take Gia into my arms and calm immediately spreads through me.

"I'd still like to help."

223

I've screwed enough women to know when one is interested in me. The look on this nurse's face is unmistakable. She sure is pretty, and dating a medical professional right now might be a wise move since I'm still figuring shit out with Gia.

But Stella crashes into my thoughts again. Christ, I want *her*. But I can't have her.

"Well, take my number in case you have any questions. Babies this age can be a challenge." She strokes Gia's head while she's in my arms.

Then hands me a piece of paper with her number on it.

"Thank you." I take it to be polite. "And I can get her in the car seat. I did it while she was wailing, this will be a breeze."

"I'm Veronica, by the way."

"Charles."

She laughs. "I know. We seriously checked you out."

Which also means she knows I'm rich.

"Have a good night and thank you. Thank everyone for me." My stomach twists again and I can't imagine how parents go through this.

Kids get sick. Kids get hurt. It's gut-wrenching. To do it alone... That makes me think of Ana. How had she been managing this whole time? Why hadn't she gotten in touch with me when she was pregnant? As mad as I've been at her these last few weeks, now I'm heartbroken that she's had to go through so much on her own.

If I had to guess, she knew my reputation and thought I would tell her to fuck off, and that makes me feel utterly awful.

Maybe for a split second that thought would have

entered my brain. Yet, with the baby in my arms, I'm so glad I wasn't put into that position to do something unthinkable.

"Hey, *Charles.*" Veronica jogs up to me. "I heard you say you don't know where Gia's mother is."

Shit. Resisting an eye roll, I say, "I had no idea Gia existed or that her mother was pregnant. She never told me. We weren't dating." I'm not sure why I'm vomit-confessing. Must be nerves.

"And she just dropped the baby off?"

"Yes. She's a photographer and had to work in Alaska."

Veronica nods and rubs Gia's back. "I'm glad this little one has such a great dad. Being a new mom is very hard on some women. You know…post-partum."

I've heard the term, but never gave it much thought. All I know is it makes women do crazy shit. Like…hurt their kids. Christ, poor Ana.

Instantly, my anger toward her evaporates.

I'm glad this little one has such a great dad.

Ana must have seen something good in me to trust me with Gia. That makes me feel as good as I'm going to feel in what's just been a horrific few hours.

I walk to my car after receiving the astronomical bill because Ana *didn't* leave me an insurance card. I'll deal with that later. Gia goes into the car seat smoothly, and the drive back to my house along the coast looks so different from a few hours ago.

The house is lit up and alive with activity when I pull my car into the courtyard. I park in the garage and take Gia in through the breezeway, then straight into the kitchen.

Stella immediately rises from the island where she

and my best friends are cutting up fruit. "How is she?"

I stifle any remaining anger and know I need to get past what happened. "She's fine."

Stella reaches for the baby, not because she thinks she has to. I see it in her eyes how she's aching for Gia and that kills me. So I hand her over.

"She feels nice and cool. Did they give you any medicine for her?" Gia's head slips under Stella's jaw and they both look so at peace and happy.

I feel like shit for denying her that comfort earlier in the hospital when I held her for the first time, knowing she was okay. "No," I say. "They just said to give her baby Tylenol if she spikes again."

"We have that." Stella rocks her. "And a baby thermometer. I'm on it, Charles."

"We have all that?"

"Yeah. There's a whole drawer of baby meds. Your mom knew to buy it."

"My mom…" I mutter, knowing that situation with Griff needs addressing, but I'm wrecked.

"Still no word from your mother?" Jordan asks, being the bad guy to make sure that gets resolved for Stella.

I want that resolved too. "No. I'm gonna call her lawyer in the morning."

"She looks sleepy." Stella smiles at Gia. "I'm gonna give her a quick bath and get her settled." Without looking at me or Alex or Jordan, she whisks Gia from the kitchen with her lips glued to the baby's head.

Christ, she loves my daughter. Which seems unfathomable, but I fell in love with her instantly too.

Now, I'm not sure who the hell I mean.

I rub my face, deciding what I need to calm down. A

drink? A run on the beach? A woman in my bed? Not *a* woman. *That* woman. Stella. My...stepsister. My nanny. I just have no idea how to make that happen, other than dragging her into my bedroom and pinning her down.

I settle on a beer and while opening it, I stare at my two best friends. After a sip, I say, "So you're *both* gonna be banging her for the rest of the month?"

Alex's jaw twitches. "I wouldn't say we're *banging* her. She's not one of those strangers we bring back here. I...like her."

"I like her too," Jordan announces.

Sharing a woman long-term can't possibly work. Although supposedly, I have neighbors up the beach who live like that.

"Fine. Just don't do it around my daughter, and—"

"Hey," Jordan snaps. "That's uncalled for. What the hell do you think we are?"

Animals... But that's not fair, so I don't voice it. I'm going by how they usually act with women. And I'm the same. "You know what I mean."

"Charles, if you have a massive problem with this, then—"

"I don't." I cut him off even though I would love to know what his solution is. Perhaps he'll tell me to hire a real nanny and he'll take Stella away.

My heart thumps in my chest thinking that.

"What are you gonna do about her father?" Alex asks me with his arms crossed. "I understand you have a lot on your plate. My father's a doctor, my sister too. I can ask them to visit Griff."

"Thank you." I truly don't know how to right that wrong without talking to my mother first. "Like I said,

227

I'll call her lawyer first thing in the morning. Jordan, can a power of attorney be overridden if the person isn't in the country?"

"In a case where there's an emergency," he says, nodding. "It would have to be documented."

"We can send an ambulance to the place," Alex adds. "One look at him, and no EMT would leave him there."

What a mess. So much is adding up. I want to help Stella with her fashion line. I want to help her with her father. I have a baby to take care of. And a six-thousand-dollar hospital bill.

I need that damn contract with Tyler Pace.

And the person who can ruin that is upstairs with my baby and I dread the idea of losing them both.

*

Stella sings to Gia while kneeling in front of the jacuzzi. My daughter loves to kick and splash the water that's risen up in her plastic tub.

"Hey," I say softly and amble inside.

"Hey," Stella responds hesitantly. "I am sorry, Charles."

"I know, it's okay." I lay a hand on her shoulder as I get on my knees to sit next to her on the floor. "I'm still figuring this all out. I was upset."

"I understand. And I'm not sorry for what I did. I was off duty and your friends are adults." She defends fucking two men and Christ, that turns me on. "I'm sorry I wasn't here when you needed me. Or that I didn't tell you about the baby Tylenol."

"Shit happens. She's fine." I reach in and stroke Gia's face and when I pull back, my hand lands on Stella's arm.

She freezes and I don't move it. Tension builds between us, and something makes me start to kiss the side of her head. "I'm so glad you're here," I whisper.

"Me too," she says and turns her head.

Next, I'm kissing my stepsister. Our tongues tangle and I take her face in my hands. When she brings hers to mine, they're wet.

Shit, Gia. I stop and look down. The tub is designed to keep her in place with a bump between her legs so she doesn't get submerged. She's cooing and splashing the water.

"Is she clean?" I ask, Stella.

"Very."

"You're so good with her."

"So are you."

We stare for a palpable moment and it's the look I get when I know I'm going to fuck a woman. I want Stella more than I've wanted anyone in a very long time. Right now, I don't care about anything else, including the idea that I'm not supposed to be touching her. Okay, I care about that, but it's turning me on.

"Let's get her dressed for bed." Her eyes blink when I say bed. Christ, I'm gonna fuck Stella in my bed, aren't I?

Right after she's been with my two best friends, and I admit that makes it even hotter for me. But raw with the kind of jealousy that turns me the fuck on.

She's the nanny, but I'm the father, so I take over. I lift Gia out and kiss her face. All over. God, I love her so much. She's all mine too. Stella wraps her in a towel and my eyes wander. I'm caught in a vortex of conflicting emotions. With Gia in my arms, I pay attention to what the hell I'm doing.

I stroll to the bedroom. The routine is ingrained in me by now. Dry her off. Lotion her up. Clear out her nose. Put on the diaper. Dress her in a onesie. After a kiss from both of us, Gia's in her crib, already closing her eyes.

I set the mobile going and then drag Stella back into the bathroom. Against the closed door, I kiss her again. My cock, hard as steel, grinds into her. "I'm sorry. I'm so sorry I snapped at you."

"You're forgiven. Keep kissing me."

"What are we doing? You're my…" I struggle to say the word.

"Our parents are married, Charles. That's it. I'm no one."

"Shhh." I stroke her throat. "I know we haven't been close."

"That's an understatement."

I press my hard cock against her stomach. "Not anymore obviously."

"What's happening?"

"We're gonna fuck. That's what's happening. Do you want that?"

"Yes, please. I want that."

"Oh yeah? How long have you wanted me to fuck you?" I hope the answer isn't anything perverted.

"Probably when I saw you get out of the limo holding the baby."

"Really? And if I just swaggered out alone?"

"It was a nice suit, so yeah, probably if you were alone too?"

"Good." I kiss her again and it turns wild and frantic.

Screw the bed, I might take her right here on the bathroom floor. Or standing up. I reach under her tee-shirt and cup her breast. "You're not wearing a bra?"

"I didn't have time," she moans into my mouth.

I thumb over a hard nipple and then pull up the tee-shirt so I can see her. "God, you're beautiful."

"So are you. Don't stop." She arches her back.

I reach down and lift her up so her pussy notches against my dick. Her tits bounce as I grind against her. "How many times did you come with my best friends?"

"Not enough. I need more."

"Fuck, yeah." I lower my mouth to lick her nipples while I dry hump her against the door. Only, it's not very dry, my dick is leaking like crazy. "Are you on birth control?"

"Yes."

"Good. I want to fuck you bare."

"You *all* like fucking me bare."

My cock twitches and I can come just like this. It's been weeks, and I'm ready to explode. "My bed. Now."

I set her down and take her hand. It's a short walk to my bedroom, and I don't care who sees us. It's my turn with her, and I don't want to explain myself, especially since I've been saying for weeks we can't do this.

No such luck. Jordan and Alex are there. Stella's nipples are rock hard under the tee-shirt and my dick tents in my shorts.

"Hey," Stella chirps, sounding happy to see them.

Christ, she wants to fuck all of us at once, doesn't she?

"This just came for you, Stella." Jordan hands her a white envelope, his face grim.

"Is it from that group home?" She takes it and tears it open.

"No," he answers and looks at me.

231

Shit, the James Pace lawsuit. *Fuck*. This is about to get really complicated. And I'm not getting laid.

"Wait… What is this? It's from a law firm." She looks around.

"Really?" Jordan and I make eye contact again.

I shake my head so he doesn't act like he knew all along. That we knew she was getting sued and didn't warn her.

"How does anyone even know I'm here?"

"Law firms hire private investigators," Jordan informs her. "Cameras everywhere can track license plates." He takes the papers in his hands and reads it. Or pretends to read them.

"Oh…" Stella sounds frightened, and that kicks me in the gut.

"Okay…" Jordan begins. "It seems you're being sued by James Pace." His voice is absent of emotion and very lawyerly.

"What?" Stella screeches in contrast and tries to grab it.

I pull her into my arms, staking my claim on her. "Let Jordan look at it."

"It's a hush agreement. With a settlement offer."

"A hush agreement?" Alex chimes in, sounding just as invested in protecting Stella. "What the fuck is that?"

"You're not to make any public statements about him."

"In what regard?" She loosens herself from me.

God, what a day she's had.

"It references an investment proposal dated three months ago."

"Right. He offered to invest in my fashion line then called me fat and my clothes ugly behind my back."

"I'm guessing that's what he doesn't want you to say in public." Alex holds her now and the way she sinks into his arms crushes me.

"When I confronted him about what I overheard, he didn't bother to fight for our relationship because he was using me. He had a whole speech prepared, telling me to keep my mouth shut. Pretend to still be his girlfriend and take his investment money. He wants the good press of being inclusive by investing in a plus-size line. And dating the plus-size designer. Only, it would be fake." She sniffs. "I told him to fuck off."

"Good girl," Jordan says and kisses her forehead in Alex's arms.

"Do I have to take his money?" she whines. "Am I really being sued to *take* money?"

"No. He can't force you," Jordan tells her.

"Good."

"But there's a contingency in here that says if you talk about *why* you're not taking it from him, you're liable for ten million dollars."

She gently breaks from Alex and grabs the paper. "Libel? It's the truth what he said. Sorry, if that's an inconvenient blow to his reputation."

"So just—" Jordan's eyes say he's losing control of her.

"How dare he come at me with this."

"Stella…" I try to reason with her.

"No. I need to go public with what happened so someone else will invest in me to spite him. I'm gonna shame that motherfucker all over social media." She disappears behind her bedroom door.

I lower my head.

Fuck…

thirty-six

STELLA

"Did any other investors get back to you?" I ask Bernadette from my cell phone while standing on the beach. It's been a week since I got James' threatening order letter.

"Not yet," she says, and I hear papers rustling.

"This lawsuit is out there, isn't it? James wants people to know I'm his, so no one is daring to cross him, right?" We showcased my line in January at a ritzy downtown hotel. Bernadette collected interest cards from five investors who are now avoiding us.

"Maybe they're just busy." Her hopeful voice doesn't soothe me this time around.

"I can't believe this."

"How's it going with the baby?" Bernie distracts me.

"Good." Gia's been wonderful. No sign of another fever.

"And the daddy?" she chirps.

Every night when I bathe Gia, I wish Charles would come in so we can have that moment again. But he hasn't touched me since that night.

"*He's* busy."

"And the others?"

"Charles and Jordan are working on a project for his tour company. They don't say much about it. I don't even know who they're trying to promote."

Charles also asked me not to out James until he gets back to his office in a couple of weeks. He doesn't want paparazzi swarming his house with Gia there.

I agreed.

In the past week, Alex and I fooled around. We do it in front of Jordan who dominates me into submission, but it's like meditation. It's so freeing to lose myself and get out of my head. I'm not sure what the hell I'm doing, wanting Charles too when I have two men who make me boneless and mindless every night.

I also gave Bernie the run down about my dad. We still can't get a hold of Katherine. The lawyers are dragging their feet. Alex's dad said, despite being a doctor, without a court order from a judge there's not much he can do.

"What are our next steps?" Bernie asks me, and I can hear the concern in her voice.

It kills me to say this, but… "Bernie. Save yourself. You don't have to stick around. I'll figure something out."

Even if it means offering to be Charles' full-time nanny. The smell of the ocean thrills me. This isn't exactly a shitty life, even if it were the last resort.

"You have enough working cash to pay me for another two weeks," she reminds me.

"Okay. But please, start looking for something else." Tears build as I say this.

"You know the best place for both of us is New York." There's a certainty in her voice I've never heard before. Like she's taking charge because she thinks I'm falling apart.

Because I am.

I squeeze my eyes shut. "I know. But with my dad here…" I wouldn't have an issue moving to New York if he were lucid. We could talk on the phone.

"I know, Stella."

"But you're right. Make some calls, Bernie. Fly out to New York. I'll pay for it."

"That's a tempting offer."

"That's me, the tempting-offer-queen."

"I have a tempting offer for you," a voice whispers in my ear from behind.

I might have swung around and punched the guy in the balls, but I recognize not only Alex's voice, but his scent and the heat of his muscular body. "I have to go, Bernie."

"Someone needs you, huh?" she asks with humor in her voice.

"Something like that." I hang up and when I turn around, Alex kisses me.

"Hi, baby." His kisses breathe life into me again.

"Hi. And where were you before?"

"The gym, with a client."

"For three hours?"

"It was a two-hour session."

"Woman?"

"Yep."

"Beautiful?"

"This is L.A." He pinches the strap of my bikini top under the cotton dress I wore to take the call on the beach.

"So that's a yes."

"They're all beautiful."

"Lucky you."

"I am," he says and then kisses me before I can keep going. "I'm lucky because I have you."

"Good answer."

His kisses taste like heaven. It's so easy to forget my

troubles when these men touch me. But something still feels empty. I want Charles too.

Alex drags me down to the sand. "Come on. Let's be bad."

"There's bad and there's lewd. It's a public beach." While talking to Bernie, I wandered about a quarter of a mile from Charles' house.

"Actually, it's private."

"Meaning, anyone from these houses can walk by."

"So? I don't mind people seeing me fuck you." He lifts my dress right off. "God, I want you so much."

I wore my triangle black bikini with a thong bottom. It's flattering on big asses *and* small ones. Alex pulls on the back, and it rubs against my hole. "Has Jordan taken you here yet?"

"Has he taken your tight hole?" I nip at him.

"Maybe he should line us up." He licks my lips. "Is that a no?"

"You're usually with us when we fuck."

"Really, he doesn't sneak into your bed at night?"

"No. Gia and Charles are right across the hall. It doesn't feel right."

"I get it." He puts my hand on his hard length. "I wish you'd sleep with me at night."

"Maybe Saturday I will since technically, Sunday is my day off."

"Fine. What about now?"

"What about now, what?"

"Can I take your ass?"

"Right here on the beach?" I look around, feeling a little startled to do something so filthy in public.

"Can you think of anything dirtier?"

I bite my lip and spot the jetties about one hundred

feet down the beach.

"Now that you have me thinking… Come on." I pull Alex that way.

thirty-seven

ALEX

Stella leads me to the jetty and then sits her gorgeous ass on a flat rock. "I need to get you nice and wet."

"Can't say no to that." I pull my cock out of my shorts and lower them so my ass is visible. Jordan told me how hot it is to watch me fuck Stella's mouth just looking at my ass.

Stella's lips close around my length and I brace my legs. My toes sink into the wet sand as my cock slides across her tongue and down her throat. Christ, it feels so damn good. And the fact that we're in public makes it even hotter.

I found our kink, she and I. If I'll be sharing her, I want Stella and I to have something special. Just for us.

Us... I love how that feels in my heart. I love how Stella has healed my heart.

God, I have to fuck her ass. Really make her mine.

I pitch my hips and her mouth feels almost as good as being deep inside her pussy.

Fisting the base of my shaft, I pull out, and glistening saliva attaches to the head from her mouth. I push the tip across her lips as she smiles. "Open, baby. Keep it open. I'm gonna fuck your mouth until I come. Then I'm gonna make you come with my mouth."

"Please..."

I step out of my shorts, fully naked now. I set my foot on the rock she's sitting on and then thrust in and out of her mouth. It's the view someone might be getting that makes me blow. Stella cups my balls while I come, and it's mind-altering.

She swallows me down so beautifully and when I'm depleted, I pull out and kiss her mouth. Holding my wet, limp dick, I say to her, "Go stand over there with your feet in the water and strip. Like it's a photo shoot."

"Sounds more like porn." She glides over, her ass bobbing. "You know sometimes they turn into pornos."

"Is that true?"

"I've met a few photographers. They get caught up and next they're fucking." She unties her top and teases me.

She's got beautiful, full, and perky breasts. Pulling the string from the bikini across her hard nipples, she's a fucking natural.

"Cup your breasts." I love it how she listens and seems to get off on being this playful. "How do you feel?"

"Amazing." She twirls, topless. Scooping water and coating herself, she says, "I love this."

I love you.

My heart pounds. How? How can I love her? I've only known her for a few weeks. But I've seen her every day. That's the equivalent of twenty-one dates. So maybe I really do. I've never felt this before, the constant heart thumping, lighting up when I see her. Rushing to get dressed in the pool house every morning to get to the kitchen sooner so I can make her breakfast.

"Take your bottoms off. Show me your pussy."

Without even telling her to turn around, she shows me her ass and slides the thong off. Tossing it to me, she giggles. "You like?"

"I love," I cough. "I love how you look. You're

beautiful."

This makes her blush. Shyness seems to come over her as she glances around. I sneak a peek too, but this part of the beach is empty. I jog up to her and kiss her mouth. We're both naked in the sun with the water lapping at our legs.

I lay her out, and say, "Stay on your elbows and watch me."

With the water cresting around us, I lick her pussy. The salt and her sweetness drive me crazy as I lap her up until she comes.

Then I flip her over and massage her ass with my knees deep in the wet sand. It's the most erotic thing I've ever done.

"Alex, that drives me crazy," she moans, pushing against my fingers.

Dropping a wad of spit right in her hole for lubrication, I push my cock all the way in, and my head explodes. "Fuck, that's tight."

She's on her knees, but low to the ground with saltwater splashing up at her pussy and my balls.

"You okay, baby?"

"Don't you dare stop."

"No way." I pump in and out, watching her puckered hole take all of me.

Jordan's gonna hate me.

I come in a rush, my entire body shivering. I pull out and coat her hole with the remaining squirts. "Sore, baby?"

"A little, but damn, nothing's ever felt like that." She twists around naked, full of wet sand, her hair a beach wave mess as she kisses me.

I don't think I've ever been happier.

We're both naked, and I'm lying between her legs, kissing her like my life depends on it. It's the most exhilarating thing I've ever felt.

I stand her up and bring her deeper into the water to get rid of the sand. She jumps into my arms still naked and kisses me.

"Are you enjoying your summer?" I ask her.

"I certainly am now." She licks her lips and then asks, "When do you go back to work?"

"The end of the month. Charles closes the office every July. Gives people a chance to enjoy the summer. I run the gym, so that means I'm off too."

"And when it's open, do you work nine to five?"

"Five to nine, baby." I smile, but realize I might sound unavailable. "I still find time for fun. What about you? You sound like you're gonna be busy once your line launches."

She nods, and doom overtakes her. "I guess."

Shit, why did I bring up her troubles? "Where are you getting the clothes made?"

"Kansas. If I make my window."

"Shit, are you *moving* to Kansas?"

"No." She flicks water at me. "I'll have to go there about once a week to check samples. It will all depend on the actual orders placed. I have requisitions from several stores based on my showcase."

"Sounds exciting. I hope it works out for you." I wish I can make it happen with a snap of my fingers, but I'm a working-class guy. Jordan and Charles have cash to burn. I'd ask my family, but Stella already said she wants a professional investor and not private money. I respect how she wants to burst out of the gate looking one-hundred-percent legit. "Where will you live when we leave here?"

"That's the part I have to figure out. Charles said I'm welcome to stay in the house. But with everyone gone, it will be lonely as hell." A shadow darkens her blue eyes. "Who knows, maybe I *will* live in Kansas. Might be cheaper to live there and fly back and forth here. But…"

"But…" I can't imagine anything more awful than having her live one thousand miles away.

"My assistant thinks we should move to New York. Run the company there."

My stomach twists, hearing that too. It feels like either way, in a couple of weeks when we leave here, I'll lose her. We'll lose her.

Not happening.

I can't imagine she'd turn down staying with me while she figures stuff out. I take her hand and bring her back to the shoreline to get us dressed. It's close to Gia's noon feeding.

"Um. Where are our clothes?" She breaks from my hand and looks around.

I glance up and down the shoreline too, and panic. "Oh shit."

"Alex… Did someone actually steal our clothes?" Stella breathes heavily, covering herself.

"Okay. Get back in the water, I'll walk back to the house."

She scampers in and sits down so she's covered. I love how open she is with her body, and I don't mind sharing her with Jordan and Charles. But that's it. It's like Jordan said, she's *ours*.

"Are these yours?" A voice behind me stills me. I can tell it's a male adult. I turn around, not bothering to hide my dick. "Apparently so. Holy shit."

Standing there is Jaxson Steele, rock god extraordinaire.

One of the three men living with Lacey Wilde down the beach.

"Yeah. Where did you find them?" I take the stuff from him and glance at Stella in the water. If she recognizes him, she may come running out, forgetting she's naked. He's that fucking famous.

And shit…even hotter in person.

"I saw two kids running with them," he says, grinning. "I recognized them. They're little pranksters. They live a few houses up from us. Jax." He reaches out to shake my hand.

"I know." I smile and his hand in mine feels electric. "Alex. And that's Stella."

She waves, her body covered by the water. "I love your music," she yells playfully over the crashing waves.

"Thanks." He waves back and gives me a knowing grin.

I step into my swim trunks, then jog to the water to hand over Stella's bikini. "Here. Put this on. You're mine." Even though I'm sharing her with Jordan.

I get back and notice Jax stuck around, so I ask, "Kids, huh? How old?"

"Ten, I think."

I hold my head, wondering if I should admit I was fucking Stella in the ass when they took our clothes. Kids. Christ, I have to be careful, but this woman makes me lose my mind. "Thanks."

To my surprise, Stella defies me and walks out of the water completely naked. "I'm sure this isn't anything you haven't seen before."

God, her confidence is as deep as this ocean.

"I used to get crazy on tour." Jax holds up his left hand with a gold wedding band. "I'm married now."

"Yeah, I heard. Lacey Wilde?" I stand in front of Stella. "And two other guys?"

He laughs. "We were a little nervous when that got out. No one seems to give a shit."

"We got a little threesome playtime going on," I say quietly.

"Something must be in the air. My partner Nate's sister has the same thing in New York."

"No shit." I wonder where the hell I've been.

He leans in. "Four guys."

"Four?" I glance at Stella behind me and wonder where the hell four dicks would go. Pushing the dress over her head, I say to Jax, "Hopefully for her sake, not all at the same time."

thirty-eight

STELLA

I immediately check on Gia and find her smiling in her crib. Not crying, even though she probably needs a diaper change.

I get her taken care of, then bring her into my bathroom where I put her in her bouncy seat while I take a shower.

As I touch my body, I remember Alex's hands on me and how his cock felt so damn good in my ass. I take my body wash and massage my hole. It's a little sore, but fiery to my touch. God, I want more of that.

With my wet hair combed out and a print jumper on, I amble downstairs to feed Gia lunch. I take the long way to pass Charles' office, and my heart sinks seeing the door closed. Again.

Jordan's not hanging around, so I assume he's in there too. When Alex waltzes into the kitchen with his hair wet and his body smelling of soap, I assume he showered as well.

Twirling my wet hair, he kisses my neck. "We should have showered together to save water."

"I don't think Charles would appreciate you and I getting it on in the shower with Gia right there."

"Why?" He takes her from me so I can prepare the bottle easier. Lifting her in the air, he adds, "Where do you think parents get other babies from? Clearly, they're doing it with the kids around."

I smile. "We're not Gia's parents."

"Obviously. Unless…" He trails off and rocks her.

"Do you want to feed her?" I ask since he doesn't look like he wants to let her go, and it's so hot to watch him and all the guys with this tiny baby.

"Sure." He takes the bottle from me.

"Unless… You were going to say something. I'm curious."

Holding the bottle, he says, "It's that relationship those rockstars have. They're all committed to one another."

I freeze at what he's implying. "You think because I'm sleeping with you and Jordan, we could have something like that?"

He shrugs. "Too soon?"

I agree with the philosophy *when you know, you know*. But in my experience, women get there first. My focus is solely on getting my line in production. Regardless of who I marry, I want a career. And the man, or *men*, in my life will have to accept that.

"Your theory has a hole," I say, instead of addressing if it's too soon for us to speak about getting serious.

For one, it's only been a couple of weeks, and there are three of us in this. That might be harder to figure out since it's unconventional. I didn't become a fashion designer to be famous. In fact, ninety-nine percent aren't famous. But if for some reason, a spotlight lands on me, how would that bode in the media if I have two lovers? Or…three. Rockstars get away with shit that a lot of people don't.

"What's the hole?" Alex struts up to me and against my lips, growls, "Because I'll be sure to fuck it."

"You're bad." I kiss him and then lay a peck on Gia sucking on her bottle. "As far as your assumption that it would be okay for us to boink in front of Gia if we were committed, you're forgetting that Charles is her father and isn't part of what we have."

"Not yet," he says with confidence.

It's been a week since Charles kissed me and ground his massive erection against my core. A week since I got served with those papers from James. And we still can't find Katherine.

Working as a nanny has wiped out a good chunk of what I owe her. But now I can't even ask her to invest more. I'm coming close to breaking down. I should put my pride on the back burner and ask Charles to invest, but I can't stop thinking of fucking him. I can't repeat the mistake I made with James.

While Charles would never do that to me, I am family after all.

But I don't want to think about that right now. Watching Alex feed Gia is a much better thing to concentrate on. His comment about me, him, and Jordan taking our relationship further has my mind churning.

"I get why guys would want to share a woman for fun. Something temporary. But why would you want to share me in some kind of permanent relationship?"

He doesn't answer right away, and it makes me think I interpreted his earlier comment wrong. Maybe the word permanent hit a nerve. Finally, he says, "I like you. Jordan likes you. Why make you choose?"

Right, I don't want to choose. Smiling, I continue to watch him, until Charles waltzes into the kitchen.

Sigh.

This doesn't feel right. Talking about a permanent relationship with Jordan and Alex. I want Charles too.

*

The next few days crawl by and not much changes. I take care of Gia during the day with Alex, who's teaching me how to cook. Jordan and Charles work all day behind closed doors. At night, Charles takes Gia from me. Then Jordan, Alex, and I fool around in the pool house.

It's Friday, and I expect the three of them will go do happy hour in a little while.

Charles and Jordan amble into the kitchen, looking stressed from their project. Before Charles says anything to me, Jordan sweeps past him and lays a spicy kiss on me. "How about steak tonight? There's a great butcher down the road. I'll grab some ribeyes."

"I don't *eat* steak," Alex grumbles.

"I'll get you some veal filets."

"That's baby *cows*," I argue.

"Right. Then I'll grab you some fish." Jordan lays a smile on him that makes Alex blush. Then with keys in hand, he leaves through the kitchen door. A second later, the turbo engine of his sports car fires up.

"How's your project going?" I ask Charles, who's making himself a sandwich for lunch.

"Fine," he says.

"Whose tour are you bidding on, by the way?"

He stops mid-swipe of mayo across a piece of hero bread. "I can't say. It's part of the NDA I signed. Sorry."

"Really?" I cross my arms. "You trust me to take care of your daughter, but not with that information?"

"It's not that I don't trust you, Stella." He cuts the hero in half. "People's brains these days are overloaded.

249

You can say something without realizing it."

"Hmph," I mutter. I'm still hurt, even though I get what he's saying. When I look back at Alex, he's mouthing something to Charles. "You know, don't you, Alex?"

His neck turns red. "I *am* upper management."

"What about me? I work for you, Charles."

"It's not the same thing."

"Thanks a lot." Now I just feel like being bratty. "I'm gonna see if I can catch Jordan. I'll let you two gossip girls talk shop." I grab my wristlet and leave out the kitchen door in time to see Jordan sitting in his car looking at his phone.

For a moment, I wonder if he's texting another woman. A Sub. A *real* Sub.

"Hey." I wave at him, and he smiles, his eyes crinkling in the corners. "Can I tag along?"

"Of course."

When I get in, he kisses me in a way he doesn't in front of Alex. Feeling like I have nothing to lose, I bring up what Alex said about taking this relationship into the real world when they leave Malibu in a couple of weeks.

"Alex thinks we can make it as a three-way couple."

"He does?" The surprise in his voice makes my stomach twist.

"I had the same reaction," I lie. "I'm sure you can't wait to get your hands on a Sub."

"What makes you think that?"

"Come on. This can't last. Plus…" I steel myself. "I'm gonna be very busy once I get my line in production. I'll have to travel a lot."

"Sounds like you don't want to continue seeing us,

kitten."

I bite my fingernail, debating a response. "We saw Jaxson Steele on the beach the other day. Did you know he's committed to Lacey Wilde *and* Nate Domenico?"

"I hadn't heard that." Jordan keeps his eyes forward.

"Jordan, Alex has more than just the hots for you, you know that right?"

He blows out a breath. "Alex and I are bending the rules of our friendship because we're on vacation. When we leave here, we'll return to being best friends with no benefits."

"If we make this three-way relationship work, and you and he are a couple too, then no one's left out. What if I'm not available and you both need sex?"

"I can control myself, kitten." He kisses my hand.

"Do you have a philosophical reason for not wanting to be with Alex that way?"

"No," he snaps.

"Is *he* just not your cup of bisexual tea?" I can't imagine he can do any better than Alex.

We pull into a very posh-looking strip mall with valet parking. Jordan gets in line and looks at me. "What are you getting at?"

"You and Alex have something. I feel it between you. He clearly...*wants* you."

"You know this?"

"We...talked about it."

Jordan's face goes even for a moment, then he smiles. "Honestly, I've been enjoying you too much to think about sticking my dick in someone else. You keep us satisfied, kitten." His kisses make my head swoon, and I can't think of a rebuttal at the moment.

thirty-nine

JORDAN

We get back to the beach house with three ribeyes and two stuffed chicken breasts for Alex since he doesn't eat red meat. My mind's been whirling at Stella's comment that Alex wants us to go further than just kissing and rimming.

Alex messes up my head. We've been lost, enjoying Stella. Looks pass between us when we're both inside her, especially when I feel his cock through the thin membrane separating her ass and her pussy.

It's forcing me to consider how much further I want to go with Alex. She's sleeping with both of us. Either we all go our separate ways when the month is over or we make her choose.

Or not.

That leaves me sharing her with Alex. Connecting me to him, keeping this open question of will we or won't we. Will Alex and I be together? And do I want to have that experience in front of Stella? What if I choke and can't go through with it?

The kitchen is quiet as we put the food away. Through the row of windows over the sink, I see Alex swimming in the pool. A cry upstairs captures Stella's attention and then after a peck on my lips, she bounces away to take care of Gia.

Walking out to the pool, I recall a Dom from my club. Nolan exclusively takes on men as Subs. They're not in short supply. He has a fucking waiting list. He's very open about his sexuality and almost always fucks them in public.

It's hot to watch because Nolan is a Viking with shoulder-length dirty-blond hair and neck tattoos. His subs aren't twinks either. He's big enough to take on guys with girth. Like Alex. The idea of him going into my club to find a guy to dominate him has my feet moving faster.

Alex swims laps using the butterfly stroke. His tan and sculpted arms chopping through the water and his chestnut wet hair in his closed eyes make my cock twitch. He's fucking beautiful. There's one thing I'm sure of. I don't want to do this in front of Stella. I'm not sure I want her to see how I would fuck Alex. How rough I would be. It might scare her off.

I circle the pool, watching him. When he reaches one side, he pinches his nose. His eyes widen, seeing me outside the door to the pool house. I lean against the wall with my knee bent.

My hands shoved into my pockets, I watch him. I don't know how to start this. I don't want a lengthy conversation about it, either. If it's going to happen, I want it to start naturally.

Animalistically.

Alex gets out of the pool, and the sight of him sends sparks through my body like never before. I must have been mentally holding back, pretending he didn't affect me. Now I don't have to lie to myself anymore.

"Hey," Alex says, grabbing a towel. "What's up?"

"My cock," I answer.

His eyebrows raise and he looks around like he expects I'm waiting for Stella. When he doesn't see anyone else, he saunters to the outdoor shower with pinched, full lips. Fucker is gonna make me wait for it.

With his back to me, he slips out of his swimsuit, and all I see is his ass. Makes sense, he wants me to fuck it. He's also making sure I want it. Maybe he wants us to start out here, but I won't do that.

If he wants my cock and makes me wait, he'll get me feral, and may not like it.

The view is amazing until he turns around, and my heart stops. The water cascades down his body and it could be a scene from a movie. His stiff cock juts out from his body, and I know there's no going back.

My feelings for Stella beyond making her a Sub have opened me up.

I break first, but only to open the door to the pool house. "Inside. Now," I order him.

He shuts the water off and ambles to me, but there's nothing submissive about it. Fuck, he's hot. And he's...mine.

"I believe that's my line," he says and pinches one of my nipples.

The pain shocks me, but it sends a jolt right to my dick. I close the door and since he's already naked, and I'm not, I have a decision to make.

"Undress me."

His cheek ticks up, and he walks toward me. "I'm not your Sub."

"You don't want me naked?" I run a finger across his wet chest.

"I didn't say that." He grabs my finger and puts it in his mouth. "I don't want to be ordered around."

"Are you sure?" I smile and watch him suck on my finger, his tongue laving the sides.

Fuck.

I step back and kick off my shoes. My shirt is barely off my chest when Alex's mouth latches onto a nipple. A moan escapes me.

"You like?" he asks, gruffly.

"Yes."

"Are you sure you want this?"

I answer him by getting on my knees, my nails scraping his body on the way down. The curves of his muscles are the sexiest thing I've ever seen on a male. My lips skim his abs and the cuts in his hips.

I close my hand around his dick first and then lick the tip. Without any hesitation or mindfuck going on in my head, I part my lips and let him slide right in past my tongue. Having a cock in my mouth isn't as jarring as I thought it would be. Then again, it's Alex. My best friend.

"Fuck," Alex groans as I take him deeper into my mouth.

The control dynamic turns me on the most. I get into sucking Alex because damn, I like it. I like the power having his cock in my mouth gives me.

Alex glides that amazing dick out of my mouth then drops to his knees to undo my dockers. When they slip below my ass, his mouth closes around my cock. It's mind-blowing. His light brown shorn hair, buzzed on the sides, feels so coarse when I run my fingers through it.

I manage to get a grip and pull him up so I can kiss him. It's not a kiss. It's a devouring. Something snaps, and I let go of all I hid. Even I didn't know until now how I really felt.

"Let's do this in the bedroom," I rasp out.

"How romantic." He spins around and waltzes that

way, again teasing me with that ass.

Inside the room, I undress and push him onto the bed. We're both naked now, his body smooth, mine rough with short coils of hair.

I kiss him again, and his passion stuns me. I sit up and suck him some more.

Alex bucks in my mouth. "Fuck, that's good." His large, meaty hands grabbing fistfuls of my hair feels amazing. "Lay back," he orders me.

How adorable…

I lean against the tufted headboard and Alex crawls toward me, pushing my legs apart. He goes to work on my cock, stroking it, licking it up and down. Christ, I'm so hard. He's fucking amazing at this.

When his lips close around it and he deep throats me, I almost lose it. I struggle not to come, so I pull him up to kiss me. But he licks his way up my chest first, running the wet tip of his tongue across every plane of muscle.

He straddles me and next, his cock is in my face, so I suck it again. With a leg bent, he begins to fuck my face. No, he doesn't fuck it, he makes love to my mouth. His rocking hips look so sexy in the mirror across from the bed.

Christ, I'm not sure how long I'm going to last.

"Can I come in your mouth?" he moans. Shit just got real. "Please, I want to come in your mouth. Then you can fuck me. Fuck me for hours."

Sounds like a good deal. I pull off and then lick the side. "Come for me. Come in my mouth." I close my lips around it again and hot cum shoots down my throat.

It makes me so fucking hard as I swallow and watch

my best friend fall apart like I never watched him lose it before.

forty

ALEX

Jordan finds my lube in the nightstand drawer and coats his cock. He's fucking gorgeous with that rumpled, sable hair, and that trendy beard makes him look sophisticated. The way it felt against my skin when he sucked my cock drove me crazy. I never imagined he'd be into this with me. Yet, here he is, lubing up his dick to stick it in my ass.

Our relationship is about to change. I hope it can withstand the weight of this moment.

He lays on top of me again. With fire in his eyes, he kisses down every inch of my chest and sucks on my dick some more. It's springing back to life. I needed to come, and I wanted to do it in his mouth. Test him to see what he can take.

He positions himself between my legs as I lay on my back like he asks. It's more intimate this way.

"Ready for me?" he says in a voice lower and richer with more gravel than before.

"Fuck me, goddamn it."

"Impatient little fuck. You asked for it." He rams me with no hesitation, no second-guessing, and I see stars. "Fuuuck,' he says, and grabs my hips with bruising strength.

He grows even bigger inside me and then starts to move. He lifts his leg on the edge of the bed to get more leverage and really gives it to me. He's feral and out of control. I want this to last, so I try to slow him down.

"I like being on top," I mutter.

"What?"

I ease him out of me. "Sit on that chair. I want to ride your dick."

"Oh." He brushes his lubed-up hard-on. "Not saying no to that."

I'm fairly certain I weigh more than him, but I don't care. I get right on top of him and push my very hard dick into his stomach. He reaches for the lube and oils me up to jerk me off.

"Christ, that's incredible," I murmur.

"Now sit on my dick."

"You're fucking bossy," I whisper, and guide him into my ass.

"I'll make sure you love it." He glances at the mirror across from the bed. "Man, that looks so hot. Your back and the curve of your ass. You're gonna kill me."

"You like watching me fuck Stella."

"No." He smiles. "I love it."

I kiss him again as I lower my asshole onto his dick. It's so filling and sends chills through me. I can't take it. I don't do this without a condom so usually, the guy railing me lasts. Jordan looks ready to lose it.

We go wild for a few minutes, really being who we are. Alphas and rough. My balls ache to come and I dump onto Jordan's chest right as he comes in my ass. We're both moaning and slick with sweat.

For a second, I remember the camera and wonder if anyone's watching us. Stella? Charles? Stella *and* Charles with his hands down her shorts, stroking her to a fever?

I lift off Jordan and lay back on the bed.

"Christ, that was intense," he says.

"Good intense?" I ask, feeling a pinch to my heart.

I want this again. I want us to have what I had with Pierce, but I understand the risks. Jordan's my best friend. Pierce wasn't. Losing him hurt. Losing Jordan would kill me.

"*Very* good intense." He leans over and kisses my mouth.

I didn't expect Jordan to be so open with the kissing. He's very stingy with his mouth. "What do you want to do now?"

He turns his head, and I can't guess what he's thinking. "I'm wondering which hole I want to stick my dick in next. I have a choice of four."

"Four?"

"Stella."

"Right."

He frowns. "You don't expect me to push her away, do you?"

"Fuck no." I get up and turn butch for effect. "I love fucking her too. I guess the question is, what do we do, the three of us?"

"Four." He tilts his head.

"Charles?"

He nods. "He's conflicted as hell. Who we're bidding on will come out. We're gonna get that deal. We've been talking to Tyler's people. They sound jacked-up to work with us. They're leaving it to him, but he's finishing his record, and no one wants to bother him."

"And James Pace is about next in line to the pope, so it will be broadcast everywhere, won't it? Harlow Productions Presents…" My throat goes tight, seeing the carnage in my brain. How it will tear us apart from

Stella.

"Exactly."

"I… I'm crazy about her," I freely admit at this point. "I can't wait to see her fashion line get produced. She needs someone strong in her corner. Someone who adores her and supports her." I brush down my slick chest and get the irony of my words since I just fucked someone else. "I'm not a decisionmaker at Harlow. I'm willing to walk away. For her. If it turns into a war."

Jordan bolts up. "You think she'll start a war?"

"It will if she sees it on a damn billboard before Charles tells her."

Jordan pushes his hand through his hair. "I'll talk to Charles. We didn't do anything wrong. It was a wild coincidence."

"One that you've been keeping from her."

"You too."

"It's not my secret to tell."

"I don't know whose secret it is anymore. Keep in mind, she's really helping Charles." Jordan puts his shirt back on. "We don't want her taking off. Plus, she has nowhere to go."

"She can stay with me," I announce, loving the idea of her brightening up my townhouse in Studio City.

"You think she's gonna sleep on your couch?"

That sets me back, like he thinks what I have with her is just friendly fucking. "No. I want her in my bed." I exhale, seeing my path in front of me. "In fact, I'm gonna ask her to move in with me this week."

Jordan slips his shorts on. "She won't move in with you. She wants to be independent."

"Then how the fuck do you have a relationship with someone who wants to be independent?"

"Who the hell have you been dating?"

"No one."

"Obviously. You missed it. Women don't want to be tied down right away."

"Then I'll offer her one of the spare bedrooms and let her split the rent."

"How romantic." Jordan shakes his head. "I'm sure Charles will let her stay here. The house basically sits empty for eleven months."

"How is that not giving up her independence?"

"He's her brother."

"*Stepbrother.*" I get in his face. "And he's days away from fucking her."

"You know what? Then I have no idea. Do what you want. Ask her, but I don't want to see you hurt again."

Fuck, the guy cares about me.

"Yeah, neither do I." I twist my fingers.

"What?" Jordan notices, and strokes my arm.

"Let's get back in the house. I miss her."

He smiles. "Me too."

forty-one

CHARLES

I overhear Alex and Jordan telling Stella they fucked. I'm not sure who's more shocked. Her, that they didn't let her watch, or me. Christ, my two best friends are now having sex.

Some kind of magic is all around them. Like someone lit a match and the whole house is ablaze.

I'm standing in a puddle of cold water.

I'm not one to feel left out. I make my own good times and people flock to me in the club, fancy bars, and when I host dinner parties in my penthouse. *This* isolation is nearly unbearable.

I grill the steaks and Alex's chicken while Stella makes a salad that could have been a meal by itself. She also prepared cubed sweet potatoes on skewers for me to roast.

Jordan holds Gia, who loves grabbing his beard while all of this is going on. I swear I don't know this guy anymore.

I half expected Alex and Jordan would go about their usual whoring here at the house. Or they would bail when they saw I showed up with a baby. And that my mother hired a nanny for me. They stuck around because of Stella and are having an even better time because of my baby.

My phone buzzes as I plate the steaks, but I ignore the call. I don't care who it is because everyone I care about is right here. Then I remember I've been trying to reach my mother.

Only, it wasn't *my* mother who called me.

It was Ana.

My fingers feel numb as I call her back. The call goes to voicemail, so I text her. Again.

Saw you called. Call me back. Right now.

The phone doesn't ring again, and I don't get a response to my text.

Fuck!

"What's the matter?" Stella taps me on the shoulder.

Where the hell do I begin? "Ana just called me. But I missed it."

Stella goes rigid. "Did she leave a message?"

"No. I texted her to call back. Nothing so far." I toss the phone on the counter and lean my butt against it, waiting for the sweet potatoes.

"Have you figured out what you're going to do when she picks Gia up?"

"*If* she picks her up. She gave me no specific date."

"Seems odd…"

"What does?"

Stella forks the salad into separate bowls. "One month to photograph a sun that never sets?"

I think about that. "I don't know."

She bites her lip. "What kind of relationship did you have with her?"

I eye Stella carefully. "I met her at a fundraiser and brought her home with me. I was leaving for Hawaii the next morning, so I asked her to come with me."

Stella scoffs.

"What?"

"Your world is so different than mine."

"You were dating a rich investor."

"Yeah, for six months, and I didn't get a trip to Hawaii." She shakes her head. "Of course, now I know why."

I hate that prick for hurting her. Something makes me twirl her hair. I've seen the guys do it, and she likes it. "Maybe for Christmas, the three of us will go."

"Three of us?"

My eyes slip closed. "Me, you, and Gia."

"As her aunt." Her voice sounds sad and that kills me.

I bite my lip, pushing away this fantasy I've got buried in my head that she and I can have something once we get this Pace Brother Apocalypse out of the way.

"Something like that." I wink because I'm not giving up that she and I can have more.

She's made me feel something I've never felt for a woman. My brain can be completely compromised, however because of Gia. But…

A thought burns through me. I grip Stella's elbow softly as the conversation with that ER nurse pops into my head. "Can I ask you something?"

"Sure," she answers me while watching Alex and Jordan bounce Gia, who's laughing and kicking.

"Do you know anything about post-partum depression?"

"I heard it's very intense." Stella stares at me. "Can make women do insane things. Do you think Ana's going through that?"

"She didn't give me a chance to ask. She dropped the baby off and practically ran out of my office. I couldn't tackle her, now, could I?"

Stella bites her lip and then draws a long, steady

breath. "Charles, you have a child with her. Maybe you should attempt some kind of relationship with her when she gets back."

Those words shock my heart. I don't do relationships, which is why I ghosted Ana. All of that felt firm and solid for me until Stella came along. But she's pushing me towards being with Ana.

Stella doesn't want me.

"I don't know what I did to make Ana think she couldn't come to me when she found out she was pregnant. You're assuming *she* wants a relationship with me. I'm not exactly reclusive. I own a major company. I sit in the same office every day. She knew where I lived."

"Did you know where she lived?"

"No. That's not the point. She had the responsibility and opportunity to tell me. She didn't."

"How did you leave it off with her?"

I close my eyes, knowing I'm about to look like an asshole. "My mother's jet brought us back, and I... I said, it's been fun, but I don't do relationships."

"That probably hurt her." Stella leans against the outdoor row of cabinets. "If a man invited me to Hawaii, I would be expecting something after. Not a ring. But not to be completely blown off."

Nodding, I see what she means. "You're right. But I didn't tell her to never call me. I didn't tell her I hated her or stay away from me. There was no reason for her not to tell me about Gia."

Stella purses her lips. "I see what you mean. And you were being honest. Some men just string women along." She pats my arm, and I want more of her hands on me.

"So, Alex and Jordan…" I change the subject to get the thought of her and me out of my mind.

She lights up. "I know. I'm sorry I missed it." She glances over her shoulder and frowns slightly.

"What?"

"I wonder if it's real. When you guys get ready to leave here, will Jordan say he doesn't do male/male relationships?"

That hurts my heart to think Jordan's just playing around with Alex. "I don't think so." I debate whether to tell her that both Alex and Jordan are serious about her. Funny how she's worried they won't make it past this crazy vacation, and not whether they'll want something serious with her.

Either she knows she will or… She doesn't want a relationship. With anyone.

"And no word from your mother?" Stella looks stressed now.

"No." And I know Jordan hit a wall, asking that facility to allow Stella to see her dad and requesting an outside evaluation. Courts are backed up and he can't get a judge to order Griff released.

The timer goes off, so I pull the sweet potatoes off the grill and plate them. I don't cook when I'm back in my apartment. I have a full-time housekeeper who cooks. But I go out a lot too.

Not anymore. Which reminds me, I need a different place to live downtown. Something more child friendly. Unless…

I move here permanently. Sell my penthouse for the money I need to keep my business afloat if the Tyler Pace contract goes bust. I can ask Willow to be Gia's nanny. I just can't see Ana abandoning her baby. *Our*

267

baby.

"Hey, Stella," I say, before she brings the dinner plates to the table. "I want you to know you can stay here in this house as long as you need. You're my… You're my…" I want to say sister to reinforce that she's family and means something to me in that regard. But she's not my blood, and I want to fuck her.

"That means a lot to me." She softly nods. "I think I'll take you up on that for the short term. I don't have many options." She puts the plates down and hugs me. Her breasts against my chest set my blood pumping.

"I'm also thinking of keeping Gia down here, whether it's full custody or shared with Ana. My house manager can look after her until I find a full-time nanny."

"I would love it even more if Gia were here all the time, too." She reaches up and kisses my cheek.

I hold her in place. She smells like baby powder and cinnamon. Our eyes lock and I see desire in her eyes. Why is she holding back? We came close nearly a week ago to fucking. Did she come to her senses and decide that I'm too old, or the stepbrother thing is too much for her?

"We're hungry over here," Jordan says with a knowing smile.

He would be open to sharing her with me. I can't hope to have her all to myself. By how she looks so comfortable with Alex and Jordan, I'm guessing she doesn't want one man right now.

Right now.

Would she change her mind?

*

For the last three days, I can't help looking at Jordan

and Alex differently. We finish up another dinner at home. Going out doesn't appeal to anyone. Stella sways to music I have playing from my iPad while feeding Gia a bottle. Jordan and I clean up, and Alex makes goofy faces at Gia. Fuck, I feel like we're a family. The kind of family my mother denied me and Stella.

Christ, this feels wonderful.

But it's not real.

Gia finishes her bottle and within minutes, lets loose a couple of hearty burps. "Who's a burpy girl?" Stella holds her up in the air as Gia giggles.

I think again about Ana, who never called back and didn't answer my text. Was she going through something? Did she not have this kind of joy with our daughter? Did Gia remind her of me?

It's hard to tell who she looks like. She's just an adorable cue ball with big brown eyes. I hate to wonder if she really is mine, since my eyes are blue. I'm not sure I could take finding out she isn't. On many levels, the betrayal and fraud would cut deep.

Fuck it, my name is on that birth certificate. She's mine.

It makes me wonder... Why hadn't my mother felt that way about Stella when she married Griff? She shipped her off to a boarding school.

"I'll change her and put her down for the night." Stella knocks me out of my thoughts, and I thank fuck, my mother's emotional neglect didn't do any permanent damage to her.

I'm another fucking story.

"Kisses time!" Stella does her nightly routine of bringing Gia to each of us for love and kisses.

The guys are nuts about my daughter, and it warms

my heart to see. When Stella reaches me, I'm feeling possessive, so I say, "I'll come up with you."

"Hey Chuck, why don't *you* put *your* daughter to bed, and we'll get a movie going. Come on, Stella, help us pick out something in the media room."

Fucking Jordan. But I smile and take Gia. "Go ahead."

Gia goes down easily as usual in her clean diaper. With music softly humming from the mobile, her eyes are closed, and I can tell by her breathing she's already asleep. She seems so happy here. And in no way suffering separation from Ana.

When I reach the media room, any hope to sit with Stella and cop a feel in the dark vanishes when I see her wedged between Alex and Jordan. Their arms are wrapped around her, but they're kissing each other. It's a sight that takes my breath away.

A movie is playing, but they're not paying attention to it or me.

I sit in the wing chair with an ankle across my knee and just watch them. Messing around with women in the open around here became the norm years ago, but it irks me now because this is Stella. And I'm left out.

"Stella?" I call out to her.

"Yes, Charles," her breathy moan catches me off guard.

Alex kisses her neck and Jordan licks her fingers.

"Are you okay with this?"

"With what?" She brings her glassy eyes clouded with lust level with mine.

"This. If you don't want to do this out in the open, just tell them."

"We're not out in the open," Alex purrs against her

skin.

I roll my eyes and consider leaving them alone. Not being a part of this is my fault because I'm holding back. With Alex's tongue in her mouth and those two looking like they're ready to get naked and just start fucking on my sofa, Jordan catches my stare.

A look passes between us, and his eyes turn sympathetic. Great, pity. Every man's dream.

"Stella..." Jordan brings her chin forward with his fingers. Kissing her lips, he says. "Kneel, kitten."

My body tenses.

"Jordan, come on," Alex snaps. "Enough of your Dom shit. It's just us here."

"Trust me," he fires back at his best friend and now lover.

Stella stands up and moves out of the way of the coffee table. With a languid smirk on her lips, she drops to her knees. "Yes, sir."

Jordan circles her, petting her head while looking at me. "Tell me the safeword in your mind right now."

"Green, sir."

"Good girl." Jordan looks at me. His hand runs down the side of her head and he grips her chin, a little rougher than I care for. "You love doing what I tell you, don't you?"

"Yes, sir," she says, her voice compliant.

"And you love sucking cock, don't you, Stella."

Oh shit...

"Yes, sir."

"Say it." He grips her face tighter. "Say you love sucking cock."

"I love sucking cock." Now her voice is strained because Jordan's holding her roughly.

I get to my feet. "Jordan!"

"How are you doing, Stella?"

"Green, sir."

"Yellow is slow down, by the way." Jordan eyes me. I exhale. Not yellow. She's fine.

Jordan brings their lips close. I think he's going to kiss her, but he says, "I want you to suck Charles' cock."

Her chest expands and the moment hangs in the air.

"Charles, feel free to blurt out red. That means *you* want this to stop."

Did this motherfucker just give *me* a safeword?

Stella and I lock eyes. My cock hardens as a smile creeps across her full, luscious mouth. I take control by leaning forward with a commanding voice of my own.

"Do you want to suck my cock, Stella?"

She exhales. And with her eyes closed, -says, "Yes, sir." Her lustful response leaves me breathless, and my body heats up.

"On your hands and knees, Stella."

I want to bark at Jordan to knock it off already, and get why it frustrates Alex. But damn, there she is, on her hands and knees. Fuck, that's hot.

Jordan bends down and grips her hair.

She lets go of a little yelp, and my blood rages under my skin. But he lifts her head and kisses her roughly, finishing with his thumb in her mouth. "Suck, kitten. Let Charles see what he's in for."

Alex sits comfortably on the sofa, his arm bent as he watches this. This isn't something they haven't done before. If I learned one thing about Stella, even in Sub mode, she's no pushover. Christ, I love that about her.

Fuck, do I...love her? How can I love her? I've only

kissed her. Considering I fucked Gia's mother eighteen ways to Sunday and let her walk out of my life like it was nothing, maybe I need to slow the fuck down and get to know someone.

In this confined nature.

Holy fuck, I do love her.

Because I don't want her to leave.

Stella's lips close around Jordan's thumb, her eyes fluttering like she's enjoying it.

"Let him see that tongue of yours."

Her eyes land on me as the wet tip circles his thumb, and my cock throbs.

I clearly can't get out of my own way, so Jordan is helping me out. Stella wants it. She wants to suck me off. How did I get here? I knew all along she wanted me too. I felt it in her kiss last week. I should have just slipped into her bed and entered her any night this past week.

"Good girl," Jordan says and kisses her.

They smile at each other, and I can see they have something more than just this domination game between them. Christ, he loves her too. Looking at the smile on Alex's face, I've never seen him happier. Yep, him too. She's infected us all with love.

And I nearly sent her away.

"Now, kitten…" Jordan's voice gets low again. "Crawl to him. Crawl to Charles."

Now he's gone a little too far, but next, she's crawling toward me. Her eyes are on me and she's smiling in a way that makes me wonder if she planned this.

When she gets closer to me, Jordan commands, "Take his cock out, kitten."

"I'll do it," I rasp.

"I gave her an order," Jordan barks.

My body seizes, feeling Stella's hand on my shorts. She's sitting on her heels now, and when her finger slips into my waistband and hits my dick, my cock throbs again.

I want to take my own cock out. I want to hold it and make her lick it. I want to force it in her mouth. But her doing it feels better than I could have imagined.

She unzips me, and I loosen the waistband until my shorts fall around my ankles. My cock feels like it's ready to tear out of my briefs. Looking down, I see the long and hard outline.

"See what you do to him, kitten. Suck that cock until he comes," Jordan orders.

Taking some control of this situation, I slide my briefs down, recording every second of this moment in my brain. The moment I changed my relationship with my stepsister. My cock springs free and her breath hitches.

She licks her lips, and I see Jordan about to bark another order, but I bark first, "Enough. Give this moment to me, all right?"

Jordan bows his head to me. "Yes, sir."

Smart ass.

I take my cock in my hand, but hold Stella's head. "Do you want this?" I whisper. "It's just you and me right now. You don't answer to him."

"I do want it," she hisses. "Do you?"

"Fuck, yes. Open your mouth, my dirty girl."

Her lips part and I get my wish by sliding my cock inside her mouth myself.

"Fuuuck," I mutter, feeling my dick drag across her

wet, hot tongue.

We begin a slow rhythm with me rocking my hips, getting so damn deep in her mouth. I hit the back of her throat a few times and then pull out. "You okay?" I ask her as I wipe the wet tip across her lips.

"Yes, sir."

"No. You don't respond to me that way." I choose not to go the safeword route either. That's not my relationship with her. "This is you and me, Stella. Us."

"So, okay, Charles." Her use of my full name reminds me of the formality of our relationship.

"Good." I lean down and kiss her mouth.

She tastes so damn sweet. But my cock is aching in my hands.

"I'm close, dirty girl. Finish me off."

"Mmmm," she purrs and lets me glide my cock in her mouth again.

I brace my legs and struggle not to lose control, or I may choke her. "Yeah, Stella, suck my cock. *Fuck*, that feels amazing." I pump a few more times and my balls tighten. My climax hits me, and I gently hold her face while I make love to her mouth and come down her throat.

Stella holds my nuts and massages me, prolonging my orgasm. I keep my eyes on her, watching my cock slide past her lips. I don't dare look at Alex, who is getting on his knees in front of Jordan.

When I know I'm empty, I lift her up and kiss the shit out of her. "I want you. I want to fuck you right now. Do you want that?"

"I want that so much."

Kissing her again, I finger her hair. It's soft and smells of perfume.

"Come on. My bed. Now." I take her hand and glare at Jordan and Alex. "I assume there's no objection. It's not like you two can't keep yourselves occupied."

Jordan's already unzipping his shorts. "Have fun, kitten."

"I will," she answers, and the confidence in her voice seals the deal.

I'm in love with my fucking stepsister.

forty-two

STELLA

Heat builds between my thighs, and my pussy is soaked as Charles leads me up the stairs. Every part of me feels alive, and I'm suddenly sweating in the loose tank top I wore for dinner.

We get inside his bedroom, and he gently pushes me against the door, but I see hesitation in his eyes. His brain is talking him out of this. He already came, and I risk losing this chance.

I plant my feet and want to clutch my throbbing center. Charles isn't just breathtaking, he's majestic. Elegant. Manly. Even his restraint gets me hot. But we're in his bedroom, and I just sucked his cock. Made him come.

We crossed the line, and I want to take it further.

"It's just you and me," he finally speaks. "*Do* you want this?"

"I've always wanted you, Charles. You have no idea," I say with a shaky voice, as the heat in his eyes and how he's raging underneath has me ready to explode.

"And this is real? I won't speak to what you're doing with Jordan and Alex."

"I care about them…too." I reach out to him, but he catches my hand.

"Good." He licks one of my fingers.

God, this is torturing me. My pussy clenches, and I'm just molten goo at this point. Begging him to fuck me sits on the tip of my tongue, and I wonder if he'll get off on that.

I expected Jordan would have told me to get naked, but I'm glad he didn't. I've had moments alone with each guy. My first time with Charles should be between just us.

"What about me, do you care about me?" I ask, my heart racing.

He thumbs the bottom of my shirt. "Take this thing off and I'll show you how much I care about you."

My trembling fingers lift the tank top over my head, and I'm not wearing a bra. Or underwear. My nipples pebble as Charles stares at me with fire in his eyes. My entire body heats up, and I truly can't take it anymore.

I lower my shorts and Charles' eyebrows arch downward. "No bra *or* panties."

"Jordan's rule." I smile.

He rubs his chin. "I think I may want to make some rules of my own. This is my house, after all."

"Name it. I…" I almost say, I'm a tad more obsessed about him than the others. It's just different how I feel about him.

Charles is more intense than Jordan and Alex. Even more than Jordan with his possessive orders, but that's not who the guy really is. Charles *is* that alpha.

His shorts are still undone and hanging low on his hips. The outline of the tip of his cock catches my eye. He's hard again.

I'm naked and let him take me in. I'm not his usual stick-figure fuck bunny. But his wide smile tells me he loves my body.

That fire hasn't dulled. He looks ready to implode watching me. When he rubs his hard cock, he mutters a curse under his breath.

"I'm dying to know how you taste." He rests a hand on my hip. His fingers feel like fire.

"I can get a written reference from your best friends," I tease.

He cages me against the door with one hand next to my head while the other teasingly crawls toward my pussy. "Aren't you the slutty nanny?"

"You like that, don't you? That your friends have fucked me and now it's your turn."

"I sure do." Out of nowhere, he slides a finger into my folds, and his eyes flutter. "Fuck, you're wet."

"I'm standing here naked with you, Charles. You make me wet." I take in his beautiful blue eyes.

The arm he used to rest against the door now lifts one of my legs, spreading me wide. "Fuck…" He adds a second finger and then pulls it out to rub my clit.

My legs buckle and he catches me.

I feel myself drip onto my thighs. I won't last long and feel ready to snap in half.

He steers me to the bed, and I sit on the edge. I kiss his stomach and inhale his scent. He takes the tee-shirt off while I'm breathing him in. I reach up to feel the ripples of muscles, and smile at Alex's work of art.

It's ironic, Charles will fuck me so athletically because my other lover got him into shape.

His fingers wind through my hair, pressing my face to his stomach. Jordan pulls my hair a lot and I like it, but Charles does it softer. After kissing me again, he loosens his shorts and briefs until they fall to the floor.

He steps out of them and lets me get a look. I'm in utter awe.

"*You* want this too, don't you?" I ask him, letting a

touch of doubt take over for a moment.

"From the minute I fucking saw you, Stella. I'm yours. I felt something immediately a few weeks ago. I didn't know what it was. But now I know it's this." He pushes my hand against his broad, sculpted chest. His heart pounds against his ribs. "I can't say you're mine, because my friends have claimed you too."

"I belong to each of you, but I'm yours right now, Charles. This is me and you."

"Us." He mutters, and reaches for me. "Lay back. Show me your pussy."

I spread my legs, and he licks my clit. "Fuck, that's good. I can stay here all day."

"Oh yeah? Well, sorry. I can't wait anymore." He drags me to the edge of the bed and right onto his cock. "*Fuck.*"

Holy fucking shit.

I could barely fit it in my mouth before, he's so fucking big. Long. Wide. It's the deepest penetration I've ever felt. He's hitting parts of me no one has.

"Wrap your legs around me." He fills me up, and I feel him everywhere.

He sits up and holds my hips, looking down at his cock impaling me. "Son of a bitch, you feel so fucking good. So damn tight and hot."

My body blazes with heat. "Don't stop," I mutter, feeling out of my mind.

His stiff length thrusts in long strokes, driving me mad with each rock of his hips. "Jesus, you're wet. My balls are soaked. We're gonna have to wash these blankets." He says *we* with a sneaky smile.

He grabs my ass, lifting me, using my pussy for his pleasure. It's devastatingly beautiful watching him fuck me. As if I can't take any more, he pulls out and then sucks my clit, fingering me. "God, you taste even better after my cock's been inside you." He breathes on my skin and then licks me a few more times before he enters me roughly again.

"Uhhh," I mutter from the fullness.

My body loses control and I clench around his cock. One of my feet comes up and smashes into his chest. I feel like I'm caught in an F5 tornado as everything inside me upends.

"Look at that gorgeous cunt coming around my dick," he utters with the tips of his hair dangling in front of fiery blue eyes. "You're my bad, dirty girl." His cheeks redden and he blows out violent breaths. "Aren't you? Fucking your stepbrother like this."

Wow, he does get off on us being related this way. God, that makes my orgasm even more powerful.

"Come in me, Charles. I want to feel your cum in me."

He thrusts harder, as I continue to orgasm. Howling, he folds himself on top of me, and his tongue fills in my mouth as he hisses and grunts.

"Fuck. Fuck. Fuck." His face buries in my shoulder, and he drenches my skin as he pumps through his release.

forty-three

STELLA

I wake up in Charles' bed just when the morning light peeks through the elegant, translucent shades on the row of windows that overlook the ocean.

The moment is *surreal*.

He sleeps soundly behind me, passed out from fucking me hard most of the night. I'm sore all over, but my body wants more. I can't believe what's happening to me. How I can't get enough of these men.

The ache between my legs is too great, so I actually reach under the sheets and touch myself. Just one stroke of my finger against my clit makes my sex thump. I'm so needy and will come in a matter of seconds.

A brawny hand under my pillow hangs off the bed, so I tug it close to me. Charles' hands are amazing. Large, veiny, and masculine, with perfectly manicured nails, making me wonder who takes care of that for him.

Who I am to be jealous? I've been fucking his best friends for weeks.

I bring Charles' index finger close to my face and lick it softly. I want something of his in my mouth, but he's got me pinned against his chest.

Licking his finger and sucking gently, I begin to stroke myself. When I let out a moan, Charles stirs, and whispers, "Are you playing with yourself, you maniac?"

"Yeah, got a problem with that?"

He pulls his hand away and pushes my shoulder so I'm flat on the bed with him hovering over me. "You want to suck on something more substantial?"

"I won't lie, it hardly fits in my mouth."

"Fits in your pussy very well."

"Are you saying I'm loose?"

He laughs and avoids the obvious dig. Alex and Jordan are also huge, and have been stretching the size of my slit from so much sex. "You're fucking tight as hell. Are you sore?"

"A little. That's why I figured I'd get this one out of the way."

"This one? You need to come, huh?"

"Yes, now are you gonna help me with that, or are we—"

He stops me with his mouth. "Sit on my face, maniac. I'll make you come."

His words shock me. "Sit on your face? I'll smother you."

"You won't." He lays back. "Let me put it another way. Ride my face and let my tongue make you come."

Who is this guy? I'm stunned at how playful he is in bed. Especially with me.

We're both still naked, and he pushes the covers away to show me his glorious morning wood. "I'm waiting."

"Are you sure you don't want me to just ride your cock?"

"You said you're sore. I'll deal with him while I'm making you come."

"Him," I giggle. "You mean the beast."

"Don't let Jordan or Alex hear you call my dick a beast." He kisses me. "They'll get jealous."

"I wouldn't dream of it," I say, climbing over him, considering how I should angle myself. I can't literally sit on his face with all my weight.

I pitch my thighs and crank my hips until my sore pussy reaches his mouth. His warm and wet tongue goes right to work. "Fuck, that's good."

"Mmmm," he agrees, gripping my ass and spreading the cheeks. "But seriously, get lower. I want your juices on my cheeks."

I have too many questions, so I just lower myself. Wow, the extra friction is more than I can handle. It doesn't help that his finger is probing my back entrance. It all has me crying out in less than a minute. When I go to move, he pushes me further toward the headboard and licks my ass.

Good lord, he can be dirty too. Euphoria shoots through my veins.

"I have bad news for you," he says, and I'm not sure I want to hear it.

"How bad?"

"Very bad." His tongue spears my hole, fucking my ass with the tip. "I'm still hard."

"That's not bad if…" I stop and realize where this is going. Or rather where that hard cock is going. "Oh."

"Yeah, *oh*. I need to fuck you here." He pushes a finger inside me, and it feels so damn full. "I have oils that will make it feel amazing."

Again, the questions pile into my brain, but I don't care. Charles isn't using me. He wouldn't have taken this step if I didn't mean something to him.

"Do you want that, dirty girl?" His finger probes me deliciously. "You want your stepbrother to fuck you in the ass?"

My pussy throbs at his acknowledgment again of being my stepbrother. It had been holding him back, and now he's using it to make things hotter between us.

"Yes, please fuck my ass. Be dirty with me." I lift off him and nestle into the sheets face down.

His kisses down my back, all while squeezing my ass cheeks apart. "They fuck you here too, don't they?"

"Uh-huh."

"Do you love it?"

"Uh-huh. But…"

"But…" His breath hits my neck while he reaches into the nightstand beside me.

"But it feels extra filthy with you," I moan. "I want it so bad."

The cap clicks open and the gel lands right on my hole. Oh God, he's going to lube up my butt instead of his dick. Next, the head pushes past my puckered ring of nerves, and my body seizes. I'm ready to explode all over again.

"Fuck," he mutters, entering me slowly. "I don't do this without a condom. Ever."

"Good."

"Hold on, I can't be gentle." He nudges my thighs apart with his knees and slides all the way in and all the way out.

One hand pushes my head into the mattress, the pillow gone. In furious beats, he fucks my ass so hard, being a little rough with me. I moan in pleasure because it's so damn good. I love out-of-control Charles. Dirty Charles. My filthy stepbrother fucking me in the ass.

I'm drenched and on the verge of coming again.

"Jesus, I'm close. Are you close again?" he groans. "Your pussy looks drenched."

"Don't stop."

"Not stopping." If anything, he goes faster, and I feel the entire shaft leave my channel, and it's as dramatic as when he slid all the way in. "I'm fucking coming so hard," he grinds out with my cheeks spread open with one hand as his warm cum lands right on my hole. "So fucking beautiful." He pushes his cock in again while he's still spasming. "It feels fantastic with my cum inside you like this. Jesus, you're a bad girl, letting me do this to you."

"I'm also your nanny. Another reason you're not supposed to be fucking me."

"Don't get me started on that one..." He kisses the back of my neck. "You're incredible. Thank you. Thank you for this. For everything."

Tears build up and I'm not sure what he means. But I'm hit with an epiphany I didn't see coming. I want this. I don't want to stop. I want to be someone special to Charles and *not* his nanny. Not someone who's hanging by a thread. I want to be someone he's proud of.

He lifts out of me and whispers, "Don't move. You need some aftercare." I watch him walk into his bathroom, and the vision makes my heart pound. The long, lean line of him is a picture of stunning male beauty. Why didn't he become a male model?

After the water is turned on and then off, he comes back with a washcloth.

"Turn over," he says.

I do, and always wait for that hesitation in his smile when he looks at me naked. I know he's not used to someone my size. That's just reality. I follow him on social media, stalk him, really. I see who he keeps on his arm.

He can't help but smile at me. "Spread your legs, maniac." Obeying him, I groan at the warmth on my pussy. "Feel good, dirty girl?"

"Feels wonderful, my dirty stepbrother."

"God, I'd love us all to just take turns with you. Lay you out and fuck you until you're filled and covered with our cum."

Wow, *he's* a maniac. I had no idea. God, three of them at once. I smile and then feel warmth on my ass. He's rimming my hole again with the washcloth.

I exhale and want to get my thoughts out there before he sticks his dick in my mouth and invites his friends to double-penetrate me. Call me weird, but I find it hard to think of anything when one of these guys is inside me.

"That sounds like a good after-dinner plan. But can I talk to you about something?" I gently close my legs.

A blush runs across his shoulders. "Sure."

"I'd like to formally ask you to invest in my company. With James gunning for me, no one will invest, and maybe no one will notice you're my…stepbrother."

Charles goes still. "I see."

"So, for three hundred thousand dollars, you'll get 50% of the profits until the investment is paid back, plus a 10% stake after."

"Sounds generous." He pinches the bridge of his nose. "I haven't seen your portfolio, but I assume your clothes will be a hit."

"Thanks," I say, realizing he hasn't said yes. "I have my showcase video in the cloud, we can watch it later."

"I'd love that," he says, breathily.

"You didn't answer my question. Would you consider it?" Not only do I not want James' hush money, I don't want Katherine's shame money.

Charles gets off the bed, and I assume it's because he knew he wanted to fuck me and now doesn't want to mix business with pleasure. "I'm ashamed to admit this, Stella, but my company is in trouble."

That jerks me to my feet. "What? How? What happened?"

He chuckles. "You sound more concerned for me than yourself."

"I guess I am. You have…" I look around. "You have Gia."

He glances at the watch he wore to bed. "I should go get her."

While he dresses, I say, "But Charles, what happened?"

"Two years of lockdowns, that's what happened. No one toured. I don't have another revenue stream. We tried doing some pay-per-view concerts. Those were a bust because some asshole films the show on his phone then uploads, and people can watch for free." The heartbreak in his voice gets me.

"I'm sorry." I slide into his tee-shirt. "I don't want your mother's help. Not after what she did to my father. I won't give her the satisfaction of buying me off."

"Good for you." He stands at the door, smiling, his dark blond hair adorably rumpled and askew.

"Is that an official no to investing with me?"

"We shouldn't have that between us. Since we're… You know…" He bites his lip. "Can I make a suggestion?"

"Please. But not your mother."

"She *should* give you the money, but we can't find her, and you have a deadline."

"Right. What then?" I'm dying to know.

"I think you just should just take James' money."

My face goes hot, and I swear, I feel claws pop out of my knuckles. "Why?"

"It's the path of least resistance. He can bury you if you lash out at him in public, right?" When I nod, he adds, "Plus, isn't this right up there with living well is the best revenge? You get what you want. You get your dream."

"Interesting." I don't love this plan, but I consider James might slip up and call me *big* or say my clothes are for fatties. Get himself in massive heaps of trouble anyway.

"Think about it, okay?" Charles leaves, and a few minutes later comes back with Gia.

She giggles as they climb back into bed, and we cuddle with her between us. The moment is so heavy with emotion that my heart almost can't take it. It screams with an intimacy I never expected. So intimate, like… He really would want me for himself.

Just us.

The three of us maybe, if Ana either gives Gia up or…shit…never comes back for her.

"This feels so amazing, Charles," I whisper with Gia squeezing my finger.

"I know," he whispers and kisses me, then her.

"But I don't want to give up Jordan and Alex," I deadpan. "I know that sounds bizarre. This isn't The Bachelorette for me. I didn't come here to choose one man. You all have something so incredibly special." I take a breath, and then whisper in his ear, "And you're extra special to me. You do things to me that—"

His phone rings, interrupting the thoughts of how I might love him. The words feel like gumballs ready to fly out of my mouth without any control.

"Shit, it's my mother's assistant." He swipes the call. "Michaela. Where's my mother?" He pinches his eyes and I take Gia to make her a bottle.

I'm surprised to see Alex coming up the stairs with one already made. "Hey."

"Hey…" His dirty smile makes my cheeks redden. "How was last night?"

"All right."

He slaps my butt. "You're so bad. Just all right? Come on, tell me the dirty deets."

"Well, it was most of the night." I take the bottle and before we get into the nursery to feed Gia, she's gripped it and pulled it to her mouth. "And then this morning he…" I bit my lip.

"He…" Alex looks salivating for details.

I turn and stick my butt out.

"That fucking animal."

I laugh, "Shhh. Gia will be talking soon."

"Right."

"What about you? Did you and Jordan get busy?"

He stretches, making me stare at his bare chest. And then slaps his butt.

"Good Lord. We're some crew, huh?"

"Are we? A crew? All of us?"

"I made it clear to Charles." I lean in and kiss him, realizing I hadn't done so yet. "I want all of you."

"Good. That's what I want too. But he's a controlling and possessive son of a bitch."

"You talking about me behind my back?" Jordan

appears, dressed almost identically to Alex.

Despite these two admitting real feelings for each other and acting on them, their eyes on me always let me know that I'm part of what they have. "No. Charles."

"He christened every hole," Alex announces, like he's shocked.

"Atta boy, Charles," Jordan says to him, standing in the doorway.

"Morning," his voice is low.

"Anything, Charles?" Our eyes lock and he smiles. "Did you find your mother?"

"No. Michaela called to tell me I have to go to a fundraiser tonight for her." He looks furious.

"Lucky you." Jordan kisses me, then brings Alex and Charles into a huddle while I feed Gia on the rocking chair.

They glance over their shoulder with devilish smiles until Alex leans toward me and kisses me on the side of the head.

He leaves, but comes back a few minutes later with a plate of cheesy eggs and whole strawberries. Next, he's feeding me while Gia eats, and Jordan rubs my feet.

The strawberries are so juicy. Taking a bite releases bursts of juice that stay on my chin. Alex licks every drop and then kisses me. He alternates feeding me and Jordan, who tears into the strawberry flesh like he's a lion. His eyes are on me, but winks at Alex.

It's not a heavy breakfast, just enough to hold me over.

Charles comes and scoops Gia out of my arms for a good burping. After she lets loose some nice ones, she's wiggly.

"She wants her playpen," I tell Charles, so he places her in there, tummy side down.

Jordan gets to his feet and goes into Gia's bathroom, where I hear the jacuzzi tub jets running. "I believe I told you how you're completely my responsibility, Stella. That includes bathing."

"I believe the word you used was hygiene."

"That's the clinical Dom speaking." He takes my face in his hands. "This is beyond any of that. You're not my Sub. Never were. I don't...fall for Subs. This... This is real. You and me." His kisses make me see stars. "And them. You belong to each of *us*."

I relax, part of me waiting for a shoe to drop and being forced to choose. "I want that."

"Good. We want you. All of us." He runs his lips along my neck. "Fucking you. Together, right now."

"We're not fucking her right now," Alex says. "Charles rammed both holes like the maniac we know he is. She needs aftercare."

"That's what the bath is for." Jordan tugs my tee-shirt off.

I'm fully naked while they're each in some form of dress, gym shorts, and tops, but Charles is shirtless.

Jordan scoops me in his arms and it's as if I'm light as a feather. But he's jacked-up and not breaking a sweat. The smell of eucalyptus and lavender hangs on the steam floating off the water bubbling in the jacuzzi.

Jordan lowers me in and even though the temperature is near scalding, it's soothing beyond words. My ass screams in relief the most. Charles took me so hard, but I loved it.

Alex sits on a stool at the top of the oval and rubs my shoulders, his hands slipping into the water to pinch my nipples. This is the unexpected part. To be unbelievably turned on so soon after coming. In fact, the orgasms are relief valves popping, the desire and force of lust barely receding.

I'm already curling my hips, wanting someone to fill me or suck my clit. But Alex called it. I'm damn sore. Instinctively, I reach between my legs and close my eyes at the tension my touch eases momentarily.

My eyes slip closed, and I'm content to get myself off with Alex's lips on my neck and his strong hands massaging everywhere else.

A buzzing sound forces my eyes open, and Charles is standing there naked with a hard cock in one hand. In the other? My vibrator.

"Where did you find that?" My heart races, staring down my clit massager with a vibrating dome head.

"In your nightstand, dirty girl. I was tempted to throw it out. You don't need this with us taking care of you." He puts the vibrating dome against my inner thigh. "But I realized in times like this when you're sore… And you will be sore from the three of us. A lot. We need a teammate with this specialty."

"Like special teams?" I chirp.

"Exactly." Charles laughs at my football analogy.

I throw my left leg over the side of the tub, exposing my sore pussy to him while Alex kisses my neck and holds my breasts.

"Make her come, Charles," Alex groans in my ear.

My stepbrother lowers the vibrator against my clit while gripping my thigh. My explosion is almost immediate given the entire scene.

"I've never done anything like this," I whisper to Alex.

"We'll do everything, baby. You just open yourself to us. And then tell us what you like." He stands and lowers his pants until his thick, long cock springs free.

"I'd like this bad boy in my mouth." I twist around and get on my knees, still submerged in the water. I kiss Alex's cock and lick the head.

"Fuck," he groans. "This is fucking hot."

The water rises and arms close around my waist. The body behind me is undoubtedly Charles. He kisses my back while Alex thrusts his cock in and out of my mouth.

"How does he taste, kitten?" Jordan whispers in my ear, sitting on the side of the tub.

I let Alex's dick slip out. "Taste for yourself."

Jordan swallows Alex's cock, and he moans, bracing his hands against the tub. "Fuck, man. That's not fair, you two."

Jordan releases him and licks the sides. "Don't want you blowing your load yet. Keep him hard, kitten." Jordan licks up Alex's torso and next, they're kissing.

I resume sucking Alex's cock, my concentration wrecked by Charles using my ass cheeks to get off. "I will never get enough of this ass. Even this has me ready to blow."

Just when I think it can't get any more intense, Alex lifts his leg, and I see Jordan's dick disappear into his ass.

Alex throws his head back, his body being held up by Jordan who fucks his ass like a pro.

"How dare you not tell me how fucking good this feels." Jordan's deep voice sounds dangerous, and the force of his drives has Alex losing it. "I could have been taking care of you all this time. *Me!*"

"You... You two. You're killing me," Alex groans, looking down at me.

"I'm here too," Charles whispers in my ear, and I wonder if he'll suck Alex's cock as well. That could give the guy a heart attack.

Maybe someday, but I don't think Charles is ready for that. I'm thrilled with this dynamic, especially since Alex gets exactly what he needs from our relationship. Fulfillment from a man. His best friend. Someone he can trust.

Now Alex doesn't have to choose either. He gets to have it all.

We all do.

Warm liquid lands on my back and down my throat at nearly the same time. Alex steps into the jacuzzi. Jordan is there, rinsing his cum off Alex's back.

Charles gets out and Alex takes me under his arm, his eyes barely open. "We got you," I whisper to him.

"You sure do, baby. You sure do."

forty-four

STELLA

I'm not sure if anyone knows who I am at this fundraising event in a swanky downtown L.A. five-star hotel, or that I'm Charles Harlow's stepsister.

Who he's fucking. I needed a night out and practically begged him to take me.

The line I'm so desperately trying to fund includes two evening gowns, one over the top with sequins and feathers, and the other a sleek plum shimmery, one-shoulder, asymmetrical business-dinner knockout.

I decided to wear that one and show it off at the fundraiser to possibly scare up another investor before crawling back to James.

Charles and I walk a mini red carpet, and he looks devastatingly handsome in his Tom Ford classic black tux.

"Who are you wearing?" photogs yell to me.

"It's mine," I coo back. "Stella Raven. Write it down."

"You're fucking incredible at this," Charles whispers in my ear, and I'm blinded by the flashing lights.

I wonder if his mother will see these anywhere. What in the world would she think?

The photogs ask a few more questions, and I invite them to call me for formal interviews next week.

Next, we're ushered straight to a table dead-center in the room before I get to make eye contact with any of Katherine's rich friends. The table is an insult to be honest, if Katherine gives away as much money as I think she does. We should be on the damn dais.

Feeling Charles' hand ride up my thigh, though, is worth sitting here in obscurity.

I'm feeling lost when his fingers tap the entrance of my thong, but he pulls his hands away abruptly and muffles a smothered curse. My heart sinks, thinking he saw an ex. Ana! I look up and freeze, watching James sit across from us at the table.

"Stella," he greets me coldly.

I swallow and want to bolt. "James."

"That's it? No, hi, how are you?"

"Hi, how are you?" I ask robotically and the people at our table look delighted that a fight might break out and make their boring lives fun for a change.

"I'm great." He reaches across the table to Charles. "James Pace."

"I know who you are." To my shock, he shakes the guy's hand.

I'm ready to jab my fork into his thigh, when his hand lands right back where it was between my legs.

A text buzzes on my phone and I look down to see it's from Charles.

Relax.

Then a finger slides under my thong.

Open up for me.

"Charles Harlow from Harlow Productions?" James asks, then swigs a glass of champagne like it's cheap beer.

"Yes." His one-word answer surprises me. I want him to gush about his company.

"He's working on a big deal." I boast about him instead. "A two-year tour. Right, Charles?"

He growls, circling my clit. "Something like that."

"Indeed," James says and stares at us.

I lift the vodka soda with extra limes and suck on the straw, letting James watch me as I'm getting fingered by Charles under the table.

Lick that straw all you want while I play with your pussy. You're mine.

"You look great, Stella. Is that new?"

I roll my eyes, since it was part of the collection he called stupid and ugly. Yet willing to fund to save his ass. "No. It's mine."

"Really?"

"Someone once called it ugly. But those photographers outside loved it." I look around. "I'm sure I can scare up some financial interest."

"You don't have to," he says and then looks at Charles, who's typing.

Keep that jackass talking... Make him crawl to you. You'll get better terms.

Why? I quickly type back.

I want his eyes on you when I make you come.

"He won't recognize me coming because I faked it with him," I say like a ventriloquist, keeping my lips pursed as much as possible.

Charles snorts a laugh.

"I want someone to fund my clothes who actually likes them," I snap at James.

His eyes go beady. "You got my paperwork, didn't you?"

"Sure did." I lean back and spread my legs more.

Careful.

"Stop playing games, Stella. Take the damn investment."

"Let me think about it. I thought about it and…" A wave hits me and I'm coming so hard.

James and I lock eyes. Does he know what's happening?

Charles isn't trying to hide it. He leans in when I'm finished, and says, "Was that good?"

"Oh. My. God," I breathe, and am about to lick Charles' face.

James utters, "I would think you could do better than your stepbrother."

We both freeze, and the table's conversation comes to a halt. Yeah, this just got even better for them.

"That's none of your business," I bite out to James.

"Ha ha." He leans back. "You're not some anonymous worker bee, are you Charles? You're the CEO of Harlow Productions. I wonder if *your* investors would like to know you're banging your fat stepsister."

Charles lunges across the narrow rectangle table and grabs James by the throat.

"No," I clutch his arm. "He's not worth it."

"Smell that?" Charles growls, ignoring me. "I please her so easily. She told me she faked it with you. Every time. I may be her stepbrother, but I know how to satisfy her."

"Charles?" A man's voice sounds behind me, and I'm sure it's a bouncer of some sort.

But Charles closes his eyes and releases James who noisily falls back into his seat. Charles quickly wipes his hand and turns around. "Tyler. Hi."

"Is there a problem?" The man in a slim-cut, shiny blue tux and a silver bowtie stands there looking horrified.

"No," Charles says, red and flushed.

"Then why did you have my brother by the throat?"

"Because he insulted *me*, his date," I jump in and go to shake his hand. "Stella Raven. I used to date your brother."

"Oh…." Tyler stares at James in confusion. "He never mentioned you."

"Well, turns out he was using me. So no, you wouldn't have heard about me." I'm only wondering why I never heard of… Tyler… My heart stops. "Tyler Pace, the…singer?"

"Yes. Charles is bidding on my tour. I want to make sure there's no real problem here."

The room sways around me. This is why Charles wants me to keep my mouth shut about James. Why he wants me to take his money. So the whole mess goes away and he gets Tyler's contract.

My phone buzzes, and I look down.

Open, a message with a zip file sits there.

I grab my phone and walk away. My hands tremble, seeing still photos that look hacked from Charles' security cameras. They're of me, naked, getting railed by all three of my guys. Together and separately. Not that I care. Heck, sex tapes make people fucking famous these days.

"No one might care if you let three men fuck your ass in a row," James' voice lingers in my ear. "Charles could get some really bad press for fucking his stepsister, a girl fifteen years younger than him, who also happens to be his nanny. A homeless piglet who I believe went to him for help, only to be sex trafficked to his friends."

My stomach violently flips, realizing how my situation can be spun that way. What would that do to

Charles' business? Jordan's law license. Alex's private training clients.

I swallow, seeing Charles talking to Tyler like he's explaining. He needs Tyler's tour to save his business and I threaten that.

"Take my money." James breathes in my ear, and I want to throw up. "Let me look like a good guy, investing in a fat girl's clothing line. Then I'll make sure my little brother hires your big brother. You can fuck *him* all you want. I certainly couldn't stomach touching you. I don't know how those three great-looking guys fuck you."

I bite my lip and wrench away from him. "Your negotiation skills suck. How are you a billionaire? You should stay out of your brother's business. Charles' production company is the best. Your brother should be begging him to produce his tour." I straighten my back. "That's got nothing to do with you and me. I'm not taking your money."

"Stella," Charles snaps at me. "Can I talk to you for a minute?"

"Get her to take my money and you'll have my brother's contract in your inbox by the time you get home." James pats him on the back, making Charles' neck vein throb and look ready to burst.

Charles takes me by the arm and leads me away with the room buzzing around us. My confidence is shattered, and I feel every ounce of fat clenched in Charles' fist.

I have to pull away. "I can walk. When were you going to tell me Tyler Pace was the artist you were wooing? You had to know he and James were brothers."

"I told you, I signed an NDA."

"You can fuck me in the ass, but not trust me with your secrets?"

"Please don't be vulgar like this." He pushes a hand through his hair. "You have a lot to learn, Stella. You're young, I get it. Rule one, don't piss off rich people. Extreme wealth is a small world."

"I don't need to be your age to know that. I understand your business is in trouble, but James Pace is evil. I don't know Tyler, but if James can make Tyler hire you, he can make his brother fire you. Not pay you. Screw you over."

"I've done a lot of research on someone who's offering me tens of millions to produce a two-year *world* tour. He's never stiffed anyone."

"We don't need them in our life." I say this to declare that I intend on having a relationship with Charles. We're not just fucking. "If you're in bed with Tyler, then you're in bed with James."

"My bed was crowded this morning. I'll get used to it." His words are like a slap in the face. "I need this deal. And you need financial backing. Put your big-girl pants on and sign with James."

"*Big* girl?"

"It's an expression, Stella. It means you're a grown up. Time to deal with grown-up shit."

"*Everyone* is touring again, Charles. You can get another deal."

"No, I can't. Artists and bands are hiring full-time tour managers who work directly for them. I'm a middleman. A dinosaur. I need this, Stella. I'm gonna have to fight for Gia."

"Don't you put that kind of pressure on me. Your

mother will cut her wrist to help you."

Charles just blinks at my comment. "I'm sorry she did you wrong, Stella. I told you I had no idea."

"Because you weren't around."

"You were eight when I met you. I was twenty-one. Figuring my own shit out."

"I assume a free ride to Harvard made that difficult." I fold my arms stubbornly. "I want to leave."

"I'm here for my mother. We have to stay. *This* is what I'm talking about being grown up."

"I'm not sitting at a table with James. How did he even know I'm here?"

Charles doesn't answer, but looks over my shoulder. I glance that way and roll my eyes. Tyler Pace is waving him over. Shit.

"I'll be right back. Do *not* leave," Charles mutters angrily and then stalks off.

"Fine," I say, but bolt toward the lobby to hijack one of those limos outside.

"Excuse me." A man in a light gray suit with sandy blond hair struts up to me.

"I'm sorry. I know we're being loud." I assume he's security, and scoff at how even bouncers in L.A. are fucking drop-dead gorgeous.

"It's not that. I overheard part of your conversation." He holds his hand out to me. "Giancarlo Byrne, I own this hotel."

"Nice to meet you, Giancarlo Byrne." Christ, this guy is breathtaking.

"You were saying you wondered how some guy knew where you were."

"Right." I fold my arms, feeling goose bumps just looking at him.

"Guys are putting trackers on girls' phones lately. Can I see yours?"

I smirk at him. "How do I know you won't put a tracker on my phone?"

He stares at me. "I'm married. My family has roots in New York and Boston. We own hotels on both coasts, and I handle all their security."

I shudder at the words family, New York, Byrne. Fuck, this guy is Irish Mafia. Here I go handing him my phone.

"Yep, here's the tracker app." He shows it to me.

"I never saw that."

"It buries itself in a folder. Did this guy James have access to your phone?"

"I dated him for a while, so yeah."

"New rules, sweetheart. Don't leave your phone unattended. Ever." He swipes a few times then hands the phone back to me. "It's gone, and I added a blocker to uninstall anything with similar code."

On his hand, I see a diamond-studded wedding ring on one finger and a silver etched ring with four colored stones on another. Same hand though. His kids maybe? "Thank you."

Charles comes back and pulls me to his side, possessing me in front of Giancarlo. "Can I help you?"

"He owns the hotel, he's a security expert here too. He found a tracker on my phone that James probably put on there."

"I see." Charles eyes him suspiciously. "Do I know you?"

"I don't think so. Giancarlo Byrne. I live in New York, but my brother-in-law lives in Malibu."

"Oh, maybe that's where I've seen you. Charles

Harlow. I have a beach house in Malibu."

"Who's your brother-in-law?" I ask him.

"Nate Domenico."

I gasp, remembering what Jaxson Steele told us about Nate's sister having the same polyamorous relationship. With *four* men.

My head is spinning and while I have a year's worth of questions, I thank Giancarlo. I also consider asking him to invest in my fashion line, but he's gone before the words form on my tongue.

I'm left staring at Charles. "I'm still mad at you."

"I know."

forty-five

STELLA

"Can I sleep here?" I say to Alex after Charles and I get home.

I checked on Giana and took one of the monitors with me, but I can't sleep in Charles' bed tonight. Or any other night. Even being across the hall feels too close, like he owns me somehow. That might be irrational, but I'm not thinking straight. I just want arms around me. Thick, meaty arms that will hold me down when I'm being fucked without having to kneel on command.

If I weren't responsible for Gia, I'd leave and go sleep on Bernie's sofa. But Alex's warm arms feel much better. I'm in a relationship with him too.

I just have to figure out how to balance everything.

He's welcoming and makes gentle love to me before I can say anything about what happened.

"What happened tonight?" he asks. "You felt extra tight, baby." Alex strokes my forehead. I'm naked and panting.

"I'm not taking James' money. I have my pride."

Alex brushes my lips with his. "If only more people were as honorable as you. You're really willing to die on the hill over this?"

"Yes." I painfully swallow. "*Especially* this."

Alex gets up and paces in front of the bedroom's white-brick fireplace. It must be nice to have when the weather cools in the fall. "Did Tyler give any indication of what he's doing about Charles' proposal?"

"No." I utter on a sob, "And James said he'd tell his brother to not hire him if I don't take his money."

Alex's face goes pale. "Oh, Stella…"

It's all he says.

"It's not fair to be put in this situation."

"Fuck," he curses under his breath. "I get it. It's those Pace brothers playing with our lives."

We all have a stake in this, and now Charles' business staying open rests upon me taking money from a man who called me fat. I thought I had developed tougher skin, but insults always hurt. The biggest one was that he was cheating on me and using me *because* he thought I was fat.

I suddenly feel so lost. There's no one I can turn to because everyone around me has a dog in this fight and can't be impartial.

Of all the people though, Alex perhaps has the least to lose. He's a certified trainer who would probably make just as much, if not more money working on his own or another company. I put my fate in his hands. "Do you think I should take the money?"

His eyes are filled with pain, given the responsibility I just laid on his shoulders. "Stella…"

"What would you do?" I sit up. "What if you overheard Pierce say he never had any feelings for you, that he was only using you, and then comes around and offers you a great job?"

"I'd tell him to go to hell," he says quickly. "But other people's lives are at stake. Think of Gia."

"I know." I let loose the tears I'm holding back, and Alex cradles me. I've gotten myself into a delicate situation, sleeping with three men. When Charles packs up and leaves here for his penthouse downtown, I'll have to make a choice. Continue to see all of them, or none of them.

Unable to make any decisions, I sleep with Alex for a few more nights. Jordan understands why I can't be under the same roof as Charles, and slips into the bed with us deep in the night. Fucking me, then fucking Alex.

During the day, it feels like the movie *Groundhog Day*. Get up. Make Gia's bottle. Ignore Charles. I play with her in the pool, watch her take a nap, change her diaper, and feed her when she wakes up. It's a military-regimented schedule, and I'm glad I don't have to think much.

*

With four days left to go before the month is over, I face reality. I'll miss the deadline with the Kansas factory.

That means letting Bernie go.

When I call and ask to meet her at our favorite diner because I won't do something so important like this over the phone, her response shocks me.

"I'm in New York," she says.

"Oh. A Broadway show you were dying to see?" I pray she says yes.

"Um." She hesitates. "Stella, I'm sorry, I just interviewed with Prada."

My heart pounds wildly in my chest. I know I planned to let her go, but her leaving me first hurts. She's been a great friend and I want the best for her. "How did the interview go?"

"Great. The marketing manager used to be a model. God, he's tall and gorgeous. His wife works there too, but they travel back and forth to Milan and want someone who's more permanent in the New York office."

I can hear the excitement in her voice. "If he needs a reference…"

"Can I make a suggestion?"

"Sure."

"Come with me. We'll get a cozy two-bedroom apartment with a great view of the entire city. You have a niche that's unfulfilled. I can't imagine other fashion houses won't want your designs. There're so many opportunities here."

I bite my lip and yes, I *want* to get on a plane to New York, but the other reality slaps me. "I have to get my father's situation settled. We've not heard from Katherine, and all legal attempts to see him and move him have failed."

"Right." Bernie sounds sad and it guts me. "Well, the offer stands."

"Thank you, Bernadette."

"Oh… My apartment has a few more months on the lease. It's yours if you want to pick up the rent."

The idea that I have someplace to go on my own terms settles my nervous stomach. It's best I don't live in this house. For all I know, Charles might have to sell it. According to Jordan, Tyler Pace hasn't formally declined Harlow Production's offer. Yet.

James is waiting me out.

Playing chicken.

This sucks.

Jordan storms into the pool house looking ravenous.

"Bernie, I have to go. Call me… Don't forget about me."

"I won't. Love you." Bernie hangs up.

I drop the phone so Jordan and I can devour each other.

Panting and sweaty, he says the words I don't want to hear. "We're heading out of here in a couple of days. Are you staying? I know Charles won't make you leave."

"How is he?" I can't believe we haven't spoken in four days. Or how broken I feel without him.

"He's wrecked."

"No word from Ana?"

"No. He…" Jordan squeezes his eyes shut. "He hired an agency to find him a full-time nanny."

Nodding, I say, "Good. I want him to have Gia."

"What about you?"

"Bernie might be moving to New York. She said I can stay in her apartment. Jordan, is there really nothing we can do about my father?"

"I'm sorry." He kisses my forehead, and Alex comes in wet from a swim.

"That was quick," he smirks, and I want nothing more than the two of them inside me. "Fuck me. Both of you."

They do, and it's heaven. Especially the way Jordan and Alex kiss each other with me sandwiched between them.

When we're done, Jordan says, "So where's this apartment?"

"Not far from where I lived in Glendale."

"You don't want to move in with me?" Alex says, eyeing Jordan.

"Not yet. It's too soon." I snuggle against them.

"Too soon to be serious?" Alex asks.

Do I want two boyfriends when I have unresolved feelings for Charles?

"You want to be serious with me?" I ask, looking from Alex to Jordan. "Both of you?"

After an exchange and a nod, they smile. "Yeah," Alex says and kisses my lips. "I love you, baby. That's how it happens. Love doesn't go by a calendar."

His words choke me up, and my heart swells. "I love you too." I know it's real because when I could have just left here a few nights ago, I went to him. I needed him.

And how can I not love him? He's gorgeous, he can cook, and he's a nice man.

"What about you?" I challenge Jordan, who I know can go back to his old life and find a Sub to keep his bed warm. "Do you love me? Because I love you." The same reasoning applies. He's brought out a side to me I never knew existed. I felt confident before I got here, but now I feel damn near unstoppable.

"I do, kitten." He smiles. "I hope you'll let me bring you to my club and show you off."

My body tingles at that idea and just like that, I have two boyfriends and we're in love.

I just don't have a job. Or a place to live. Access to my father. A way of saving my career...

A knock on the door is followed by Charles standing there with the baby monitor. "Gia's napping."

I'm naked, and so are the guys.

Blushing, Charles adds, "Stella, I need to talk to you."

"Talk." I sit in a chair and at least cross my legs. The man's not had sex in a few days, and I really want to hear what's in his heart and not what his dick is telling

311

him to say in order to fuck me.

He kneels at my feet and reaches for my hand. "I'm so sorry. I should have immediately stuck up for you Saturday night."

I close my eyes, understanding he had to protect himself because that includes Gia. "You did lunge for James."

"But I should have told them both to go to hell when James threatened you."

"It's not important now."

"Yes, it is." He grips my knee. "Stella. I love you too." *Too* meaning he pressed his ear up to the door and listened to our conversation.

I hold back tears and want to yell how much I love him from the rooftops because I do. I think I've always been in love with him. But it was the fairy tale love of a young girl. "Charles, you and I, together, are complicated."

"I know. I took care of the one thing I can change to uncomplicate it." He takes a deep breath and leans into me. "I just told Tyler Pace's people I'm withdrawing my bid. For you." He kisses my hands.

Jordan gasps and Alex covers his face.

"Charles!" I'm breathless. I never imagined he'd turn Tyler Pace down. For. Me.

"I don't want this insane imbalance between us. Now we both have to figure our careers out." He puts his hands on both sides of the chair, caging me beneath him. "Now... Do you fucking love me or not?"

"Yes. Yes, I do." I kiss him passionately, my heart filled with joy.

He roughly holds my face. "Say it. Say you love me."

"I love you."

"Good. Now spread those legs so I can eat your pussy and make you come. I'm dying for you, dirty girl."

I do, and his mouth on me has me crying out almost immediately. He fingers my ass and I'm coming again in a manner of minutes.

When he kisses me with my juices on his lips, he's never smiled more brightly. "What now?"

Getting my breath in check, I say, "Go sit on the couch. Naked." Glancing over his shoulder at Jordan and Alex, I add," All three of you. I want a cock in every possible hole."

It doesn't take long to decide who I'll ride and who'll be in my ass. Alex sits down and pats his legs. "Come on, baby. Give me that pussy. Your stepbrother needs your ass more than we do at the moment."

His words make me tingle. But then there we are. I'm grinding my pussy on Alex's cock with Charles' cock buried deep inside me too. Jordan sits on the back of the couch and feeds me his cock, then lets Alex suck him off as well.

We're totally debauched and feral. One by one we all climax, Alex sucking down Jordan's release, and I feel him pulse in me as he does it. It's so fucking hot. Charles is holding my breasts as hot cum fills my ass.

He kisses the back of my neck, and whispers, "I want you to sleep in my bed tonight."

It's a new beginning for all of us.

It's going to be amazing.

The door to the pool house crashes open, startling me.

"What in the hell are you boys doing?" Katherine's

voice screeches from the doorway.

"Fuck, Mom," Charles spits out, tucking my head against Alex's chest. "Don't you knock?"

Jordan holds his dick and yanks his shorts on without saying anything. He's too stunned, watching Katherine charge into the living room as if we all weren't naked.

"I thought with your daughter here, Charles, you'd show some restraint. And your *sister* is living here with you. Do you know what I had to do to make that happen? Have you no shame, mister?" Just then she spots me, *his sister*, wedged between them.

We're gonna have to call an ambulance because it looks like Katherine's about to collapse from an aneurysm.

forty-six

STELLA

Katherine storms out of the pool house.

"Stay here!" Charles warns me, dressing quicker than I've ever seen anyone put clothes on to catch his mother before she falls in the pool.

Alex and I dress as well, but watch the show from the window. "I wonder what the hell he's saying to her."

Then it hits me. "My father!" I bolt away and head for the door.

Charles eyes me as I charge him and his mother. He holds up his hand, trying to stop me. But I ignore him.

"Katherine," I bark at her.

"What in the world do you want? You…"

"Watch it," Charles snaps at her. "I'm in love with Stella."

"You're sick. She's your sister."

"Oh, so now I'm his sister." I get in her face. "Now I'm some important relative because it suits your moral outrage." I feel Charles pulling on my arm. "Well, lady, I'm in love with your son too. And what we do is none of your damn business. The real issue is what did you do to my father?"

Her face contorts. "I don't know what you mean. I cut my trip short because I got all these crazy messages from the facility he's in. Saying some absurd woman showed up."

"That would be me." I fold my arms.

"And they're getting threatening legal letters."

"That would be me." Jordan struts over from the pool house dressed in his shorts and a tee-shirt.

"What in the world is the matter with all of you?" she asks, throwing up her hands.

"They wouldn't let me see him," I answer.

"That's ridiculous. You've seen him plenty of times."

"Yes, at Parker House. He was moved to some dump in Van Nuys. Why?"

"It's not a dump. It's a highly recommended hospice facility."

My stomach twists, hearing hospice. He was sent there to die.

"Mrs. Harlow, with all due respect," Alex jumps in. "That place was a complete dump."

Charles lowers an eyebrow at her. "Did you even go there?"

Katherine swallows, looking at the four of us. "No. Not yet."

I have to forgive her for not visiting him often. I stopped going too because there was no point. He's incoherent. "I've missed visits too, Katherine. You're his wife. I trusted you to do the right thing by him. My father earned that."

She takes a breath and then gets on her phone. I make eye contact with each of my men, and we're on the edge of our seats wondering who the hell she's calling. "Michaela, it's Katherine. The place Mr. Raven is in…" She doesn't even know the name! "Who inspected it? You told me you were taking care of this for me."

"She's fucking blaming Michaela." Charles shakes

his head.

"Uh-huh, I see. Thank you." Katherine hangs up. "Apparently, we were misled. I'm sorry." Her empty apology enrages me.

"We're going there right now," I say to her.

"Charles, go with Stella and Jordan," Alex says. "I'll stay with Gia."

"You can't stay here with a baby," Katherine scoffs.

"You haven't even held her!" Charles roars. "Who the hell are you to tell my best friend he can't watch my daughter?"

"You four must have had an interesting month here together." Katherine turns icy again.

"We have." I take a breath and move toward her with soft eyes. "Katherine, I love Charles. I always felt something for him. I know it seems wrong. But I never lived with him. He's my stepbrother in name only. Now he's more than that. He's an amazing man and a wonderful father."

"Have you heard from Gia's mother?" Katherine ignores what I said, and stares at Charles.

"*Ana*," Charles defends the woman who left him with a baby to the woman who won't even hold the baby. "And no."

I resist an eye roll at the absurdity.

"And Stella has done an amazing job taking care of Gia," Charles adds.

"You've really tunneled your way into his life, haven't you?" Katherine snarls. "Get him to love you by being all good with the baby."

"Would you prefer she was awful with the baby?" Charles screeches.

"Are we going to that place, or not?" I snap.

"Mother, I'm putting my relationship with you on the line over this."

"You have a billion-dollar trust coming due, Charles." Katherine folds her arms. "Are you sure about that?"

I gasp, wondering when that is. Maybe when he turns forty in two years. I don't care about his money. I love him.

"I'm so sure. Now get your ass in my car and let my girlfriend see her father for fuck's sake."

We're all stunned at not only Charles' language, but the voracity of anger toward his mother. Quite the 180 from a month ago.

"Sheesh." She spins around and walks off.

We pile into the Escalade that drove Katherine here and speed to Van Nuys. Charles and Katherine sit in the second-row captain's chairs while I'm with Jordan in the third row.

"Elder abuse is common, Katherine." Jordan tries to good-cop her. "I'm sure someone showed whoever checked the place out a beautiful suite."

"Yeah, bait and switch," I say. "But we're moving him out of there."

"I'll handle this," Katherine says and stays quiet for the rest of the drive.

Her resolve crumbles when the same staff who shunned me is even reluctant to let *her* in. She shows several pieces of identification and throws a fit before we're taken to his room.

That was a stalling tactic. He's no longer naked on a rubber sheet the way I saw him. He's dressed and under a pretty quilt.

"Katherine, this isn't what I saw. Alex was with me.

They're duping you, *please believe me.*"

She quietly takes in the room. The shitty neighborhood and the rundown complex speak for themselves. Turning to the man in scrubs who sits at Dad's bedside, she says, "Are you even a licensed nurse?"

"No ma'am."

I'm tempted to ask if he's on loan from a nearby prison.

"Fine." Katherine bursts out of there and goes back to the main office. "I'm calling a friend who's a doctor right now. I'm moving my husband out of here."

*

An hour later, a medical transport van arrives and an older man in a very nice suit gets out. "Katherine, what's going on?"

"Hudson, thank you." She kisses him on both cheeks.

"Fuck me," Jordan mutters.

"What?" I ask, alarmed at Jordan's shocked face.

"That's Hudson Perry. He's the head of neurosurgery at Faith L.A."

"*That* was her friend?"

Charles hugs me from behind. "My mother knows she fucked up."

"And you threatened your relationship with her." I finally get to address that. "That lit a fire under her ass."

"We'll address *our* relationship with her once your father is settled."

"Thank you."

He breathes in my ear. "Look, we have five days left. But when I go back to work, please stay at the house.

I'm getting a full-time nanny. That's not your job. I'll give you the money for your line. I'll talk to my finance guy. I have stock options I can sell."

I smile, even though I don't want his money anymore. I don't want that between us. I have to put aside my own dreams for the time being. My father apparently doesn't have long to live. Charles needs help with Gia. There are other factories here in the U.S. I can get my line in production somewhere else at another time.

I hug Charles and Jordan, who's on the phone with Alex, giving him an update.

We have a few more days together, all of us.

I want to enjoy every second of these men.

forty-seven

CHARLES

With each hard pounding of my feet on the sand as I run on the beach, I reflect on every minute of the last month. I showed up here in Malibu a wrecked man from having a baby dropped on my doorstep. Now I feel like a king.

Love was the furthest thing from my mind. Stella changed everything I thought I wanted and needed in this life. She loves me and she loves Gia.

I also never imagined I'd be in a four-way relationship and sharing her with my best friends. But they love her too, and making Stella choose, even if it were me, means she wouldn't be complete.

When I get back to my office on Monday, I face a big challenge with my business. Not producing Tyler Pace's world tour is a blow. But my honor isn't for sale. I also learned over this past month that money isn't everything.

And that my mother isn't the person I thought. That relationship will need some work. But I made it clear, either she respects my relationship with Stella, or she and I are through. It's only been a few days and she's been at Griffin's bedside almost non-stop. I respect that and will give her time before she addresses Stella and me.

The sun stings the top of my head as it's right over me now. I didn't get out as early as I wanted because I made love to Stella most of the morning. I can't get enough of her.

A man with wavy brown hair wearing a wetsuit and carrying a surfboard steps out onto the sand from one of the many palatial houses on this part of the beach. Something is so familiar about him that my ears start wildly ringing.

Wilde...

It hits me like a brick from Alex mentioning that he and Stella ran into Jaxson Steele, who's in a very public polyamorous relationship with Lacey Wilde. And that her ex-husband Aidan Marx is part of that relationship.

I met Aidan on several occasions when he ran the A&R group at Thompson Street Records. He's now the COO of a new label called Fortress Records.

He looks my way and I wave. It takes a moment for him to recognize me. When he does, he smiles and stands his board up in the sand to come say hello.

I wipe the sweat from my hands on my shorts before shaking his hand. "Aidan."

"Charles, how are you?"

"Good. I didn't know you lived here."

"Yeah, I moved in about three years ago." He nods. "I heard you didn't get the Tyler Pace contract."

Good news travels fast. Music is also a very small world.

"I turned it down actually." I cross my arms. "I had a conflict."

"Really." He tilts his head at me. "It's funny me running into you."

"Why?"

"Come with me." He turns and heads up a set of stone-carved steps leading to a long, narrow backyard with a pool, laid out much like my property. Only, the actual house is nearly twice the size of mine.

Silver-blonde hair with pink streaks catches my eyes and I admit, my heart flutters at the idea of meeting Lacey Wilde. She's sitting at a patio table with two other men. The intensely dark-haired man is Jaxson Steele and the other… I go breathless, recognizing Nate Domenico.

Lacey stands up and I see she's pregnant. Her swollen belly under a long, pink sheer coverup takes over her tiny body.

Aidan greets her with a kiss. "This is my wife, Lacey." He sounds so damn happy saying that. "She's the CEO of Fortress."

"Nice to meet you, Lacey. Charles Harlow." I shake her hand.

"Yeah, Aidan said you're *the* Charles Harlow of Harlow Productions."

It hits me.

I'm a rock concert promoter, and I'm staring at four rock gods. Two of which are still touring.

Stella's words whisper through my brain, *Everyone's going back on tour*. I'd been so narrow-minded, focusing on Tyler Pace, that I forgot that.

I'm in a tank top and shorts, sweating like a beast, but I manage to convince Jax and Nate to use me for their next tours.

And I set up a meeting with Aidan and Lacey at their office to discuss partnering with them on their 360-contracts for other artists. Record labels now sponsor and take a cut from artists' tours.

I leave there, and any thoughts I had about how my situation would look being in a relationship with Stella, Alex, *and* Jordan doesn't feel weird. It seems normal.

I run back to the house at top speed to tell the news to my family.

The yard is empty and I'm wondering why no one's in the pool since it's such a gorgeous morning. I'm tempted to dive in and cool down, when I hear Gia laughing and my heart tugs.

I go inside and expect to see my daughter in Stella's arms because she giggles and coos the loudest when she holds Gia.

But it's not Stella holding the baby.

It's Ana.

forty-eight

STELLA

I get to my feet as Charles comes in through the kitchen door. He left nearly an hour ago for a run and I've been waiting for him.

We've been waiting for him.

"Hi," I say to him, but his eyes are on Ana holding Gia. "Look who's here."

"Yeah, I see." He sounds harsh.

I move toward him. "She got here around forty-five minutes ago. We've been talking. She's... She's so *nice*, Charles." Something made it easy for me to connect to Ana.

Mostly the way Gia lit up seeing her. Ana cried, Gia cried, and so did I.

"Hello, Charles." She's bouncing Gia, who's giggling. "We should talk."

"You're damn—"

"Charles," I cut him off and hug him. "Listen to her."

"Talk," Charles says, gripping me firmly like he's proud I'm his. Of us.

The guy who didn't do relationships chose me.

"I didn't mean to keep Gia from you," Ana starts, already sounding upset. "You made it very clear you didn't want a relationship with me."

"I didn't want a relationship with anyone," Charles corrects her. "It had nothing to do with you. You told me you were on birth control."

"I was. You're very virile." Ana grins at me. "Watch out."

I squeeze Charles again and then let him go. "I'll keep that in mind."

Ana already knows Charles and I are in love. We had a lot to talk about.

"Anyway, I thought you'd accuse me of trying to trap you, Charles. I was just as surprised by this little one. I was confused. And scared." She kisses Gia's head. "I had a difficult pregnancy. And if you haven't noticed, I didn't exactly lose the baby weight. I went through some emotional stuff. When the job in Barrow came up, I needed to get back to work. But that was no place for an infant. I'm sorry."

I tug his hand to talk to her. She'll be in our lives forever because of Gia. I want him to have an amicable relationship with Ana. There's another reason now too...

Charles leaves my side and strokes Ana's arm. "I'm sorry you felt you couldn't reach out to me. I wouldn't have *accused* you of anything." He pets Gia's head. "It doesn't matter. She's here and I love her. I want us to have shared custody."

Ana smiles. "I want that too. I hope the schedule can be flexible. I met someone in Barrow."

"Are you moving there?" Charles asks with panic in his voice.

"No. We're gonna do the long-distance thing for now. I already told him I wouldn't take Gia away from her father. As long as you want her..."

"I want her." He smiles so assuredly. "Completely."

We're silent, and then I say to Ana, "Can I tell him?"

"Tell me what?" Charles says, looking like he might

get more startling news.

"When Ana got here, I had my sketches laid out so I can start making new presentations. She loves the line." I look at her and nod, so she'll continue for me.

"I do. I've felt so off these past four months with the changes in my body. I figured out it's because all of my clothes didn't fit," Ana explains, and the pain in her voice is so real. "I didn't want to buy anything plus-size. I know that's very shallow of me." Her cheeks redden.

I appreciate her honesty, and it's a roadblock I was always familiar with in my niche. "But then I showed her some of my samples."

"They're amazing. Look at this woman." She points to me in my dark blue and red trim wrap dress. "You look *gorgeous*. I want that. And I want other people who aren't size two to feel great in their clothes. *And* their skin."

"Okay…" Charles looks confused. "So did you hire Ana as a photographer?"

"No." I smile and show him the check she wrote me. "She's investing in my line."

"That check is for five hundred thousand dollars." Charles sounds exasperated. "You carry that much around in your checking account?"

"I don't mean to be crass in front of your new girlfriend, Charles, but if you had talked to me a little more during our week fucking in Hawaii…" Ana blushes, and I can honestly say I don't feel jealous because I believe with all my heart that Charles loves me. "You would have found out, that I have a sizable trust fund."

"I see." Charles looks at me. "You said you only

needed three hundred thousand."

"That's for six lines. She's investing in ten."

"Ten?"

"That's six years of working capital." I grab his shirt. "Jordan is amending the agreement I had with James. She also doesn't want the same payout. I just have to give her a free set of every line."

We show Ana the house, Gia's nursery in particular, and mention she will live here when she's with us. We ask if we can have her for one more night and that we'll bring her home to Ana's house in Marina Del Ray tomorrow.

I'm already guessing Charles will be a mess, and he'll need some extra love.

Ana cries again, saying goodbye to Gia and we watch her leave in a BMW. Just as she leaves, Alex returns with the Charger.

Jordan kisses him before I do, and then we tell him what happened with Ana.

When it's just us, the four of us, Charles drops a bombshell of more news. He'll be working with Jaxson Steele and Nate Domenico on their tours. And he's meeting with Aidan Marx at Fortress Records to discuss signing a contract as an exclusive promoter for the small record label.

We have a lot to celebrate, and I'm so glad Gia is here with us. Even if it's only one more night. It will hurt not having her full-time, but she needs her mother, and I know what *not* to do as a stepmother.

Plus, I have a fashion line to get into production!

On Monday I'll call the Kansas factory and tell them I can wire them the payment they need to start the process. I'll have to travel there once a week at first to do inspections. It hits me, and for a moment, self-doubt creeps in, thinking I'm not ready.

"What?" Charles says, holding my face while I cuddle Gia against my chest.

"I'm feeling overwhelmed. I don't have Bernie. I have to staff up."

"You need a design assistant, right?" Alex says, rubbing his chin.

"Yeah, if she's a great designer and knows the plus-size market, I can focus on the business end for a while too."

"I'll help you with that." Charles hugs me.

"Do you know someone who designs, Alex?" I ask him.

He blushes and then stands in front of the floor-to-ceiling kitchen windows before saying anything.

"Alex?" Jordan crosses the room and massages his shoulders. "What's going on?"

"I was with Pierce."

We all gasp, and my heart lands in my throat, thinking he's going to leave us and go live with Pierce. With *them*.

Oh, *hell* no. He's ours and I will fight for him.

"God, look at you three." Alex laughs. "It's not like *that*. He called and asked me to work for his mobile training company. He signed with another movie studio. His guys show up in a van with weights and other equipment to help celebs work out in their trailers."

"Are you giving me your notice?" Charles asks, choking up.

"I listened to him, figuring I had to keep my options open. Charles, you don't need the expense of an in-house gym with a trainer. You did that for me because I needed a job." Alex swallows.

"Well, my business is no longer on the skids. I don't want to lose you," Charles says proudly. "I have good people working for me, for us. I want to offer decent perks to keep them."

I'm glad that's all settled, but I want to get back to the part about Alex knowing a designer I can hire. "Alex, who's the designer?"

He takes out his phone and shows me an Instagram profile. "Who's Selena Eldridge?"

"Cooper's daughter. She was at the diner with him when I met Pierce. She just graduated from FIDM and needs a job. I think she knows what she's doing in the plus-size market."

I look closer and her beautiful, round face and curvy body make me smile. Another woman who embraces her figure and even wants to help women feel more beautiful is all I need to see. "She's hired!"

"That won't be weird?" Jordan interjects. "Stella working with Cooper's daughter?" He pulls at his beard. "I don't want to be the bad guy here, but I don't think I like this. I don't want something like *this* between us."

The emotion in his voice stills me as Alex stomps over and plants a kiss on Jordan that has me and Charles holding on to the kitchen island, it's so hot.

"I'm fucking yours, you feel me? I love you. *You*."

Jordan looks so unraveled, but that's what love does. Pulls you apart and then puts you back together piece by piece. "Christ, I love you too."

They kiss again, then Alex takes Jordan's hand. "If you don't mind, I need to show my boyfriend how much I love him."

Without waiting for our answer, they leave.

Charles and I glance at each other, Gia sleepy in my arms.

"So…" He strokes my cheek. "We could take a nap with her."

Nodding, I say, "We could do that. Or…"

"Or…" Biting his lip, he says, "We can watch those two on the security camera while fooling around."

My heart pounds, and right there I know how much fun this is going to be. The four of us. "I'll put Gia in her crib and meet you in the security room."

"Remember Jordan's rules. No bra, no panties," he growls while kissing his daughter and then me.

"I'll never forget. I love you."

"I love you more, you maniac."

epilogue

One year later
STELLA

"Stella Raven Designs, please hold. Oh, Stella, I was able to move your interviews with *Vogue* and *Elle Magazine* to next week," my assistant says to me as I pass her desk.

"Thank you, Paige." With the massive success of my first two lines, I opened an office in a converted warehouse right in the heart of the L.A. fashion district.

"And I got you a flight back from Kansas earlier like you asked, so you'll be home all weekend. Then you fly to New York that Monday."

"Great!" I smile appreciatively, and text Bernie that I want to see her when I'm there.

Noticing the time, I pick up my pace to reach the private client salon. Inside, the walls are covered in pearl-colored textured silk, and the room glows, thanks to the crystal chandelier above. I cross into the dressing room and stare at the dress form. Anxiety swirls in my belly, wondering if the custom wedding dress I was hired to design will satisfy the bride.

Whoever she may be.

The request and the deposit came from a personal assistant who wouldn't give me the client's name for security reasons. Either a celeb or a politician's daughter who might be having a shot-gun wedding.

According to the measurements I was given a month ago, the bride is about my size. I found doing custom pieces here and there is extremely lucrative. Hence, the posh room where I can do fittings.

I didn't say yes right away, feeling out of my depth because I hadn't done a wedding dress since fashion school. Charles, Jordan, and Alex encouraged me. With an outrageous budget and the freedom to design it however I wanted, I agreed, and really dove into the project.

I went nuts, basically. Italian silk, handmade Israeli lace, and Swarovski crystals.

Selena struts into the dressing room wearing one of her designs, a red and white print dress with a high elastic waist. "That gown is stunningly gorgeous, Stella, stop worrying." She's been an utter godsend to me. I hired her as soon as Alex told me she was looking for a job. She designs with an edge that has made my brand really stand out in the early-twenties market.

"Thank you, Sel." I always get choked up at how Selena looks at me with gooey eyes. I've tried to be a good mentor for her.

I miss Bernadette terribly, and offered her a huge raise to come back, but she hasn't answered me yet. Maybe she met a man in New York and is just caught up. I know the feeling. My men adore me to the point I can't think straight.

This past year has been so amazing. Charles and Jordan kept their places closer to the Harlow Productions office, but stay in Malibu when Charles has custody each week from Wednesday to Sunday. Alex lives with me full-time at the beach.

With great joy this year came great sadness, however, when my father passed a few months back. For a man whose strength and stamina defined his very existence, he became a shell of his former self. With no mobility, a sketchy memory, and nearly no verbal skills, that wasn't the man who raised me.

While I never said this out loud, I take comfort that he's with my mother now, and hopefully at peace. Katherine plays the dutiful widow and even gave me all of my father's money.

She's not thrilled about Charles and me, but he's her sun, moon, and stars. She won't give him up because of me. So she pretends he and I aren't fucking like rabbits every chance we get. We haven't dared to address Jordan and Alex fucking me too. But it's so much more than that. We're in love. We're a family.

"Oh no," Selena says, reading from her phone. "The model can't make it."

"Shoot." My heart sinks. Selena found a student from FIDM with the same measurements to model the dress for this wealthy client.

I stare at the beautiful gown on the form.

"I know what you're thinking," Selena says as I look at the dress longingly.

Marriage may be in my future, considering what I found out the other day. But I'm also happy with my guys just the way we are.

"What am I thinking?" I ask.

"That nothing does a dress justice more than one draped on an actual body, showing how the piece moves."

Especially a curvy body and she's right.

"You have to model it, Stella."

"I'm not a model." I feel my neck getting warm, and my ears are ringing all of a sudden.

"We don't have a runway, so you don't have to

worry about working the audience. Just put it on and twirl around so the client can see how it hugs your curves and how the crystals catch the light. We can tie up the train if you're worried about it."

Hearing tied up immediately makes me think of Jordan and that shibari rope he uses on me. "I don't know…"

"You know it will look a thousand times better on you than the form. I'm not the right size or I'd wear it myself. Just put it on. I'll pin anything we need to. You'll make the client happy and who knows, maybe this will be the start of a new business. Stella Raven Bridal."

"Wait a minute, Sel, you're getting ahead of yourself."

"Stella, the client you're waiting for is here," Paige notifies me through the two-way radio I keep on my hip because I spend a lot of time on the production floor.

"Thank you, Paige." I glance at the dress again, something giving me pangs about it all of sudden. "Please get her situated in the salon. Then offer her champagne along with the cheese and fruit plate I brought in. It's in the breakroom fridge."

Alex made it up for me this morning, smiling the whole time. That could have been from Jordan keeping him up all night. Those two… I swear, the foundation rocks when they have sex. But no matter how far gone they are in each other, the minute they see me, they pull me right into their scene and make me mindless too.

"Will do, Stella," Paige answers, and the connection fuzzes out.

"I'll go say hello and explain about the model canceling." I turn to leave, but Selena stops me.

"Really, you won't put it on?"

"No." I fold my arms.

Her adorable smirk is so transparent. "Stella. Raven. Bridal."

Shoot, I do like the sound of that. And I only received a deposit, and still need the final payment. I laid out more money than that deposit on the fabric and trimmings. I also sewed it myself. Looking at it finished, I feel if I put this thing on, I may not want to take it off.

Now that I'm handing it over, a feeling of unease settles over me. The model canceling is a weird omen.

"I don't recall if I committed to the client that I would provide a model for the reveal." I take out my phone and call Jordan, who does all my contracts, but it goes right to voicemail.

My options are limited right now. Paige is close to six-feet tall with lots of love in her trunk. Selena is much shorter than me with wider hips and a very ample bosom.

Shit, I'm gonna *have* to put this thing on. In the walkie-talkie, I tell Paige, "Stall her, please." Living here in L.A. I know how rich people hate to wait. "Okay, Sel. Help me get the gown off the dress form."

Twenty minutes later, I'm staring at myself. A revelation wallops me. I grab Selena to keep me steady. I look so much like my mother. This gown, with a boxy neckline, cap sleeves gently sloped off the shoulders, and drop waist with inverted pleats *is* Mom's dress. The memory must have been buried somewhere in my brain, but came out with every detail I added to this gown.

"It looks amazing, Stella," Selena says, zipping the

back, unable to contain her giggling.

"Thank you. What's with you?"

She blinks, and says, "I just can't wait to meet this mysterious client." Her words come out in a flourish.

"I hope she doesn't mind that *I'm* wearing her dress. Let's not mention the model who blew us off."

"No way." Selena fluffs the cathedral-length train, which in design and crystals took more time and cost more money than the bodice. The silk was so gorgeous, I only pinched a few pleats here and there and didn't have the heart to cover the fabric.

Christ, this thing is gorgeous, and I almost don't want to show it to the client. I want it for myself, damn it.

But the door that leads to the salon is open, and Selena is holding my train like an eager page boy.

So out we walk. I don't care who the client is at this point. The dress will sell itself. Once the sale is final, I'll have her try it on so I can alter it for her.

In the salon, my brain twitches when I only see a man in a tux. Good Lord, it's the groom who ordered this dress for his bride. He's going to surprise her with it. Like an engagement ring, but better. I can't think of anything more romantic and start to feel tears prick my eyes.

Then I notice it's...*three* men in tuxes.

I take in their faces, and I can't breathe.

Charles. Jordan. Alex.

They're *all* standing there in tuxes, gawking at me.

Selena is now crying and laughing, and it hits me instantly.

"You set me up!"

She nods enthusiastically. "Thank God this part is

337

over. I couldn't take it anymore."

"And the model you said you found?"

"Yeah, there was no model." She waves me off.

"You look like a model, kitten." Jordan takes my hand first.

Charles is to his left and Alex to his right.

"Guys… What's… What's going on?"

"It's not obvious?" Charles says and gets down on one knee. Jordan and Alex follow.

Holy. Shit.

I stare down at them.

"Wait. How…" I step back, feeling overwhelmed. "How do we get married? The four of us?"

"We have to ask you first, baby." Alex winks at me and seeing him in a tux, when he's usually in tee-shirts and track pants, blows me away.

Ask? As if I'd say no.

Charles presents a blue velvet ring box.

I open it and I'm expecting a three-stone setting, something similar to what I saw Giancarlo Byrne wear, but that was a man's ring. My eyes pop, seeing the humungous, round stone. It's like our love. Never-ending.

"Guys, this is huge!"

Jordan smirks and takes the box from me. "Sounds like we're at home."

"I second her huge motion, counselor," Alex says and kisses Jordan while Charles kisses me.

But soon we're all tangled up and I'm kissing Jordan and Alex too.

The door leading to the reception area opens and Ana peeks her head through. "Can we come in?"

"You were in on this too?" I say, turning to her, and

she doesn't look the least bit surprised that I'm standing here in a wedding dress.

"Of course, I was." Ana is my investor, but she feels more like a great friend now.

"Is Gia here?" I ask, ready to take her into my arms.

"I don't want you all to freak out, but this happened last night." Ana, wearing one of my asymmetrical hemline coat dresses that matches her hairstyle, opens the door completely.

Gia wobbles in and we all gasp, because she's walking.

Gia's walking!

I stare at Charles who is now ready to lose it from the emotion building up. Wearing a cute, pink lace dress, Gia goes right for her daddy, and he scoops her up the second she reaches him.

It never gets old seeing how he utterly adores that little girl.

"What's that in her hands?" I notice she's holding a white box.

Charles takes it from her. "Can Daddy have Stella's present?"

"No!" Gia coos and tries to gnaw on the box.

"I'll take her," Alex says and holds her close, so lovingly.

"What's going on, Charles?" I say softly.

"You'll see, you maniac, relax."

Jordan chuckles because he knows how strung-out I get and how I want to control everything all the time. When I get over the top, he takes me away for a few days and it's all hardcore discipline and so much dirty, rough sex, I can barely walk when he's done with me.

Speaking of *done*... He canceled his club

339

membership. He's all mine. And Alex's.

"Can I stay?" Ana asks with her hands clasped.

"Of course." I love how she and Charles have become great friends too. It means a lot to me that he opened his heart to her in a way that is pure, showing he is a man of forgiveness and grace. That he puts Gia first. All without ever giving me a hint of worry.

He's mine.

And I'm his.

It also looks like he wants to make this permanent between us. All of us.

Charles opens the box, and the tissue paper makes me think of the baby clothes I unwrapped for Gia a year ago. How that day in the nursery led to this moment.

"I truly can't take waiting, Charles." I bounce on my heels.

He laughs. "Close your eyes, maniac." He calls me *dirty girl* when it's just us.

Figuring I'm outnumbered here and ready to collapse from the excitement, I close my eyes and hope I don't fall over.

Something tugs into the top of my head.

"What…" I open my eyes before I'm told to. Charles never disciplines me. Just sticks his cock in my mouth when I get my freak-out on.

But all thoughts empty out of my head when I see that familiar, stiff tulle and pearl applique I remember from my parent's wedding photos.

"Is this…"

"Yes, Stella." Charles breathes into my ear and kisses my neck. "It's your mother's veil."

"Where did Katherine find it?"

"*I* found it. I went through my mother's storage unit

after your father died." His voice is tight. "I've kept it hidden in my office. I knew... We knew... This day was coming. That we'd want to make you ours officially."

Jordan and Alex huddle tightly in our circle, and I immediately take Gia from Alex. I catch us in the mirror. I wish today was our wedding day because I can't imagine any of us looking happier.

"You look gorgeous, kitten," Jordan says and kisses me.

Gia taps our faces and laughs. I blow raspberries on her cheek to make her cry out in laughter.

"Is one of you going to ask me to marry you?" I bounce Gia on my hip with no plans to let her go.

"We're all gonna ask you," Alex says, pinching my earlobe and then kissing it.

"Stella," Charles begins.

"Kitten," Jordan adds.

"Baby," Alex finishes.

"Will you marry me?" they say in unison.

They also don't say *us* because they each want me in their own way and for their own reasons. But together we are very much...*us*.

"Yes, Yes, and Yes!" I squeal and we melt into an amazing group hug.

Next, I hear snapping and Ana photographs us, wiping tears away. She melts into the background, as I take in this moment with my men.

We're all breathless and excitement hums off our skin. I want to run to find someone to perform a wedding ceremony right now.

We probably should because this dress won't fit me for long.

Guess it's the right time to announce my baby news...

"Hey, um...guys?" I address them collectively because I honestly have no idea whose child is growing inside me. I also don't care. We're a family. We share Giana when she's with us. This baby will be no different.

Charles, Jordan, and Alex stare at me with such love, and if I had any doubt about bringing a baby into our world, this surprise washes all of that away.

"I have something to tell you..."

The End

THANK YOU FOR READING

SHARING HIS NANNY.

Tori Chase

Tori Chase is the ultra-sexy side of award-winning author Deborah Garland.

If you're looking for very explicit reads where anything goes, Tori Chase is your new favorite author.

You can follow her exclusively on Instagram @torichaseromance.

Made in United States
North Haven, CT
13 November 2024